The Legend of the Gamesmen

The Agben School

Book 2 of The Legend of the Gamesmen

Jo Sparkes

PORTLAND, OREGON

The Agben School - Jo Sparkes -- 2nd Ed.
ISBN 978-0-9853318-6-3

To Sue and Audrey and Bart

and Scott and Chris and David.

Also Annie Tapper Blem and Mike Terlizzi.

Prologue

MIK WAS ALL OF ten years old, and had responsibility.

At least that's what his mother had told him this morning, when it was time to open the shop. His grandfather was ill, and needed her help.

"Just keep it closed for half the day," Father had suggested.

"Not with four ships in port," Mother had snapped back.

So it was Mik's job to mind the store.

He'd done everything before, of course. Poured out the herbs, wrapped them in paper. He knew to keep the items close to himself until the customer paid in coin. "A poor little Mid Isle shop taking credit would go broke in a month," his mother smilingly explained to any who asked.

Yes, he'd seen it all and he knew what to do.

Until the pretty girl walked in. She was Trumen, like himself, and maybe 17 years old. Trumen were the smaller, weaker race, while Skullan ruled the kingdom. Being Trumen would rule her out of any other position of importance – except that Agben seemed to treat both races equally.

The girl's clothes weren't as nice as many before her, but nicer than some. She had that desert air, right down to the sandal shoes, but her hair was long in the Missean fashion instead of the short cut of the Flats.

She didn't seem Agben. But she didn't seem not Agben, either.

Her hair was dark red and braided down her back. When she turned in the sunlight from the door a scarlet strand flashed. Little wisps escaped and curled around her face, making her seem too soft.

Women of Agben were never soft.

Mik realized that responsibility did indeed have weight, just as his father said. He was feeling that weight on his shoulders this very second.

The girl looked over the shelves carefully, and he didn't interrupt her.

And then she turned to him, and smiled. The smile alone was almost enough to prove she wasn't Agben. Almost.

"Illsmith," she said. "Do you have any?"

Mik nodded. "In the back, Miss. How much do you want?"

"Just a handful, please." Her eyes were blue, he saw, but not the faded blue of his mother and baby sister. Hers were a deep blue, like the sea's depths as evening fell.

He hurried to fetch her Illsmith.

"And Musk Oil?" she called after him.

Ah hah! The girl must be of Agben, Mik realized. Illsmith was a desert plant, and Musk Oil from the Great Continent. Those two went together, he knew, to rub on sore muscles and strained shoulders. He knew because one of the Agben women had told his mother so when his father hurt himself pulling in the big swoopfish.

Mik grabbed a tiny glass bottle of oil – all of ten copper, he remembered – and then the crock of Illsmith. Returning to the girl, he set both on the counter, and produced a paper to hold the latter.

"Twelve copper," he said, as he plucked out a handful of the herb and wrapped it proper.

Some people frowned when the price was mentioned, but this girl merely drew coins from a pocket.

Mik stooped low to open the box he wasn't supposed to know about, and snatched the pretty bauble from inside.

He carefully wrapped it in a soft cloth, the kind used for fragile glass on long trips. And then presented it to the girl.

"What is this?" she asked, starting to lift a folded corner.

Mik stopped her, because old man Tanner strode into the shop. "Take it," he whispered.

"Mik, my boy," Tanner grinned. The old man always wanted advice on a new ache. "Your mother not here this morning?"

The girl hesitated, still staring at him. He snatched up the coin she'd placed on the counter, and tugged the step ladder over to just beneath the Stomach Cure jar.

"That's right," Tanner told him. "Just a swig, my boy. Just a swig."

Mik felt the pretty girl's eyes on him. Surely she knew no one else was supposed to see that thing. Surely she knew to stick it in her pocket and pretend it didn't exist.

The girl gave him a last frown, but said no more. By the time he'd wrangled the tonic down from the shelf, she'd gone.

1.

MARRA STEPPED OUT into the sunlight and smiled.

She had no idea what the boy in the shop had given her, but then the island practically burst with strange customs. Most had turned out to be very pleasant.

When the Trafalcon first docked, friendly people had rushed to toss flower necklaces over their heads, while kissing cheeks and clasping hands. A sort of laughing welcome. It was a giving place.

The change in her circumstances from a year ago seemed impossible to believe.

Marra had apprenticed with a potions maker on the desert flats, until Mistress Britta suddenly died. With so little time in her study, she found herself in the power of the mistress' brother, a bad man involved with worse fellows.

And then she made the Birr Elixir from a recipe in her Mistress' old book.

Now she was Brista, Potions Maker to Drail and the Hand of Victory, traveling to the Skullan city of Missea. Drail and his men were gamesmen, victors of the famous Port Leet comet game. Their goal was to follow the legendary footsteps of Drail's grandsire – to win on the Great Continent itself.

The others were eager to reach the city. But Marra was content to wait, when waiting meant strolling on a sunny street with colorful shops and light sparkling off the. She savored the early morning warmth of the oddly soft air, like a warm sweater caressing her skin. Such a feeling this humidity, as Tryst had called it. Water actually living in the air.

Mid Isle was between the Wavering Continent and the Great Continent, although the Captain assured them it was much closer to the latter, and that they'd be in Gold Harbor in just a few weeks. Apparently other islands existed, but Mid Isle was most used by trade ships, as it had a reputation for preparing you for Missea.

"Why do you need to prepare?" she'd asked. Tryst had smiled, but everyone had fallen silent to hear the Captain's reply.

"Missea is a place of moods," he had said, when he'd plucked a pipe from his mouth. "As winds change the ocean, tides of events change Missea. It's well to know which way the wind is blowing."

It was a small isle. Not content with their allotment of land, the islanders had spilled out onto the sea, constructing platforms and rafted buildings with rope bridges connecting it all together. It made for a delightful floating world.

The Captain claimed it was the long time at sea and not the Island's attractions that made people fall in love with it. But then the Captain hadn't wanted to sail that trip at all. Apparently he made more money when his ship was borrowed by a Skullan Captain and crew. They only traveled now because the Skullan had changed his mind after contracting for a special cargo.

"We'd have made a ton of gold without leaving home," the Captain had sighed. "The Skullan was going to take her twice as far as a Gold Harbor run."

"Where would he be going?" Tryst had asked.

The Captain shrugged. "He wouldn't say. Just suddenly found himself without the promised cargo."

Now Marra hurried through the deepest part of town, high on solid land. Somehow Drail had found a comet game, and the Illsmith was for any injuries the men might incur. For how could you be confined to a ship for five moons and not be affected when you played your first game on solid ground?

The comet field was as nice as any she'd seen outside of Port Leet. As with everything on the island, it had a small town-size with a touch of city sophistication. Good construction, quality details. Such as signs printed with actual letters, indicating the citizens could read.

Marra had walked the entire town just to practice her reading. She'd even purchased a book in a shop to improve her skills. The more she learned, the better she hoped to be at interpreting Mistress Britta's book of recipes.

Reaching the edge of the field, she realized she was late. Marra barely stepped beside Old Merle, Drail's mentor, before the four comet balls were hurled out onto the field of play. The four teams sprinted into action.

She watched Tryst weave – trying to shake a defender – but the man was tenacious. When Drail charged past, Tryst hurled the ball to him.

Drail launched the comet ball toward the tail, and Marra stretched her neck to see if it went in...

BOOM!

Tremors shook the ground, people screamed. A giant splash from the water nearby – and Old Merle grabbed Marra's shoulder. In the stands around them, the crowd heedlessly ran.

One woman tumbled into the running mass, her shrill scream abruptly cut off. The shriek spurred panic in the spectators.

They fled like desert hares, blindly leaping without thought. As likely to jump into danger as away.

Old Merle urged her towards the center of the field, and she ran to Drail. It seemed the one place no one else wished to go.

Tryst knew a cannon shot when he heard one. But no answering volley followed, no battle horn blared. He assumed it was some sort of exercise.

The crowd panic startled him. They must not be used to cannons, he realized. And cupped his hands around his mouth.

"Stop!" he shouted. "Don't run!"

No one seemed to hear him.

A man on a local team did the same thing, shouting at the stands. "Calm down! Please!"

And a third gamesman joined in. "Everyone stop!"

The words slowly rippled out, penetrating one mind, then another. A few people hesitated, a few more slowed. No more shots rang out, aiding the notion that perhaps they were safe. The panic ebbed.

People still hurried, but they no longer raced headlong in terror. Some paused for others, helping the old, picking up the young, where a moment before they ran over them.

Olver was staring at the other teams, one of which had already disappeared. "I think," he told them, "the match is off."

With a glance at another team captain, Drail shrugged and then grinned at Marra. "We've already had our elixir," he mused. "It will be interesting to see the effects off the field."

"I'm gonna find me a wench..." Manten began, as Old Merle joined them. Old Merle had been speaking to the field manager.

"Warships," he told them. "Just arrived in the harbor, and flying the Missean Flag. No other vessels in sight."

Tryst froze as the others relaxed.

Seeing Marra observing him, he forced a smile, even as his mind flew over the concept. The big Warships did not leave Missea lightly. They were designed precisely for war. Other military vessels traveled for various reasons, to show the flag, escort a high official. Negotiate a treaty.

Never the Warships.

"Ships?" He asked, keeping his voice casual. "As in more than one?"

"Five."

Tryst would have assumed whoever called it a Warship had no idea what they were talking about – except for the cannon shot. When a Warship approached with any intent other than battle, the cannon was fired to announce its arrival. The tradition was meant to empty its cannon, a gesture of disarm. Of course, with eighty cannons on board, one less loaded gun did not exactly render it defenseless.

In Tryst's whole lifetime he'd seen perhaps three Warships leave Gold Harbor. As fast as his mind raced, none of the possibilities that occurred to him were good.

Olver dug out Drail's scoring ball from the comet tail in the center, and wiped it clear. "Five-spot. We got the five ball," he announced. "Such runs our luck today - perfect score, and no one left to see."

Tryst only hoped their ill luck ended there. Turning, he hopped over a wood rail to climb to the top of the arena benches.

To see the ships for himself.

Watching Tryst ascend the stands, Drail sprinted to follow. They reached the top bench as the first Warship glided towards the pier.

The sheer span of her four masts impressed him, even with her sails already stowed. Skullan sailors tossed something over the side – seemingly another sail – and it dragged through the sea to slow her even more. And as she slipped past the Trafalcon, which had been the largest ship docked, he gasped aloud.

The Trafalcon looked a child beside its mother. Its length was less than half that of the larger vessel, its height a mere third. The three masts were as toothpicks compared to the four on the Warship. Like comparing one of little Marra's fingers against his own.

"I only see one ship," he murmured. And Tryst pointed out at the sea. Squinting, Drail could just make out a second ship, more than a quarter hour behind the first.

Even as he watched, the high sail arms on the distant ship folded upwards, and then rolled down the mast.

"I don't understand. Are they attacking?"

"They'll not fire cannons again," Tryst replied. But something in his tone showed the man didn't welcome the arriving vessels.

'Warships,' Drail said aloud. He'd heard the word, but really knew nothing about them. Now, seeing one so near, he felt a shiver trickle down his spine. "Is there a war looming some place?"

Tryst's hands dropped from shielding his eyes. "So it would seem."

The second ship's gangplank dropped into place as Tryst strode up the floating wharf.

Gangplank was a misleading term, for a Warship's plank was wide enough that five men could travel abreast. He'd walked them before, to inspect or tour. To be royally welcomed. He'd never boarded one outside of Missea.

And never alone. He wasn't even sure of the protocol.

Tryst, though no one knew it, was a prince, son of King Bactor, heir to the Skullan throne. Almost a year ago he had awakened on the Desert Flats to find himself surrounded by Trumen – the smaller, weaker, race. A race he usually interacted with as servants.

Not only had they failed to recognize his face, they

hadn't realized he was Skullan. Well, he was a smaller specimen perhaps. His father had promised he'd grow taller, but now – at the age of twenty-one – he doubted that would happen.

Beyond his size, his hair had grown out in the long, unnatural sleep, obscuring the truth of his race from a people that rarely saw his kind. Skullan males shaved their heads completely, and few Trumen realized they had hair to shave.

Now Tryst had a whole ship of Skullan before him, men who took an oath to serve the King. In theory he should be safe and finally out of this wild adventure.

In theory.

In fact, he doubted anyone could recognize him in his humble Trumen clothes. But he had to try.

Tryst strode to the top of the plank and paused at the three steps down to the Warship's deck. Waiting for permission to step aboard.

Across the huge wood expanse, the Captain spoke with a Lieutenant. The sheer size of the officer struck him – it had been months since Tryst had even seen another Skullan. Now every head before him was completely shaved and oiled, every sweat-covered body a third more massive than the average Trumen.

He'd forgotten how small he was amongst his own kind. Or perhaps it was the lack of royal trappings, standing here alone instead of surrounded by princely companions.

The Captain looked up and stopped speaking. For

an instant Tryst imagined himself recognized, as he indeed recognized the Captain. And then he saw the sneer, and realized it was merely contempt at a Trumen daring to approach a Warship.

Any thoughts of revealing his identity evaporated.

He forced himself to relax, waiting to see what the Captain would do.

The man turned his back.

After listening to his Captain's instructions, the lieutenant rushed over to Tryst.

"You may not stand there," the lieutenant said. Firm, but not unfriendly. Tryst felt the full weight of appearing a lowly Trumen instead of a Skullan prince.

And equally realized the impossibility of proclaiming his identity. He might not survive long enough to prove it.

Forcing a nod, he turned away. And then couldn't resist asking the question. "Where are you heading, Lieutenant?"

The Lieutenant raised his eyebrows.

"Warships do not travel lightly."

If the Skullan thought it odd that a Trumen on an island knew this, he didn't say. "We sail for Port Leet. Trumen have kidnapped the Prince."

Ten blinks of the sun later Tryst stood on the deck of the Trafalcon, urging they all leave immediately. But the Trafalcon's Captain, though very much in sympathy, couldn't set sail for at least twelve hours.

"There's the tide, you see. And the men, and

supplies. Aye, we'll go. But the morning's light is the soonest we can do so."

Drail, standing beside Tryst, smiled. "It may not be that important. After all, the Warships haven't really done any harm."

Standing at his rail, forty paces from the first Warship, the Captain did not return the smile. "I've heard disturbing tales," he muttered. "Things changing in Missea, they say. More restrictions for Trumen, more exclusions. More suspicion."

"Because of the Prince?" Drail asked. And Tryst bit his tongue to keep from uttering foolish things.

The Captain shrugged. "Skullan don't need excuses for that. Circumstances have been deteriorating for years. But lately it's accelerated."

The last of the Warships neared, heading for a berth on the far side of the Trafalcon.

"Never seen one of those outside of Gold Harbor," the Captain added under his breath. "Ugly thing, ain't she?"

As the sun fell below the island's west ridge, Drail set torch to timber. Their campfire blazed to life.

The Trafalcon had been in harbor three days before the Warships arrived. And while everyone in the Hand of Victory had berths in cabins of reasonable comfort, they all chose to sleep here on the hill. Even little Marra, after the first night, had found one of the colorful island sleep-slings and attached it to a tree.

The sling dangled from a sturdy branch, the bright cloth tied to either end of a pole. Marra said it was very comfortable, that the yielding cloth cradled you. But there was a trick to climbing in that eluded Drail.

Besides, he preferred his back pressed to earth. Something about feeling solid land beneath you gave comfort. A ship pitching with waves, even in the relative calm of the harbor, got very old.

Tryst licked goose fat from his fingers. "Tonight, I think Passing the Attack."

He'd been teaching them battle techniques, which had turned out to be very useful for gamesmen. Somehow the balance, efficient movement, and discipline improved one's comet form.

Tryst now faced off with Manten.

"The key is to consider the direction of the attack." Feet planted square to his teammate, his hands poised between them. "Whether the opponent has a weapon, such as a knife or stick, or just his hands and feet, he will direct a force at you. Men have a tendency to try to meet force with force.

"Instead, slip that energy past you."

Manten blinked – as confused as Drail felt.

Tryst saw their faces, and frowned. And then pulled Marra to her feet.

Marra had watched the drills carefully, yet she never participated as Drail expected. He'd thought she wanted to learn to protect herself. Perhaps the size of the men intimidated her, or maybe she just felt more secure these days. Whatever her reasoning she never tried the moves.

"Watch," Tryst said now.

He strode toward Marra threateningly, hands out to grab her. She held her ground, which made Drail smile, even as Tryst shoved her backwards.

"He can defeat a girl," Olver said. The others chuckled.

Tryst whisked Marra up off her feet, swinging her back to her original spot. He whispered in her ear as he set her down again.

Her eyes grew round.

Again his palms came up; again he purposefully strode toward her. Marra waited till his fingers just touched her shoulders, and suddenly pivoted, slipping to the side as her hands swept his past her. She'd sidestepped his attack.

"Marra cannot hope to out-muscle me. Instead of meeting force to force, she simply slides out of the way, allowing my energy to pass by rather than trying to stop it. If she does this fast, and at the proper moment, I'll be beyond her before I see her strategy."

Olver scoffed, but Drail was on his feet. "Try me."

And soon they all worked it, over and over. Faster and faster, until no one could lay a hand on another without resorting to more sophisticated technique.

Marra, Drail realized, watched intently. She never spoke, never asked for another turn. But where before she'd merely observed their drills, she now studied carefully. Very carefully indeed.

Early the next morning, Marra gathered herbs.

After living on the ship for so long, she'd been slow to return to performing the task. But once she'd rolled out of her sling bed and slipped away from camp, she found the task soothing somehow.

She enjoyed the solitude of the early morning, as the wild colors of dawn roasted the sky. For the few hours before breakfast, the world was hers.

Marra explored the wooded circle – a valley brimming with greenery, set between the island hills. The trees exploded with leaves, so many that their branches dipped low from the weight. Grasses and wild bush sprang up everywhere, some so deeply green that surely they couldn't survive anywhere but this lush, watery isle. Exotic blossoms, huge and vibrant, covered everything in breathtaking colors of yellow, blue, and bright red. No wonder the desert seemed monotone to outsiders, she realized.

Now if only she knew what properties these plants contained.

Long ago Mistress Britta had started a talk about new ingredients. A method for classifying herbs by their taste, which could hint at what they did. But that talk was never finished.

Regardless, she gathered all the healthy plants.

On her way back she heard a branch snap. Marra froze.

A second noise came from the same direction.

Creeping silently through the foliage, she peered past a tree dripping with ivy – and saw Tryst.

He was practicing with the sword he'd won from the Trafalcon's Captain in a foolish card game. Waving the blade through the air as he moved in a sort of rapier-dance. Slow, then fast, then slow.

She had watched Tryst perform dances like that – forms, he called them – without weapons in his hand. Now the slender blade seemed part of him, an extension of his arm, moving with an intricate rhythm. Gliding across the grassy carpet in a clearing in the trees, with the early island mist clinging to his feet, Tryst seemed more a vision than a man.

It was hard to slip away, but Marra felt wrong spying on him and withdrew through the ivy.

"Marra."

She froze, rolling her eyes at herself. And then stuck her head back through the green vines.

With the sword tip resting in the grass; Tryst beckoned her. She sighed and emerged into the green clearing.

"Have you come to practice?" he grinned. "I'd intended to work the drills with you today."

In response she touched the herb sash tied at her waist. Drail and the others would wave her away at this point, but Tryst merely cocked an eyebrow.

"It's best to pick herbs early in the morning," she told him. "Before the sun heats everything."

He held his hand out. She untied the sash, laying it carefully across his palm. He used the same care in setting it on the grass. "Now that you're here, you can practice Passing the Attack."

She frowned up at him, suspecting a joke. But his face seemed sincere.

"Why?" she asked.

"I thought you wanted to learn to protect yourself."

Now she knew he must be joking. "You taught me things already. How to make a fist."

He gestured her to proceed him, obviously expecting her to practice.

"Can a girl really protect herself?" she sighed. "From anyone who truly intends to harm her?"

Tryst blinked in surprise – whether surprise at the question itself or that Marra had asked it, she could only guess. But he pondered his answer. "Yes. Perhaps not infallibly. Maybe not against every foe. But she can study and practice techniques. Every skill learned, every ability developed, improves her chances. Adds an arrow to the quiver."

"I can't fight men," Marra scoffed. "I can't floor a drunk at a bar, or stop a Skullan from grabbing me."

"If you have a bit of anatomy knowledge, and a little skill, you can slip away. To flee, Marra. Not stand and exchange blows."

She suddenly remembered a Skullan long ago, who snatched her up off the street. She'd flailed wildly, and her foot struck him below his waist. To her surprise he'd dropped her, and she'd escaped.

Tryst waited. She moved a little away from him, shifting her weight to balance evenly on her feet as he'd taught the others to do. And she nodded.

The lesson began.

Tryst had not really taught before.

He'd been taught – by some of the finest teachers on all the Great Continent. And while he had instructed Mauric, one of the prince companions, on a few occasions, it had always been at Jason's insistence and under his watchful eye. Jason, the Defense Master, believed that true mastery began when one taught the art.

Drail had learned much from Tryst, but then Drail intended to learn. The others had picked up a few things, but seemingly more from Drail's example than from anything he himself did.

Yet here was Marra, so tiny and fragile, gazing up at him with a readiness. And she understood nothing, he slowly realized. Apparently there were many things males grasped from growing up – how to make a fist, what vulnerable spots to strike. She knew none of these things.

And she had faith that he could teach her. That he would teach her. She had *trust*.

They worked Passing the Attack over and over, until Marra slipped past him once without his being able to stop her. As he'd let her win several times at that point, she didn't realize the difference. And he couldn't tell her without admitting she hadn't succeeded earlier.

"That was well done," he said. She nodded once, barely acknowledging the praise, and set to do it again. He laughed and sat, stretching his legs out on the grass.

After a moment, she joined him.

"Are there other things to learn?" she asked, tying her sash around her waist.

He nodded. "Many. But this is enough for now. You must practice."

She looked at him, and he saw the thoughts in her eyes. The doubt quickly veiled, doubt of how she could manage to practice. She'd never ask any of them to help her, he realized.

"Find your training in everyday life, Marra. As people approach you on the street, slip past them at the last instant. Watch their movements – be able to predict them.

"When you see Drail and the Hand drill, pretend you're drilling with them. If Drail attacks Manten, pretend it's you. Feel yourself there – see your reactions in your head. In a tavern, outside in a crowd, alone in the woods. Conjure up the situation, and let yourself react. See yourself slip past every time."

"Practice – in my mind?"

He nodded. "It's almost as good as physical practice."

She digested this, her expression so serious. Smothering a grin at her reaction, he stretched. A shoulder muscle twinged in protest, and he rubbed it automatically. "I must have pulled that in a drill last night."

Marra dug into her cloak pocket and withdrew two cloth items. "Illsmith," she said, as if he'd know what that was. She lay a packet in the grass between them, and then weighed the second one in her palm.

"And what do I do with Illsmith?"

Hastily she untied the string, spreading the paper of herbs before him.

"A pinch in your hand," she told him, and plucked a tiny vial from her pouch.

Eyeing her with a rueful grin, he gingerly took two leaves, and lay them in his palm.

She poured a few drops of oil on top. "Rub vigorously, until it feels hot. Then apply."

He was very tempted to ask her to rub his shoulder – but teasing her at this point might make her wary of future lessons. And if there was one thing he could do to repay her for waking him that day in the desert – for probably saving his life – it was this.

Months back, on the Wavering Continent, Tryst had awoke from a drug-induced sleep. Far from home, and surrounded by Drail and the Hand of Victory. Marra, this little half-trained apprentice of potions and elixirs, had discovered the combination to wake him. Where he'd be if she hadn't – if Drail hadn't plucked him up from a backroom floor – he could only guess.

Now, as he massaged green mush into his shoulder, Marra unwrapped the second package. The contents gleamed in the morning sunlight -- a small, intricately bound book.

A book that, it dawned on him, was a fit gift for a prince.

"Herb lore?" he asked, watching her face.

Her fingers turned it over. He saw that the pages were edged in gold – with a tiny lock set in them. She tugged, but the book did not open.

Not a book at all, he realized. A clever box, apparently locked. For an instant he wondered what intrigue she was involved in – and then saw, from her widened eyes, that she was more baffled than he.

"Where did you find that?"

Her finger brushed the tiny lock, and withdrew as if burned. Marra then offered it to him.

"The boy in the herb shop gave it to me. He insisted."

Tryst found it heavier than it looked. And painted with gold. It had to be gold, as gold was one of the forbidden items. It was not allowed to fake gold nor silver in any way.

The top was expertly etched with a glowing image of a dark horse poised atop a cliff. Individual strands composed the mane, some lighter than others, and the stallion's eyes blazed with emotion. A raw sort of power.

This was no simple gift.

"Do you have the key?"

She shook her head, and shivered. He tried pressing the lock – but it refused to yield.

A messenger box. In the Palace, such boxes were used to deliver letters or small items to nobles far away. The boxes themselves were impervious to tampering. If the box was delivered whole, the receiver could be certain the contents within had not been disclosed.

He studied Marra's face – but she was genuinely startled.

"This," Tryst told her, "is a very expensive box. Few could afford such a thing."

"Those of Agben could."

At her words he noticed a tiny mark on the back. It was indeed the mark of Agben.

"The Herb Shop?" he asked. She calmly nodded.

But when she looked up, he saw the fear in her eyes.

"The boy probably thinks you're Agben. It's nothing to worry about." Unless Agben preferred to keep their communications quiet, of course. But Tryst wouldn't mention that.

"You can simply deliver it to the School when we get to Missea. It should make a welcome introduction."

She met his gaze then, and he saw she wasn't

fooled. She knew very well Agben might not welcome an unknown girl having stumbled upon a messenger box.

Truth was, the King's own boxes were on a par with this – some of them not as cunningly crafted. Whoever waited on this message was very wealthy, or very powerful.

Tryst rewrapped the cloth, and placed it in her hand. "You can always sneak it back to the boy, tell him he made a mistake. Just don't let anyone see you do it."

He stood, and flexed his shoulder, surprised to find it already easing. With an acknowledging grin, he reached a hand to help her up. "Shall we see if breakfast is ready?"

She hesitated, as always, before touching him. Then her hand grasped his, and he pulled her to her feet.

Dignity, the thought flashed through his mind. She had a careful dignity, probably hard won and definitely precious to her. He knew the bare bones of her life, but nothing more. Marra always answered direct questions, but she never elaborated.

As she moved up the hill ahead of him, and he watched the curves beneath her skirt, he realized where his thoughts were going and stopped them. Dalliance with a prince was supposed to confer an honor. But then she didn't know who he was.

And, he admitted with a wry grin, he strongly

suspected it wouldn't make any difference if she did.

Marra slipped the messenger box in her pocket when she saw the camp activity.

It was still early, and she hadn't expected everyone to be awake. But Olver was rolling up bedrolls and Manten shoving cooking pots into a bag as Drail untied her sling bed from the tree.

He greeted them with relief.

"The Trafalcon leaves as soon as we get there. Sooner, if we're not fast enough."

Tryst came up behind her. "Did something happen?"

Drail nodded. "There's talk of a tally today. A Trumen tally."

"Tally?" Marra didn't understand. "As in count?"

"That's the guess," Drail rolled the sling cloth around the pole, and stuffed the end in the cooking bag. "The Captain doesn't choose to wait around to find out."

Olver and Manten lifted bags to their shoulders and trotted off. She and Tryst hurriedly crammed their own items away, and followed Drail to the docks.

The next time Marra would remember the messenger box they would already be out at sea.

It was past the breakfast hour as the Hand of Victory marched along the floating docks, and Drail's stomach protested the delay. The Trafalcon, further down the quay, appeared ready to sail. Her crew shimmied up masts, hauling ropes and shouting instructions amidst occasional angry oaths.

The Warships themselves seemed ominously quiet. Docked on either side of the Trafalcon, they felt penned in, restricted. What if they wouldn't allow them to leave?

As he strode past the steel-tipped bow of the first Warship, Drail felt sheer awe. The thing loomed over him, more than four times his height. It was said that they had false hulls – which the hull you saw wasn't one at all. Stars, they were large enough he could believe it. Drail couldn't see the deck, but the sounds assured him that however early it was, men worked there.

The Trafalcon Captain hustled them aboard. They'd no sooner set foot to deck than the gangplank was pulled, moorings freed and the first sail raised.

"Best go swift-like," the Captain said.

They slowly slipped past the Warship, taking longer than Drail thought possible. As they drew abreast of the stern, a Skullan sailor all in red peered down over the rail.

The Skullan locked eyes with Drail. Watching.

Slowly the Trafalcon widened the gap, pulling farther away. The Skullan in red seemed to follow their path most carefully.

They passed the end of the wharf, and then eased by two more Warships anchored farther out. The crew worked feverishly to raise sails, hauling the lines until the sheets found proper angle and billowed with breeze. Even as the full winds of the sea thrust them on their way, he still watched.

The Warships rocked gently in the currents, making no effort to pursue.

Drail started breathing again.

2.

MAURIC DREAMT of a bewitching brunette, coyly beckoning.

He woke to a single candle and an open window. And a figure in the chair – far too big to be his brunette. He had to shake his head and knuckle his eyes before he could see.

"Jason!"

Mauric leapt up, flabbergasted. The man in the chair made no movement.

"Hello Mauric."

He slowly sat back on the mattress. It had been a year since he'd last seen this man, but he well knew that look on Jason's face.

"We thought you were dead. They said no one survived..."

The Defense Master watched him carefully, unwavering. A sudden flash of memory struck Mauric, of a time in the stables when Jason strode through in search of a ten-year-old Tryst who'd dodged sword practice. Mauric was a year younger than Tryst, Jason a full eight years older. And even then, the man had been a master of combat.

Jason had discovered Mauric in the stables, and stood gazing down without ever asking a question. The man then looked to the hay beyond, and stepped past to fish the young Prince out from behind a bale. Jason had always been very sharp, but at that age they believed him omnipotent.

Why he remembered that now, Mauric didn't know.

"You were ill the morning we left," Jason broke the silence. "So ill you sent Kellan in your place."

Mauric shook his head.

"You seem healthy enough now."

And that faint, nagging disquiet Mauric had felt a year past suddenly flared up like the sun on a morning hangover.

"No," he whispered. His mind searched for the words – but something in his expression shifted the mood in the room. Jason sprang to his feet, and punched the wall.

And stood there with his back to Mauric. "Tell me what happened."

"I was ill – so ill I couldn't move. I remember

someone by the bed, and the physician later. It was he who said you'd all left me behind. I sulked for three days."

The Defense Master turned, and Mauric felt profound relief as his tiny dimple appeared. Jason's lips never formed a proper grin, but that lop-sided dimple had enlivened many a night. "I was violently sick – food poisoning, they said. I think some suspected I'd drank too much, but none of us drank more than an ale the night before. You wouldn't let us."

Jason nodded. Pondered.

"That someone you first remember," Jason spoke softly. "Chamber maid?"

Mauric shook his head. "One of us." He thought back, remembering that damn awful smell from being sick. The bedclothes awash with his sweat. And the voice – whispering he was far too ill. Feverish. He mustn't see the Prince less he infect him.

"But I didn't ask to see Tryst," he said aloud. Jason cocked an eyebrow. "Baldar. He told someone I'd infect the Prince. Must have come to wake me."

"Baldar."

"He would, you know. We were friends – and about to go on the epourney. When I didn't turn up for breakfast, he'd seek me out."

"When did you last eat?"

"At dinner, most likely. Same as everyone else."

Jason leaned forward, staring into his eyes.

"Nothing else? No drink?"

"No – wait. Pomegranate. I tasted pomegranate – soaked in rum. Baldar claimed it a delicacy." Mauric remembered Baldar's face, teasing him into eating more. It had smelled so odd. Come to think of it, Baldar had seemed increasingly odd in the weeks before the Prince's epourney.

An epourney was the journey of manhood, a time to travel the world. A prince's epourney was a grand adventure indeed.

Except that this one had ended so horribly.

"I still can't think about pomegranate with feeling queasy."

He waited for Jason to pace – an old habit they all once imitated behind his back. But now Jason stayed perfectly still, reminding him of the proverbial viper. No one ever saw it move – but its stare could rattle an Elite Guardsman.

"Exactly when did you hear of the Prince's fate?"

"Not long ago – maybe a moon or so past. Someone found the camp site – the bodies. The Elite Guard itself marched off to examine it. Word was everyone was killed. All dead – except Tryst. The Prince had been taken."

"Who took him?"

"Surely you know more than..."

"Who did the guards say took him?"

"Trumen rebels. They found something – I don't know what. But they knew Trumen were behind it."

Mauric's mind raced, revisiting all the events, questioning anew. "I asked about you – about Baldar. The guard said everyone was accounted for except Tryst. No survivors. Stars – they said your hand still clutched a sword. The Court was told you died protecting the Prince."

Jason stood as if to leave.

"Great Constellation, you have to tell the King."

Jason shook his head. "The attack came from within. Elite Guard, Mauric. Two of the prince companions – Baldar, Kellan. Very likely their noble families. Think about it. This plot has very deep roots."

"You can't believe the King himself was involved. Against his own son?"

Jason shook his head. "Doubtful." He stepped towards the door, and turned back. "But the King's trust is seemingly misplaced with at least a few of his allies. I would know more before seeking an audience. Much more."

Mauric jumped up, striding to his wardrobe.

Jason's dimple appeared for the second time. "Just where do you think you're going?"

"With you." Mauric tossed a shirt over his head, and still not fully awake, got tangled in the linen.

He felt Jason's hand clamp on his shoulder. "Not this time, my young friend."

And when Mauric emerged from the cloth, Jason was gone.

Heavy clouds swallowed the moon, dimming the path. But Jason had already seen what he needed.

He was on the Gredge Road. Traveling west from the Crossroads Inn, where he'd spoken to a wench behind a bar. The wench had once worked at the Noble Seat of Gredge. She'd watched Baldar as a young lad, served meals when the family had guests, and had overheard some dinner discussions.

Unfortunately, she'd heard nothing of any use.

But she did know a mysterious brother of Baldar was returning to the manor from far away – it would take him a year to reach home. Mysterious because no one had known of his existence. After Baldar's death, his mother killed herself in grief, and his father had shut the manor down to travel to Missea. To be near the King, it was said. Another father suffering the loss of his son. The wench and many others had been released from service.

This new brother was most intriguing to Jason. He'd asked for details, but few were available. Jason was very willing to bet this brother would turn out to be a twin.

Crunch. His boot struck the gravel patch, and he continued, counting fifteen steps before the echoing crunch.

Jason calmly slipped around a tree, and ducked low.

It wasn't many heartbeats before the man hurried up the road. Actively looking for him.

Jason drew his knife as the moon drifted out from

its cloud cover, shining on the man's face. He tucked the knife away again, and stepped out. "What in the name of the Great Goose are you doing here?"

Mauric, slow on the draw, relaxed even as his hand touched his own rapier. "Coming with you."

"I left you deliberately, boy. This is serious business."

"It's *treason*," Mauric glared at him. Mauric, who had never dared glare at anyone. "I won't lie around an empty court, playing lawn croquette with useless fops."

"I realize you care – you want to help your friend. Laudable, but..."

"I will serve my Prince,"

And Jason found himself staring at the boy before him, impressed despite himself.

"I can't protect you, young Mauric."

"I seek no protection, Defense Master. I ask to serve my Prince."

Jason had a thousand reasons to refuse. Too young, too unknowing of what might lie ahead. But the boy was loyal and he knew it – and that was rare enough. Above all the others, Mauric had been Tryst's best friend. His companion in stunts and adventures that few others ever knew occurred. The real argument was Jason had no right to place the boy in danger.

But the Prince did.

"You will do as I tell you," he said.

Mauric nodded.

Still he hesitated. "This isn't an adventure. It may well be suicide."

"I swore to serve my Prince."

Jason studied the boy. And nodded.

Together they traveled up the road. "We'll have to get you a horse in Raggon's stables." Jason sighed. "I can see you're going to add to my expenses."

Rain smiled as she touched the velvet curtains, and the brocade canopy and glossy silk bedclothes. All handmade in cream color, with just the right touch of scarlet to add excitement.

The finery didn't impress her as much as the newness. Surely nothing in the room had been there a week ago. This chamber, her personal boudoir at the Palace, was truly her own room. Specially, thoughtfully prepared for her alone.

Rain turned to look out the elegantly draped balcony. In her mind's eye she saw not the garden courtyard, but the memory of the bustling harbor from her earlier walk. Several new ships had arrived this morning, and one must have her message. Her third and final message.

The reward for the first message had been a precious jeweled pendent. The reward for the second was the invitation to reside here at the Palace, in this wonderful room. She hardly dared think what the third reward might be.

And that itself was astonishing, for Rain was used

to good things. She was a Woman of Agben – possibly the most powerful in Missea.

Agben held more power than the Zaria Academy. And that drove those religious zealots insane with jealousy. They thought it was because of what the Women of Agben told the masses. The stories of deeds done, of miracles performed. The magic contained in their pretty bottles.

But the secret of Agben, Rain knew, was in the *not* telling. The mystery wrapped around the Agben Women, more than that surrounding the Agben School itself, served better than any story. When there was no information people tended to make up their own, and somehow those made-up tales were far scarier than truth. Something those old fools at Zaria could not see. They spent so much time yelling their silly beliefs they never actually listened.

Rain's father had been one of those Zaria zealots. Stars knew he never allowed a fresh thought to enter his head. He was always far too busy talking to think. As a teenager that had exasperated her, until she finally accepted that he would never change. He would never acknowledge her own ideas, or the logic she presented. And that had always annoyed her.

But his talking had somehow snared her baby brother. Zak had gone with the old man to the tower, the place to revere the Stars. Such towers were found in every major town on the Grand Continent.

Growing up, Rain had looked out for Zak, telling

him the truth when her father's lies weren't so apparent. She'd laughed at the old man, and made fun of him behind his back. And she thought Zak had appreciated her humor.

Then she left their home town for Missea. To attend the Agben School, which was her only choice, after all. Zaria refused to allow women within their hallowed halls. She'd studied the two full seasons required to make potions, and then the three more necessary to stand before the Elder Board to be judged a Woman of Agben. Few stood in judgment, and fewer still were so judged.

Rain had gone home in a haze of triumph to discover her mother dead, and her father raging – raging! – against her for wasting her life with defilers. Defilers of the faith, he'd called them, when she'd earned such an honor all on her own. But her father's respect was a goal she'd long since realized was useless.

It was her brother's reaction she never expected. All those seasons with her father, without her voice of reason whispering in his other ear, had turned him into another zealot. He'd set out for the Zaria Academy the day after her triumphant return, with nothing more than a harsh look for his older sister. Their father had succeeded in wresting Zak's love and respect from her.

And that was something she could not forgive.

Now, as she studied her reflection in the gilt-edged

mirror, she caught a strand of hair and tested the feel. It was soft, yes, remarkable for hair of such length. Skullan women chose the opposite of their men – they wore their hair long enough to be in danger of tripping their owners. This fate was avoided by scooping the strands into three carefully formed loops, each one longer than the last, dangling down the back. Indeed, dresses were designed to arc down in pattern, emphasizing the cascading hair loops.

Few women, truth be told, could grow their hair so long. It had become the fashion to rely on weaving lengths of Trumen hair to achieve the look. Apparently a whole industry in Trumen hair had sprung from it.

But Rain was one of the few who needed no weaving. She did, however, need her herb mistress in a small, out of the way shop. And she'd have just enough time to fetch another flask of growth tonic before the messenger could arrive from Gold Harbor.

The herb mistress, while far beneath a Woman of Agben, did have a way with beauty tonics. Her shop was crowded, but she beckoned her assistant to take over her current customer as soon as Rain strode through the doorway. Rain saw this, and smiled inwardly.

The tonic was ready for her – the mistress had counted the weeks before more would be required – and Rain didn't linger. That third message box could mean so much.

She stepped outside onto the bridge, smiling at the view. The shop was a fourth tier, the very best and highest tier a mere shop could be, and she loved looking down on the people far below her. Beneath her. Still smiling, she strode toward the spiral walk.

A hand grabbed her arm.

Rain whirled in astonishment, ready to tongue-lash the perpetrator. But her eyes caught the fox on the boot before she'd completed the turn. Even so warned, she couldn't believe it when she saw him.

Kratchett stood beside her.

Kratchett, who should be on the Wavering Continent. Unless, Rain frowned, the point of delivery had been in Missea after all. But studying his face, she knew success was not the reason for his presence. Words swam through her mind, but she held her tongue.

And he, reading her face as few could, merely inclined his head.

Together they strolled up the spiral walk.

The Trafalcon slowed near the land mass. And Tryst reacted despite himself.

The sight of the boulder face, rising skyward to tower over the ship, seemed to unnerve Olver and Manten and Marra. Even Drail watched with trepidation. It was forbidding, he supposed, that brown granite wall swelling high above the sea. But to

Tryst it struck such a chord of longing that it startled him. He'd seen it many times, of course, but only on short trips sailing his private boat, or touring on one of the King's fleet. Normally it meant the end of a little adventure.

After more than a year gone, today it meant home.

The ship nosed her way toward the channel that suddenly appeared between boulders. Dead on it looked a narrow slit, but as they came about full circle, the slit widened enough to accommodate three Warships abreast.

The Trafalcon glided the channel length, surrounded still by the towering boulders. And then the boulders stopped, and they were in the mouth of Gold Harbor.

Tryst smiled as he heard his companions' reactions. Gasps, exclamations. For Gold Harbor was leagues across, and the ship still had many blinks of the sun before they'd dock. If dock they did, for although the wharfs were four times as many as in Port Leet, the traffic vying for those berths was greater still.

"What do you suppose that is?" the Captain asked. Following the man's gaze, Tryst turned.

The mouth of the harbor was flanked on either side by what looked like a pile of giant redtree logs, with a small ship roped to each. Tryst had seen it before – on a drawing in the council room.

Preparation, he thought. For a war my father swore to avoid.

But he merely returned the Captain's look with a blank one of his own.

"Warships at Mid Isle," the Captain murmured. "And now this."

Marra clutched the ship railing as Missea grew closer and stranger.

Port Leet had had a number of three-story buildings, and she'd thought that crazy. After all, why did people need to go so high in the air with all the land at their feet? But Missea seemingly had no structure less than three levels, and many were four or five. One, if she counted correctly with the ship's rolling motion, was a full seven stories!

Surely people got dizzy so far off the ground.

Marra had to count the levels twice to be sure, because Missea was built on giant hills, as if they couldn't be bothered to find flat land. There were even dyed roofs. Stars!

When she was young, her mother made her a blue dress, having dyed the material. Everyone in San Cris wore the brown or flax hues of natural cloth, for no one would waste time nor copper on fancy dyes. In her blue garment, Marra drew such teasing and scorn that she ran home, tore the dress from her body, and swore never to wear it again. When her mother gently explained the blue was a pretty color for her, allowing her to stand out, Marra tearfully begged not to stand out. It was not good to be noticed.

Her mother never dyed another cloth for her again.

Now, as the Trafalcon drew closer, she realized the decorative rails she saw weren't decorative at all. Walkways and bridges linked the various stories, so that no one need ever touch the ground. And the roofs! Many were flat, particularly the smaller buildings, and those close to the harbor. But farther on small towers rose, with pointed cone tops swirling in outrageous color. Some of the towers themselves were round.

Round! How did you build a round room?

The Trafalcon dropped its last sail and glided toward the docks. Drail and Manten and even Olver were gawking as she must be, but Tryst's mood was very different. She'd sensed this was home to him – both familiar and welcome.

Then the Captain asked about the strange harbor contraptions, and his mood changed.

The Trafalcon found a berth on the docks. Tryst wanted to leap the rail and race toward the Palace, but willed himself to calmly wait.

When the inspector appeared, he thought it an elaborate joke.

A craggy Skullan, with a lopsided beard and a twitching hand, climbed the plank as soon as it touched the wharf. He stood there scowling and huffing, and insisting on studying each mark on the passengers – the expensive mark of health required before a Trumen was allowed passage to the Great Continent.

Tryst managed to keep his temper in the face of the Skullan insolence, but when the inspector started fondling Marra in unnecessary ways he placed his own palm on the bureaucrat's chest.

"You are finished," he said, in a tone he'd barely used in a year.

The Inspector glared at him, but finally backed down.

It was not the only incident to mar his homecoming. And as others occurred, Tryst wondered how much of this degrading treatment of Trumen was new, and how much had always been a part of Missea that he, in his ignorance, had simply never noticed.

Tryst strode past the Harbor Master's building, walking between the stone Chud and Churl, soldier statues from the first and second wars with the Trumen. He patted Churl, his personal hero, and entered the city of Missea.

He'd never actually wanted to leave. He had, to appease his father. And in doing so had seen much more than his sire could have possibly imagined. He'd experienced life not from behind a safe wall of protectors and mentors, but alone and defenseless.

How lucky he was that Drail had found him.

Royal leathers, he thought. I'll commission special comet leathers for the Hand of Victory. And something for Marra as well, though he didn't know what. He'd ask Jason – no. Not Jason. Jason had died defending him when he'd been kidnapped, the last thing he remembered before waking up in the desert.

Tryst broke into a trot, hurrying past the row of herb houses. In Missea, there was no single herb shop, but houses selling mixtures for specific needs to specific people. A Trumen remedy house, a Skullan House of Beauty. Rarely did elixirs for Trumen and elixirs for Skullan reside in the same place.

The first spiral ramp was at the end of the Wharf. It took him to the third tier, the fastest path to the heart of the city. For the Palace lay at the far northeast wall, and that was leagues away.

Before his epourney, he and Jason and Mauric would have whiled away an entire afternoon on a trip to the docks. Downed a pint at the Blue Anchor, which faced out on the water. Inspected a warship, just to feel important. Although Jason always insisted he was learning.

Probably they'd have stopped along the row of herb houses to pick up a bottle of Skin Proof, an ointment that was supposed to stop hair growth on Skullan heads. And he only just realized it hadn't worked so well after all.

He passed many familiar places, recognized a face here and there. It dawned on him that no one recognized him without his silk clothing, his dyed leather and jewels, and most especially without Jason and Mauric.

A prince is more manner than man, Jason had once told him. Tryst thought now the Defense Master had been wrong – it was the trappings that made a prince. The manner made a king.

It was at the tobacco shop he noticed the black.

Quentin's was not the closest to the Palace, but it kept a certain red leaf tobacco for Jason. Rarely had they gone out that they didn't stop in for another pouch.

Tryst smiled at the familiar area, at the same old woman sunning herself near the spiral ramp, at the fresh flowers growing in that old earthen pot. And then he saw the black cloth nailed to the Tobacco Shop's wall.

His heart plummeted. It was actually the third cloth he'd seen, and while the first two might well mean bereavement for the owners, this third hinted at someone much more important. But it couldn't be the King, he reassured himself. The King's death would have the entire city draped in black.

A prince's death would look just like this. Some would be leery of displaying black for a Skullan prince, others secretly sure he deserved it. The scattering few would proclaim themselves to be close friends – and Quentin, he thought, would be one of those. The Black may even be for Jason.

Tryst picked up his pace.

Faces and shops flew past as he sped by, his eyes

no longer on the street but on the growing Palace turrets. Turrets flying black flags.

The sooner he put an end to this, the better.

It took almost an hour to reach the final spiral. The entrance through the Palace Gates, indeed the entrance to any noble house, was from the ground. Only lesser abodes were reached by the tier walkways.

The Blue Gates were wide open, as always. But in place of the usual two Kings guards a full dozen stood, six on one side, six on the other. And two of those snapped to attention as Tryst approached. Blocking his access.

He stared at them.

The Palace gates were always open to anyone. The front gardens were renowned for their beauty; the inner welcome rooms a place to view the best of Missean art. And the famous King's Court allowed spectators to view Missean justice first hand.

Still, these guards did not move.

"Are the Palace wonders no longer open to Missean citizens?" Tryst frowned.

One of the guards stiffened at his tone. "Not since Trumen killed our prince." The man waved at the draped black upon the open blue gates.

Tryst almost reeled at the hostility in the man's voice. Hostility directed to the Trumen they believed him to be.

By the Great Goose, he'd never imagined standing on his own doorstep and barred from crossing the threshold.

"Where is Commander Gray?"

"Who?" The guard was getting surlier every blink of the sun.

"Commander Gray – Officer in Charge".

The guards exchanged a long look. "Commander Tillamen leads the Palace guards."

"What happened to Commander Gray?"

Frowning, the man called overhead, where a Lieutenant stood on the bridge across the gate opening. "Do you know a Commander Gray?"

The Lieutenant nodded. "His service was not up to Palace standards – since he ran the Palace guards when the Prince was killed."

The guard before Tryst took a step closer. "Now move along."

"I wish to see a Palace resident," Tryst stood his ground. Stars, he must see the King. "Mauric, of Canton."

The second guard frowned. Then called up to the Lieutenant, "he wishes to see Mauric of Canton, who he claims is a Palace resident."

The Lieutenant jerked a thumb, and a young sentry on the ground turned and trotted away. Another positioned himself to stop Tryst should he try to bolt inside.

It was while he waited that he really saw the difference. So few people passing the gates, guards actually patrolling outside. He'd always associated a warmth and welcoming at the Palace, although now he wondered how much of that was simply because it was his home.

There was no warmth now.

He wasn't surprised when the young sentry returned shaking his head. "Mauric of Canton is not within the Palace."

"Where is he?"

Surprised, the guard started to answer, but stopped at a gesture from the Lieutenant on the bridge. "You, Trumen," the Lieutenant called down, "have taken enough of our time."

And biting his tongue on a harsh rebuke, Tryst finally turned on his heel and left.

When they stood with the city of Missea spread before them, like the banquet feast his grandsire had described, Drail could barely restrain himself. After all the stories, every tall tale he'd ever heard, the reality surpassed them yet. Stars, what wonders awaited them here!

"Did you ever?" Old Merle grinned at his side. "Your grandsire knuckled his eyes almost out of his head, he was so stunned."

"Raston?" Manten whispered. Raston was Drail's grandsire, and a legend among them all. Raston had been, simply, the greatest gamesman to ever live.

Tryst had already left, telling Drail to leave word at the Trafalcon when they found an inn. The man had been distracted, and Olver had whispered a ribald comment about a wench waiting somewhere. Tryst had been a very dark mystery before he became a gamesman. And Missea was just the sort of place to spawn such mysteries.

Now Drail and the Hand of Victory followed Old Merle's lead, climbing the spiral walkway to the second tier. They stepped off the spiral – it continued skywards – to find themselves on a solid platform wide enough for a dozen people to walk abreast. Flower pots lined the way, large ones with pink and blue blossoms trying to trick one into feeling himself still on the ground.

The trick didn't work for Drail. While he'd enjoyed the suspended walkways over the water at Mid Isle, it was quite different to be striding so high above solid ground. To fall, he thought, would have much more dire consequences than a mere splash.

Not that there was much danger of falling – the intricate railings lining the walks were very solid. Occasional wood bridges arched across routes, but most of the tier pathways were paved with pieces of stone, like the road below. The tiers had obviously existed a very long time.

Adding to his disquiet was the population. Skullan lived on his home continent, but they were rare. A Skullan on the Flats might be intimidating because of his sheer size – but also an oddity. One might be wary, but not fearful.

Here, however, the ratio was reversed. Only one in ten were Trumen – and even less appeared on the higher tier walkways. Drail knew, of course, that Missea was a Skullan city in a Skullan land. But fables told by his grandsire were far different from actually walking the streets. Accustomed to standing a head above most men, he now found his eyes level with Skullan shoulders. It felt claustrophobic.

He glanced down at Marra, striding along beside him. Did she feel smaller still, or would she even notice? Right now her eyes took in all the sights, darting from a Skullan street hawker selling his wife's homemade pasties, to an herb shop proclaiming Male Vitality Potions, to a Skullan female in a bright blue dress.

Stars, a Skullan female. He'd never seen one before. He didn't know if any lived on the Wavering Continent.

They looked normal enough, except for being proportioned to match their men. But their hair! Drail had never encountered a Skullan with hair. And this woman's hair was incredibly long – ridiculously long. Rippling waves of it cascaded down her back, to dangle near her knee. Drail wondered how she could get anything done with all that hair hindering her.

He spotted a second female. And a third. All with the long dangling hair.

The crowd thinned a little as they left the harbor area. Old Merle pointed below, where a mass of hastily setup stalls housed vendors calling out wares to a milling throng.

"That's the Sea Market," he grinned.

And looking straight below him, Drail suddenly spied a comet stall. Leathers hung there, with decorations in hues he'd never thought possible. Wrist bands – surely that's what those were – with ribbons of color. But most astounding were banners with not just colors, but pictures on them. One with a beast's paw, another with crashing wave. Stars!

And then he saw a scarlet one with a thundercloud and a flash of lightning.

"Red Storm!" He halted, looking to Old Merle.

And the grizzled veteran gaped. "Well I'll be struck by a falling star."

Manten shook his head. "I don't..."

"My team," Old Merle grinned. "Raston's famous team that played the Skullan. It was the Red Storm. That booth is selling comet team banners – and one is the Red Storm."

"Do you think another team has taken the name?" Drail wondered.

"Doubt it," Merle could not tear his eyes away. "It's possible, but I doubt it."

And they continued on in a much lighter mood.

All his life Drail had heard about the Gold Harbor Arena. He knew it was blue/black, and made from some wondrous process of pouring stone. He knew its subterranean levels were five deep, and that a full seventy rows of spectator seats circled the playing field, allowing thousands to watch game after game while actually sitting. His boy's imagination had conjured some pretty wild pictures.

But none of them came close to the reality.

Rounding a corner, the Hand of Victory suddenly confronted the black structure, seemingly close yet hundreds of paces away. The circular wall stretched seven tiers into the sky, granted special dispensation from the Palace itself for such height. Either the color or the surface defied the eye, for it seemed to shimmer in the sun like a desert mirage. The paved stone bridge they strode upon widened so that twenty men abreast could enter. Through the open doors, the sunlight seemed to blaze as it hit the arched supports that crisscrossed the air above the arena. The building with the sky for a roof, Raston had called it.

Most comet fields were under the sky, of course. But Gold Harbor Arena was open by choice.

Drail hesitated on the threshold, and the others stopped beside him. He sensed that stepping inside would forever alter his life. For the first time he realized there were no guarantees that change would be for the better.

Then Old Merle clapped his shoulder. "Come see where Raston played."

Together they entered.

Overhead eight huge banners hung from a high arch, swaying in a breeze he didn't feel. Many smaller banners lay draped along the low wall surrounding the playing field, but the eight above had an air of permanence to them. A place of honor.

It was the sounds that caught Drail's attention. Grunts and shouts, running feet and the whack of the ball. Drail sped to the railing to see.

"It's so different in here," he heard Marra murmur behind him.

"The walls are slanted toward the sun," Old Merle spoke in a reverent voice. "It brightens the whole interior." He joined Drail to peer down at the field.

Below, two teams practiced. One man ran hard with the ball, intent on sinking it into the comet tail. A second man stood guard.

BAM. The guard rooted his feet and thrust a well-timed shoulder. Striking the runner – who flew backwards, smacking the floor in a cloud of sand.

Drail watched in concern, until the runner sprang up, spitting dirt from his mouth. And took the guard position, as the former guard snatched up the ball and trotted to position for his turn.

The drill was repeated over and over, with much greater force than Drail would have dreamed of using in a practice.

Old Merle saw his doubt. "The Skullan champions play hard. These aren't the rogue guys on the Flats, picking on novice Trumen teams to convince themselves of their worth.

"To play in this arena you must be the best."

A pinprick of doubt flicked Drail's mind. He squashed it.

Seven sets of stairs around the arena offered access to the higher rows of seats. Offset from those, three spiral steps reached lower to the arena floor. Drail chose one of those, trotting downwards to stand on the sand.

And then stood there, chin lifted to gaze at the eight huge banners overhead. The one for the Red Storm seemed to wave at him from on high.

We belong here, he told himself. I belong here.

A Skullan stepped before him, blocking his view of the banners. Blocking his view of everything. Drail was eye level with the man's solar plexus – making him the largest Skullan Drail had ever seen. The giant's jaw jutted out from his face, and a tattoo of a crashing wave rose from his neck to curl on his cheek.

"No fans on the arena floor," the Skullan told him. Firm, but not unfriendly.

"We're gamesmen," Drail replied. "The Hand of Victory – we won Port Leet. I'm Drail..."

"Another Port Leeter," the Skullan called over his shoulder. His team laughed. "Leave, oh mighty ones. You frighten us."

"You cannot play here, Trumen" one of the others called. "Athan, they waste our practice time."

The Skullan was looking down, smiling. Drail realized he was looking at Marra. "She can stay," he grinned. "Is the old man your teammate, or perhaps this cute little bit?"

"She is our Brista." Drail clamped down on his temper. "You will treat her with respect. And Old Merle was gamesman for the Red Storm." Drail pointed skywards.

The Skullan followed his finger – to see the banner flapping high above them. When he turned back, he was no longer grinning.

"That," he spat out, "is a myth. A fairy story to put happy little Trumen in their beds." Drail would have answered, but the Skullan glare cut like a dagger. "And my Brista has more important tasks than to watch our practice."

Marra actually took a step toward the gamesman. "There is no more important duty than standing by my team."

Drail shifted to protect her – and then realized the Skullan was grinning appreciatively.

"Feisty," he said. "You Trumen are feisty. What do you say, men?"

The Skullan whirled, waving an arm at the Hand of Victory. "Shall we play them tomorrow night?"

"Oh, but..."

Drail silenced Old Merle's speech with a gesture. Merle would rather they practice for months, especially after the long sea voyage. This opportunity, however, would not come again.

Drail bowed. "We shall be here tomorrow night."

Turning on his heel, Drail strode away.

"Bring the little Brista," the Skullan called after them. "You'll have need of her services."

Laughter followed them up the spiral stairs.

Athan watched the Trumen go.

Nag joined him, punching his arm. "Bit cruel, that. They have no idea what they've agreed to."

"They wish to play Gold Harbor Arena. We will let them."

"You just wish to see the little filly again." And Nag trotted back to practice.

Athan paused to look up at the scarlet Red Storm banner. His finger traced his face tattoo, the mark of the Black Tide. The team of his father.

The Black Tide banner hung behind him, on the low wall with many such banners. The teams represented there were in some favor, and would remain on the wall until a new favorite rose to replace them. Honor, here, was fleeting.

Not so the Arc Banners. Once a team's banner hung on high, it hung for eternity.

The Black Tide, under his father, had won no less than three Gold Harbor Championships. To win three in a row supposedly guaranteed Arc honor. But his father had lost a middle game, winning his third after losing the prior year. It was decided that was insufficient.

Now Athan carried on in his place, and at his instigation. It was unusual for a son to play on a father's team, under a father's banner. New teams, new men, meant a new banner. A banner of their own.

His father, however, had insisted.

The man's dying wish had been for Athan to somehow earn the Arc spot for the Black Tide. Against his own gut instinct, Athan had changed the name of his Daggit's Paw team. Even after his stepmother had warned him against it.

He should not have challenged the desert dwellers. Probably, he realized, he'd been jealous. This ignorant Trumen steps on his field, disrupting practice, with a sweet little morsel he claimed for Brista. Indeed a defiant girl with a loyalty he'd never seen in his own Brista. And then to hear that dust-dog claim an Arc Banner belonged to his own family...

Such arrogance deserves punishment, he told himself. Because it had rankled. Especially after losing the championship just a season ago. It took three championships in three years to claim a banner. He had yet to win one.

I'm doing him a favor, Athan told himself. The Trumen needs to find out just how far from Port Leet he has come.

3.

TRYST KNEW a full dozen entrances into the Palace. Private accesses for nobility, special trade doors for merchants. There was even a servant's passage. He tried them all.

Seven were closed. Two of those seven were actually walled up, including his own private entrance. The remaining five, like the main gate, were heavily guarded.

One of those was below ground, serving now as both tradesman and servant entrance. No less than a dozen guards flanked it, and each entrant was checked thoroughly. Tradesmen were forced to dump supplies outside for Palace guards to inspect before servants bore them away.

Tryst had approached that entrance asking for

Mistress Anna, the housekeeper in charge of the servants. Apparently she still worked within, but it was a gaunt, forbidding female that appeared in her stead, demanding he state his business.

After a short and heated debate, the Prince had spun on his heel and walked away. And when he reached ground level again, he'd smashed his fist against the old stone wall. Cutting two knuckles.

Proclaiming himself Prince now might get him in. But tempting though that was, members of the King's own Elite Guard had betrayed him. And while these new security procedures might stop any threat to the King, a deeper purpose could be to bar him from seeing his father, if the traitors had control of the Palace.

Probably the traitors had control of the Palace.

His only remaining idea was Magda, his nurse and nanny who had raised him from a very small boy. She'd long since left the King's employ, having married and moved to an area near the Land Market by the old gate. Unfortunately, he knew not where she actually lived, having never tried to visit her. And it was eight years past – she might not even be there now.

This emerging pattern, he thought, was not very flattering to himself. So few friends, so few people he ever really bothered to appreciate. Apparently he didn't know anyone well enough to ask their help now.

What kind of prince would be shut out of his own

Palace? Just what manner of fool had he been?

Eventually, Tryst made his way back to the Trafalcon. And was astonished to find the Hand of Victory would play the very next evening, in no less a place than the Gold Harbor Arena. He'd watched the games there, in the royal apartment with a wide balcony looking out above the field. Somehow his memories of the skills he had witnessed did not match with the level of Drail and the Hand. Certainly not with himself.

The Gold Harbor balcony.

King Bactor always enjoyed a good comet match, as indeed did First Minister Charis. If Tryst were to reveal himself on the field, in front of the entire arena, no enemy could do more than bite his lip. No rumors could hide the truth revealed to the whole of Missea.

And then, he vowed, the hunters would discover how it felt to be prey.

The Hand of Victory chose the Arc Banner Inn because it was close to the arena and because the men loved the name. There was an even grander place, the Gamesman, but Trumen were barred from its doors. The Arc Banner offered them rooms on the attic floor, reached via a back staircase.

Marra found herself in a small room with a tiny balcony high above the ground. Although with all the tiers of traveling, the ground didn't seem to mean much here in Missea.

Once unpacked, she checked her herb sash. The Birr Elixir ingredients were all there, though some of the lesser ones smelled a bit stale. And for such a challenge as they faced, she wouldn't dare use anything but fresh.

In her home of San Cris, she'd tie the sashes round her waist and tramp off to the desert. Here there seemed no place where plants grew – at least, not such that they didn't belong to someone. She didn't like relying on herb shops, but perhaps someone there could advise her.

As she unpacked the second sash, the messenger box fell to the carpet. Marra sighed.

Tryst had suggested she take it to the Agben School. Just walk right up, knock on the door, and hold it out. But someone there, she was absolutely certain, would demand to know who she was and just how she happened to have something so important on her person.

She didn't look forward to that.

So now she tucked it back in her bag, took her sashes and the coin Drail insisted on giving her from their prize money, and headed out into the city.

Tryst had told her the higher the tier, the better the shop. But it hadn't taken her long to realize that no Trumen walked above the fourth tier. Indeed, even on the fourth they were rarely seen. At least the herb shops were plentiful, once she realized what they were.

The first one she entered proclaimed itself to carry the best vitality potions in Missea. These potions, it turned out, served only males, and only Skullan at that. The Skullan shopkeeper shooed her from the premises. After two more such experiences, she dropped down to the third tier, where she soon found a "Female Health" shop.

The sight of the huge Skullan woman nearly sent her fleeing the place. But the woman approached slowly, extending a hand. "And how may I help you, young miss?"

Marra looked over the jars on the many shelves. She saw no ingredient she recognized – indeed, the few words she could read were "Hair Growth" and "De-Muscler".

"I need some herbs," Marra replied, still scanning the wares. "Do you have Ragwhort?"

The Skullan looked her over more carefully. "You are new to Missea, girl."

Marra nodded. "New to the whole continent."

"All tier shops sell potions and such. Ingredients are on the ground level – for the shopkeepers, you see."

"Thank you," Marra said, and meant it. "You've been very kind."

The woman nodded once, frowning. "Trumen shops are marked Trumen. If Trumen are not mentioned, the shop is for Skullan."

Something about her tone warned Marra not to

come back. "I was kind," the shopkeeper added, "because I mistook you for a servant."

Marra fled.

There were few ground level shops. Staring at a tavern called "The Trumen Slave", she suddenly remembered the Sea Market Old Merle had pointed out. Climbing again to the third tier, she was able to spot the harbor. And in heading towards it, the Sea Market stood out.

If she hadn't seen the Market, Marra thought, the hum of people would have pointed the way. It thrived near the docks, spilling out across old wooden boards no longer used by ships. The soothing rhythm of waves lapping the wharf enhanced the blue sky and salty tang in the breeze. Trumen mixed with Skullan here, and she didn't feel quite so uncomfortable.

Open air stalls crowded each other, seemingly with no structure other than find a space and claim it. Shopkeepers called, "Freshest fish!" and "Desert Flats cloth!" Marra marveled that the last would seem exotic to Misseans.

The paths through the stalls tangled and swelled with people.

A woman selling tiny toys offered an exotic herb she swore came directly from the Dim Continent. Marra recognized it as powerful – but she had no idea what its properties were.

Neither had the woman.

Farther on, a wizened Skullan sold many herbs

from all the continents, or so he claimed. Some were fresh, most were not, although a selection had been deliberately dried. Marra wondered if that preserved the properties, and asked him.

"Of assuredly so!" he eagerly promised, and unwrapped a single pocket herb sash to show a mass of dried white petals.

"What are those?" Even dried, Marra could smell the sweet aroma, twice as strong as a fresh cactus flower.

"Why, Peet Carnation, Miss." The Skullan seemed startled that she didn't recognize it. "Most powerful cleanser on the continent. Very much in demand – and not so easy to find, properly dried like this."

"A cleanser?"

"He means internal cleanser." A young woman, a few years older than Marra, approached. She was Trumen, and wore simple linen as Marra did. But the Skullan seemed nervous.

The young woman smiled at Marra. "It is indeed very good at removing toxins from both Skullan and Trumen bodies."

"Properly dried," the old Skullan insisted.

"So it is," the girl nodded, "for shipment away from Missea." She turned to Marra, grinning as she tossed her long brown hair over her shoulder in a practiced fashion. "Peet Carnation grows just outside the city walls – indeed, in flower pots within. You don't want this here."

Amazed, Marra stared at the Skullan – and was even more amazed when he suddenly laughed aloud.

"Your pardon, little lady," he bowed. "I know better than to push such wares at yourself."

The girl held out a hand to Marra. "I'm Leah. And I'm guessing you're not from the city."

Marra found herself smiling back, and clasped the hand so offered. "I'm really in need of Ragwhort."

The shopkeeper reached for a pottery jar, but the girl shook her head. "You'll want to buy that at the Land Market. That's a bit of a stroll from here."

Biting her lip, Marra realized she'd need to mark the route carefully. She was getting too far from the inn for her comfort, but she needed the Ragwhort. "Which direction..."

"Let me walk with you. I'll show you the fastest route."

Marra hesitated. But Leah seemed friendly, and it would be far easier to go with her than try to find it on her own. She nodded.

Leah waved at the Skullan shopkeeper, and they left.

At the edge of the Sea Market two more shopkeepers called out to the girl, who merely nodded in return and strolled up the ramp. "Faster to go second tier," she grinned.

Marra tried to study Leah without staring. She wore linen as Marra did, but her cloak was surely dyed just a tiny shade greener than natural hue. And the buttons gleamed when the sun caught them – metallic, not knots of cloth as Marra's were. Her shoes, too, were deceptively simple, merely encasing her feet and leaving her ankles bare. But they appeared to be a thick, quality leather.

"Do you like my cloak?" Leah asked. She then pointed at a tiny shop with bright wraps and mantles hanging outside. "Madame Trak has the most beautiful colors."

Marra stared as they passed. Leah stopped with a questioning look, but Marra shook her head.

They rounded a corner and paused. A large brick building ran the whole length of a block, its walls as high as four tiers, maybe more. There were no windows at all – only a single gate in the center of the block.

"What is that place?" Marra asked.

"That, my dear, is the Agben School."

Feeling Marra's interest, Leah reached into her blouse and produced a hanging silver pendant – a dove with sparkling blue eyes, perched on a branch.

"That's beautiful," Marra exclaimed, and Leah shook her head and burst out laughing.

"It's a symbol of Agben."

Leah strolled on. After a last long look at the gate, Marra hurried to catch her.

When she drew abreast, Leah gave a knowing smile. "At least you've heard of Agben. Have you come to seek schooling?"

It was a simple enough question. And it spun Marra's existence on its ear.

Old Merle had them practice all that afternoon and next morning, and then drill when the noon meal had barely settled in their stomachs. Drail finally called a halt with hours to spare, so they could rest before the game.

And Drail was never the one to stop.

No one said it, of course. No one dared give voice to the doubt that crept into the bone marrow, clinging relentlessly. But this would be the first game Drail ever walked into without feeling sheer joy.

When Marra held out the glass vial of the Birr Elixir, he found himself grasping her hand for a moment. Such a small hand, he thought. How could women – how could anyone – go through life being so small and fragile? Trusting the world to not utterly crush them? It didn't even take evil intent to do the damage. Just a careless move.

"Is there an elixir for luck?" he asked her. And he awaited her answering scorn or pity.

Instead a new light grew in her eyes. "I do not know," she said.

After Marra had given Drail and the others the Birr Elixir, they marched towards Gold Harbor arena. And her mind flew faster than her feet.

They called her Brista to the Hand of Victory.

While it was an honor she greatly cherished, she never actually used the term herself, because she felt little more than a lucky girl who managed to make one potion from her mistress's old book. She could hardly claim to be anywhere near the skill of her teacher.

In truth, Mistress Britta had barely started her training.

Marra had since combed the pages of Britta's handwritten notes, studying every word in that old book. She'd wanted to be of more use, to discover other treasures that could benefit Drail. And she had found salves and balms which soothed muscles or healed scrapes after games. But really nothing more than they could have purchased themselves for a few coppers.

When she'd first opened the heavy tome her reading skills had been weak, yet over time Marra taught herself a great deal. And once she understood some rather challenging words, she had indeed found interesting recipes. But she lacked key ingredients. Indeed, exotic words had leapt off the page, with no way to judge whether they were rare to everyone, or just rare to a humble desert girl.

From previous experience, Marra knew it could be dangerous to ask for unknown ingredients without first understanding what they were. Such questions had led to two encounters with Women of Agben, and one had not been pleasant.

Leah spoke of the School of Agben, right here in

Missea. Anyone could walk in and ask to learn. Anyone. There were questions that must be answered satisfactorily, and tests that must be passed. But if she succeeded in these, they would teach her.

Leah also cautioned that few would be taught enough to become a Woman of Agben. But Marra had never aspired to such a thing. All she wanted were answers to her many questions. For someone who understood the art to point her in the right direction.

She wanted to *know*. She'd wanted such knowledge within the first month of meeting Mistress Britta.

Now the sun slipped below the Missean skyline as the Hand of Victory approached the arena. The last golden rays sparkled off the poured stone structure, making it appear more a hole in the landscape than a real place.

Old Merle led them down a ramp to a ground level street. Drail was fidgeting, and Marra realized they'd never entered a playing field just before a game. The Hand was always early to practice, testing the surface and learning the subtle differences of the center cone. Drail used a special ritual to calm himself, to prepare.

It had all been denied him tonight.

They entered the Gold Harbor arena.

There was no roar of the crowd. Silence met them as they marched down to the sand pit. Light sprang up all around as men touched torches to braziers. The flames blazed brighter than she would have dreamed possible.

Cheers burst around them as the arena lit up.

Old Merle clutched her arm, tugging her away from Drail and the others to a side wall. Her palm rested against it to steady herself, and she felt cloth. It was a huge team banner in black and gold. Not red, the Hand of Victory's color.

Scanning the arena, she first perceived that the torchlight truly was brighter – it hadn't been her imagination. Marra had heard of burn cloth – special cloth treated with an herbed oil that made it burn long and bright – but she'd never seen it till now. It was said to be too expensive for the likes of the Flats where she grew up.

And in that bright light she realized that none of the four team banners which hung lowest - which surely marked tonight's teams - belonged to the Hand of Victory.

For a few minutes, Drail's spirits lifted.

He loved standing in this great arena as the light blazed forth, his ears thundering with the crowd roar, the newly combed sand shifting beneath his feet. The comet tail winked at him from across the field, and he briefly wondered if it, too, was made of poured stone.

Instinctively, his eyes sought his opponents.

Across the grit expanse he saw four men striding out to meet him. Beyond them fluttered the black banner with the wave – signaling the Black Tide team. As they drew close Drail saw the echoing wave on their leader's face. The Skullan they had met before.

But something was wrong. Comet was played with four teams, not two. Yet no others appeared.

Drail turned, not even knowing why until he focused on the black and gold banner behind him.

"Stars," Tryst breathed.

"Where are the other teams?" Manten hissed.

"They'll be here later, when the games begin," Tryst told him.

And Drail saw Tryst staring not at their opponents, but at a balcony above them. It was large, slightly lower and cordoned off from the rest of the crowd. A flag hung from it, not vertical as the team banners hung, but horizontal. It was the flag of Missea.

The box was empty.

A Skullan dressed in a long robe strode out to the center of the field of play. Drail frowned, for the man's robe was a dark green, not the traditional white worn by the judges.

"WELCOME!" he called out, and the word seemed to vibrate off the arena walls. As in Port Leet, one could speak in a normal tone on the arena floor, and the words carried to the highest tier of spectators.

"Tonight, we bring four great matches. Eight rising teams from the outer reaches of the continent and eight Missean favorites to show them how we win in the King's own city!"

A resounding cheer answered him, even as Drail understood. The Hand of Victory was not playing comet in the Gold Harbor arena. They were some sort of exhibition, a warm-up before the real games began.

"It's only fair to show those visiting contenders just what they're about to battle."

Scattered laughter, catcalls.

"The Black Tide has graciously offered to demonstrate."

Spectators roared approval.

"I don't understand." Manten slowly pivoted, staring up at the mass of faces as if they'd somehow provide the clue.

"We're not a challenger – we're a whetstone," Olver hissed. And the words cut deep because Drail knew them for truth.

The robed Skullan gestured and four young Skullan boys, each carrying a ball, trotted out to the center. The grinning Black Tide leader stepped over the line around the comet tail, and Drail realized just how bad it was. In a proper game, no one would dare cross that barrier until the judge gave permission.

Of course, there was no judge now. Not for mere Trumen.

Drail squared his shoulders and marched out to join the Black Tide leader. The Skullan gestured to the four balls. "Choose two comets, Trumen."

"Comets?"

The Skullan rolled his eyes. "Here in the real world, we call a disguised ball a comet. Until it reveals its spots."

For a moment he stared. And then Drail snatched up the two closest.

"Then we call it the three-spot. Or the no-spot. Or possibly the five-spot." the Skullan laughed. "In which case, it's mine."

Gritting his teeth, Drail stalked back to his team. Scoring in comet depended on more than who sunk the first ball. It also hinged on the point value of the ball sunk. All balls were coated with a sticky dirt that gradually eroded as the game progressed. As each team could only score once, the first ball in the cone did not always mean victory.

Olver and Tryst looked as grim as he felt; Manten seemed dazed.

"We play," Drail told them. "We wipe the smirk off their arrogant faces."

"BEGIN," the robed one called.

Four Skullan stepped around the cone, forming a line between the Hand of Victory and the comet tail.

It was a move Drail had never seen. In a real game, they should have started in their quadrant, as his team did. They should move to sink a ball.

The Skullan leader shot his ball – not at the cone, but at them. Spinning, it struck the ground at Drail's feet, blasting a wave of sand high in the air.

Drail shielded his eyes as the Skullan roared with laughter. "True dust-dogs – confused by dirt."

The second comet landed at Manten's feet, showering grit in a wave cresting like the leader's tattoo. To prove it was no accident, Drail guessed.

Tryst took off, circling behind the Skullan. Manten, dazed, looked to his leader, and Drail jerked his head to indicate a direction. Hesitant, Manten finally circled.

Drail sent a ball to each man just as he slipped behind the Skullan. The Skullan team exchanged a grin and turned to follow. But they didn't chase the men – just slowly moved to stay between them and the cone.

Drail snatched at the ball at his feet – but it was imbedded in the sand, such was the force used. He had to wiggle it free. Beside him, Olver had even more trouble with the second ball.

Out of the corner of his eye, he saw Manten launch a beautiful shot. It should have sunk into the tail – except that a smirking Skullan whirled and caught it with one hand.

One hand.

And continued his spin to shoot the ball at Drail – striking his own comet he was just lifting. Blinding him in the crash of sand.

When Drail cleared his eyes, both balls were now imbedded in the arena floor.

The crowd hooted with laughter.

Why weren't they shooting at the cone? The Skullan could have easily sunk two balls by now, even assuming their accuracy was worse than the Skullan in Port Leet. It made no sense.

A fourth ball, somehow intercepted from Tryst, came flying towards his feet. This time Drail dove under it, catching the thing before the sand could blind him and continuing the roll to his feet again. Drail ran, straight toward the remaining two Skullan.

Delighted gasps from the crowd were smothered in the Skullan's answering roar. Drail hoped he'd angered them, but as he leapt up, five paces before them, releasing a perfectly aimed ball, he caught the look in the leader's eyes.

The man was amused.

Drail arced high in the air, intending to send the ball over their heads into the cone. But the leader knew – as if he'd seen the move a thousand times before. And was confident he could defend it, as he'd probably done a thousand times before. Timing his own jump perfectly, the Skullan caught the ball one handed.

Stars, those hands were big. They could palm the balls, actually hold them with one hand.

Drail never saw the desert Skullan do such a thing.

And the leader threw the ball away again, this time spinning not into the sand, but against the leather covering Olver's stomach.

The sand and grit on the ball spun off, creating a tiny cloud. Underscoring the stunned look on Olver's face.

The merriment of the Skullan team and the spectators seemed to meld. It felt familiar – and Drail flashed back to a time when he was six years old, when the older boys had teased him. Showing him he was too little to play them. Too weak, too puny. Calling him a dust-dog.

Just as the tattooed-wave Skullan called him so now.

Olver stood stock still, as if he couldn't think what to do next. Manten bent over, trying to snatch a buried ball free of the sand and discovering, as Drail had, how difficult that was. Drail watched the Skullan trot past the hunched man to nail him with an elbow.

Manten pitched forward face first, causing yet another dust cloud. When the cloud cleared, he hadn't moved.

Tryst launched himself at the offending Skullan, catching him mid-body and driving him to the dust. They should have both sprawled in the sand, but somehow Tryst rolled to his feet again, standing over his quarry.

The fallen Skullan was astonished. Even the crowd fell silent.

Such a look of retribution flashed across the gamesman's face that Drail found himself sprinting to help Tryst.

The Skullan sprang to his feet, fingers balling into fists. Fists the size of a sledgehammer.

"HOLD." All eyes turned to the Skullan leader. He jerked his head significantly.

His three teammates spun on their heels and

strode off the field.

Drail gaped after them.

Tryst immediately swooped down to retrieve a ball – and send it hurling toward Drail. Snagging it automatically, he pivoted to shoot it at the cone.

The Skullan leader dove, catching it with one hand and hurling it back to Manten.

Manten caught it, pretending to launch it to Drail, but this time spun and threw for the cone. With the Skullan leader so close to center field, he had no trouble intercepting it again, and this time drove it spinning into the sand at Olver's running feet.

Olver tripped over it. The crowd jeered.

Humiliation, Drail thought. The tattooed Skullan wants to prove just how superior they are. How superior he is.

And so it continued. Manten or Tryst or Drail launched a ball; the Skullan easily caught and returned it at their feet. Three, four, five times. An entire team of men who'd won Port Leet, stymied by a single Skullan gamesman.

And then Drail launched one – and the Skullan stepped aside. Letting it pass him.

The ball missed the comet cone and the Skullan laughed aloud.

Tryst angrily hurled a second one immediately, and this time the Skullan caught it. Brought it high over his head.

And turned, pausing. The whole arena held its

breath.

He sunk the ball.

There were no victory cheers. Just laughter, clapping, as if a traveling lute player had finished a particularly ribald song.

It was the height of shame.

Drail did sink his ball in afterwards, hoping to take the Skullan off guard. But the Skullan saw it.

And actually ducked. Allowing it to go in.

The Judge moved out onto the field. He clapped the Skullan on the back, before raising his hand high in victory, without even checking the balls in the cone. The crowd cheered.

"Let the competition begin!" the Judge shouted.

And as the other Skullan teams trotted out, Drail saw nothing to do but retire from the field.

Marra realized she clutched Old Merle's sleeve, and forced herself to let go.

It wasn't a loss, it was total degradation.

She saw Drail's face, felt his pain. The team looked like small boys playing their much older brothers, who toyed with them until the novelty wore off and they chose to end it.

The Skullan with the wave tattoo trotted off the field, grinning like the kid who'd snuck a pie from the ledge without getting caught.

And he was trotting towards her.

"They won Port Leet?" he asked. Conversationally,

as if they were relaxing in a tavern somewhere.

She nodded.

"Wavering Continent's worse than I thought."

Marra's fists clenched.

"You, Brista," he gazed down from a very great height. "If you wish to be a true Brista, for an actual team, I will take you."

Her mouth fell open.

"Truly," he said. And she could not doubt the sincerity in his eyes.

It was all she could do not to kick him.

The horses galloped down a steep slope.

Side-by-side they raced, the sounds of panting steeds and hooves striking turf lending a feel of the old days, when Jason raced the younger men through meadows beyond Missean walls.

Each stride leapt farther down, farther, adding to the rolling rhythm on horseback, the sense of controlled danger, the sheer speed.

For a moment, it was enough. Enough not to think, enough just to feel.

Foolish really, this headlong flight. If he had Zyphyr, his old stallion, the risk would still not justify it. Zyphyr had been a gifted animal, but like so many things, was now lost. He'd checked the Palace stables, and found a giant Brushfoot steed in his prized stallion's old stall.

Jason stole a look at Mauric, whose youthful face

echoed his own pleasure in the run. They really ought to slow to a safer pace, he thought, even as they galloped on.

It was three weeks journey to the outlying Borden area, a small seat with a very wealthy noble. A noble Jason had never heard of until Kellan appeared at court. Borden was in the Nirr Province, and oddly enough two soldiers from Nirr hadn't heard of this lord.

This wealthy Borden peer was Kellan's father. Kellan, the prince companion of barely two months before the fated epourney. Kellan, who must have brought a letter from the Duke of Nirr, or he'd never have been accepted at court.

Kellan, who from all he could gather, was at the heart of the conspiracy against the Prince.

It appeared Baldar's return had been well-laid out. Proclaimed dead in the Prince's kidnapping, Jason suspected after a discrete passage of time that the man would return home as his own twin brother. With all the new people at Baldar's manor, it would be an easy thing to accomplish. Jason would wager his fine new horse that Baldar's father had been persuaded into the plot, probably with a nice chest of gold and a promise of royal favor. He'd always been ambitious – hence his son's becoming a prince companion. For Baldar in truth had been a bit too old, a bit too sober, and his province already represented.

In short, he'd offered nothing in the way of

education or support for a young prince. But Bactor was an easy-going liege. And possibly someone had pressed for his acceptance.

Indeed, someone must have pressed for his acceptance. It would be interesting to discover exactly who that someone was.

The slope before them now flattened out, yet Mauric did not slow his pace. This was the Draylin Provence, Mauric's home, and they were not very far from his family holdings. It was obviously familiar terrain.

But Mauric, much to Jason's surprise, never hinted at stopping by Canton manor. He seemed determined to pass on, to reach Nirr before the end of the week. At another time, Jason would have relented and called for a few days halt with the boy's family.

But not today. It was far too early to stop, and he itched with the need to discover exactly what sort of place Borden was.

Mauric had been in the Nirr Provence many times. It was a shipping port, albeit a small one, and the closest point on the Great Continent to that far away spot of legend and rare goods – the Dim Continent. Most of those goods moved through larger ports, but unusual things did find their way to Nirr shops.

He remembered first bringing the small chiseled statues of strange beasts to court. He'd been very nervous of becoming a prince companion, and desperately hopeful of being accepted. If one was invited, one was already accepted of course, but that didn't mean the Prince himself would like you.

Tryst had liked him.

As it turned out, Tryst liked most people. But he enjoyed the statues, and Mauric was closer to his age than the four prince companions there at the time.

Mauric had been all of eight when he first walked through the Palace gates, and Tryst a full year older and much more mature. Mauric pictured that solemn child prince, the serious face that belied a deep desire to play. The other companions acted as tutors and chaperones, telling him what to do, stopping him from anything deemed inappropriate. But Mauric entered enthusiastically into all his boyish escapades.

In his second week, Tryst had borrowed a necklace from the Lady Moohn. The jewel was supposedly a gift from a high priest in the Zaria Academy, the order of religious philosophers. It was said to tell the future, and Tryst wanted to see if he would become a great warrior. Jason had just assured him it was highly doubtful, since he'd been skipping sword practice.

The Lady was quite upset at the borrowing, as Tryst had neglected to ask. A palace-wide search found the necklace in the garden where the Prince had hidden it. And when the Lady demanded to know how it got there, Mauric had taken one look at the Prince's stricken face, and claimed responsibility before ever considering the consequences.

The Lady insisted Mauric be sent home in disgrace, and the King himself had promised judgment would be weighed.

But somehow no punishment ever resulted. At the time Tryst denied saying anything, but years later he admitted to going straight to his father and confessing all.

That was Tryst. Honorable, as few truly were. Mauric's father had said he'd make a great king when the time came, and Mauric absolutely believed that.

More than anything, he wanted to find out who had betrayed him.

Now, as the Defense Master slowed his steed, Mauric reluctantly did the same.

"I've seen several of the Great Continent's coasts," Jason shook his head. "But nothing like this."

"The east side of the continent is very rugged," Mauric said automatically. His father's words, he realized. How often he repeated his father's words.

But they were true here. Having seen the western beaches, strutted along Gold Harbor wharfs, swam in the calmer blue waters, he now saw Borden as his father described it. Rough boulders dotted the waterline, with the waves striking them angrily. And the colors were faded, with the sea lacking the brilliant sparkle, the foliage a darker, muted green. And the mist – the perpetual mist of the east coast. It seeped the warmth out of the air.

It was the unfamiliar that caught his attention.

Borden had but one wharf, and unlike Gold Harbor, it was unprotected from the rough seas. Rarely did more than a single ship anchor there.

Yet this evening, with the sun almost touching the horizon, four vessels swayed in the white-capped waves. Two were tied to the wharf, the other two anchored farther out. Crates winched out of cargo holds now dangled in the air. On the street, men roped wooden containers to four-mule carts.

Four-mule carts. He'd marveled at those in Gold Harbor, and here they were in Nirr.

"Impressive," Jason spoke beside him. "You never told me Borden was so active."

"I've never seen it so before."

Jason straightened in the saddle. "Has the town grown?"

Mauric scanned the village streets. His eyes passed over the buildings, the wharf. When he turned back to Jason, he was frowning. "No."

Jason's expression did not change. But Mauric felt his disquiet.

Drail reached the Arena Plaza. The Crossroad, as Raston had called it.

To the right, the Arc Banner Inn spilled light and laughter onto a night-shrouded street. The Arc Banner, where winning gamesmen drank and sang and toyed with pretty serving wenches. Where Raston had tipped many a mug.

To the left and down an alley was the Blue Bone Anchor, where the losers were welcomed among fellow losers. There they, too, drank and toyed with wenches, but every beer would be paid for from their own purse and the laughs would not come for several rounds.

The only Raston defeat Drail had ever heard tell of was the great Gold Harbor game, when his team of Desert Flats Trumen had played toe-to-toe with the greatest Skullan gamesmen of the day. They tied the Skullan, and finally lost in the resulting game to break that tie. The Skullan had been so struck by their skill and their heart that songs were written, stories told. A legend born.

Had Raston ever lost another game, Drail wondered. Had he truly been that good? Or did the losses dim in the light of victory? Was one so beguiled by a few successes that the failures were wiped clean?

Drail and the Hand had indeed defeated Skullan, on a faraway continent and against men he now doubted would ever sniff Black Arena-level play. And he'd dared assume he was Raston's equal. He wasn't fit to wipe the sand from his Grandsire's feet.

For the longest time Drail stood there, beneath a crescent moon and street torches. His mind turning him left, his heart yearning to go right. He had no place at the victor's table.

Yet when he did finally move, it was to the Arc Banner.

Inside, it was even worse than he'd imagined. Three bars against three walls, a dozen lovely girls bearing brimming pitchers to demanding patrons. Everyone laughing and jeering and celebrating.

Drail well knew these sounds of celebration. And felt all the lonelier in his defeat.

4.

MARRA AWOKE to a sharp thump on her door. Did she dream it? Or...

The knock repeated. Scrambling up, she grabbed her blanket to wrap herself modestly before reaching for the latch.

And hesitated. "Yes?"

"It's Tryst."

She drew the bolt and fell back as he strode in and then looked at her covering in some surprise.

She flushed red, realizing it was late morning and he'd expected her up and about. But sleep had been elusive last night. Honestly, she was startled that he himself seemed so unaffected.

"You still have that messenger box?"

Marra nodded.

"I want you to come with me to the Palace."

The box was supposed to go to Agben, she believed, not the Palace. But perhaps he knew better.

She turned, and unearthed the book-shaped box from beneath her straw mattress. "I'm glad to give it to you. You can present it yourself if..."

"It has to be you."

He stood waiting, seeming anxious about the task ahead rather than the horrendous loss of last night. When she realized he was waiting for her, she shook the edge of her blanket and frowned in exasperation.

For an instant he stared back, and then understood. He bowed himself out of the room.

"I'll see you downstairs."

She latched the door and dressed.

They strode along the fourth tier, where few Trumen walked. Marra had tried to suggest a lower level, but Tryst had either missed the hint or couldn't be bothered.

Missea, she discovered, was often blanketed in mist. The white vapor surrounded her now, fuzzing distances. Stores and people twenty paces away were heard before seen.

Mist didn't exist in the desert.

As they walked she munched a small cake - the only bit of breakfast she'd been able to snatch before they'd left. A cup tea would have been welcome, but Tryst had been in such a hurry.

Stuffing the last of the honeyed morsel into her mouth, she licked her fingers and eyed the man beside her. Something was really driving him, and she hadn't a clue what it was.

"How's Drail?" she asked again. She'd tried to ask twice now and honestly, Tryst had been too dense or distracted to reply.

"Probably drunk," he answered, his eyes sweeping the tier before them. Seeing things she couldn't see, most likely.

"What happens next?" What would the Hand of Victory do? What *could* they do? That had been no simple loss. They'd been humiliated in a single-handed drubbing – a drubbing that was mere entertainment before the real games even began.

How would Drail recover from that?

She'd lain awake half the night worrying – and listening, Marra realized. She had listened for their return, and never heard it.

"Next? We get inside the Palace."

Dimly she wondered if there was some sort of Palace comet game, but deep down Marra knew otherwise. Tryst had always his own agenda, and for the most part she believed it both honorable and important. But Drail was now in trouble, and Tryst owed him more than this mental dismissal.

"I meant Drail," she said, in a tone she'd never used before. It startled him as much as it startled her.

He didn't get angry, which she realized she was

unconsciously expecting. Instead a humorous twinkle grew in his eye.

"And just what are you wanting me to do?"

Her lips parted – but no words came out. There was no simple remedy, no restorative elixir. That startling realization preoccupied her for the rest of the journey.

And then Tryst steered her down a wide spiral ramp to ground level, and the Palace sprang up before her.

Most of ground level Missea was less impressive than the higher tiers. But the Palace was the soul of the city.

Wide blue gates stood open, allowing ten men to enter abreast. The walls and Palace itself were constructed of gleaming stones stacked high. She thought it far more beautiful than the poured black stone of the Arena.

Grass lush and thick carpeted the courtyard. Meandering pathways wound through the center, as flowers climbed the walls and gates. Beautiful blooms dazzled the eye with pale pinks, vibrant yellows, and deep, deep reds. Such gorgeous, unbelievable color.

Marra loved it.

But that warmth disappeared as soon as her eyes took in the second iron gate, bolted shut. A small doorway in the gate itself allowed passage for only one at a time, and it was flanked by four guards on either side.

From the corner of her eye she spied Tryst draw his hood over his head, adjust the rapier at his side. He'd once told them, Marra suddenly recalled, of three positions for a worn sword: dress, for polite occasions; discrete, to hide the weapon; and prepared, so to draw at the first sign of trouble. They thought him joking at the time, but now the hilt stood clearly visible and easy for him to grasp.

Stars, just what was he planning to do?

Instinctively her feet slowed, but he clasped her arm and kept her moving straight to the flanking men. And despite the fact she'd never been anywhere like this, something seemed familiar.

"You!" another guard called. "Trumen are not allowed to wear weapons."

"The lady brings a message for the Woman of Agben," Tryst announced. Marra would have gaped, if he hadn't pinched her flesh.

The guard surveyed her critically. She tried to look lady-ish.

"You may tell it to me."

Fumbling only slightly, she drew the gilded message box from her cloak.

The guards were visibly impressed. As one reached for it, she dared snatch it back. "This message is not for you," she told him in her haughtiest manner, copied from a Woman of Agben who'd once made her life difficult.

The guard seemed to reevaluate her. Much to her

surprise, he gestured to the open doorway.

She stepped through with Tryst on her heels.

The second courtyard seemed even larger from this side of the gate, though perhaps that was due to the lack of people beyond the iron barrier. The Palace doors were open, although more guards flanked them.

Again a Skullan stepped to block their path.

"She bears a message for the Woman of Agben," Tryst announced more firmly.

This man gestured to yet another guard, who disappeared into the Palace. "Wait here," he told them.

And Marra caught the odor again. A sweet scent on the air, with a cloying property. A smell that should entice but somehow repelled her.

One she'd smelled before. It was the reason for that familiar feel.

Glancing about, Marra saw a glass bowl on a small table. A decoration perhaps, but it seemed odd. Glass, where it could easily be knocked over.

A pink liquid swirled within.

Stepping towards it, she caught a bubbling noise. The liquid, so thick it resembled gruel, clouded to a deeper pink before clearing again.

Pink gruel?

She'd never seen its like, but the scent was from Britta's shop. Her Mistress had been making something on a bright desert day over a year ago, when Marra returned from collecting herbs. Over a powder with a similar smell, the Mistress had lectured on containers – how some things must be stored only in glass, to keep them from reacting to lesser vessels.

Mistress Britta had never told her what that powder was.

Now the gruel bubbled to the deep pink and again relaxed to the clearer color.

Eyes riveted, Marra saw the bubbles again when a pacing guard drew near the bowl. Deep pink, then clearing before he left the vicinity.

Tryst spied her interest and stepped towards her.

Immediately the bubbling began, but this time didn't stop.

And then the gruel suddenly smoothed out to a bright crimson, like a bowl of blood.

"What by the Great Goose..." Tryst noticed the liquid as Marra sniffed a new scent – less sweet, much more cloying.

She turned fast, stumbling. And as she grasped his arm to save herself, her hip nudged the table. Impulsively she nudged harder.

The bowl did not fall far, but it struck a boulder and shattered.

To her eyes, the red was still visible when a guard loomed over the broken glass. He studied her, however, and not the goo-covered flora.

"Are you all right, girl?" he asked.

She sagged in relief. Tryst watched her with narrowed eyes.

"Yes. Thank you," she told him and willed him

away.

After the longest moment, he righted the table and strode back to his post.

"What..." Tryst began, but she cut him short.

"We need to go. Now."

He shook his head – but his eyes drifted to the flower bed. Perhaps the large white petals seemingly drenched in blood got through to him. Could he guess what it all meant?

The first guard returned, bowing to her with respect this time. "Follow me, lady."

"Go back," she told Tryst loudly. And almost winced at the flash of anger in his eyes. But the guard was already leading her inside, and Tryst could hardly follow after such a vocal dismissal.

Marra knew he contrived this whole exploit to cross the Palace threshold. She knew he was furious to get so close and fail because of her.

But she also knew to the core of her bones that the pink gruel had been set to find him.

So shaken was she that it wasn't until she mounted the gilded stairs Marra took notice of the Palace itself. Stars, she had come a long way from San Cris.

Each new town, each city, had seemed so much larger, brighter. Richer. She had thought nothing could compare to Port Leet, and Missea had proved her wrong.

But the Palace tipped that feeling into surreal.

She treaded now on gold, by the Desert Crane. Or by the Great Goose, as Tryst would say. The stone flooring of the Palace was inlaid with paths of the precious metal. Just what use was gold to step upon? It did not make the walking any faster nor any easier.

People bustled through the Palace halls. Many were Trumen, and they were all servants. If a woman passed in a velvet skirt, or a man in fine leather, the height and hair declared them of the Skullan race. Marra kept her eyes fastened on the floor and the feet of those around her.

Her mind raced furiously.

Everybody that had passed that bowl of pink liquid made it bubble. The Skullan guards, she herself. After bubbling it had settled back to its original state. Then Tryst had drawn near and suddenly the pink goo changed to blood red.

Could it have been something on Tryst? Maybe his sword? Except that surely the guards would have been watching for that. Surely one of them would have demanded the weapon from Tryst.

The guards hadn't cared about the bowl, so others had set it there. How often did they check it?

Tryst had set it off, she knew. But how? What exactly did the bowl-maker seek?

Abruptly the escorting guard opened a door and gestured her through.

Marra stepped cautiously inside – and froze.

A lady faced a large window, presenting her back

to Marra. The lady's height and cascading hair would have proclaimed her Skullan, if her bearing had not already done so. She was the third Woman of Agben Marra had ever seen, but the first Skullan.

Marra had almost believed Agben to be free of Skullan.

"You have something for me?" the lady demanded.

Marra realized she was nothing more than a servant to this woman. Perhaps that was not a bad thing.

"Yes, Lady," she said, hoping that was the proper form of address. When the lady remained as she was, Marra added, "I'll leave it on the table."

She hoped to bow out before the woman got a look at her. But the lady turned, and Marra instinctively lowered her head.

If the Agben woman noticed her at all, she gave no indication. Her hand lifted, palm out.

Marra laid the expensive box upon it.

The woman produced a key. Deftly she plied it, and the lid sprang open. Marra only just realized how very awkward it would have been had the box remained locked.

She kept her head lowered, awaiting a dismissal that must surely come.

Except it did not.

The lady set the box aside to untie a ribbon around a small scroll. She read the contents carefully. Marra did not think she liked what it said.

"Who gave you this?"

"A woman, on a ship."

"She told you to bring it to me?"

"To the Lady of Agben at the Palace." Marra's fingernails dug into her palms. She half expected a rattling slap or a cry for the guards.

But this woman's fury – and fury it was, for Marra could feel its heat – was directed somewhere else. The beautiful box flew out the door, clattering against the stone floor of the hall.

Marra held her breath for a full twenty heartbeats.

Then, "Leave."

She did.

Seeing the box, Marra swooped to retrieve it as she fled. A foolish impulse, but once done she didn't dare put it back.

Instead she raced to the large stairway. Her heel caught on a gilded edge.

She pitched forward, tumbling down the hard steps. And landed in a heap on the impressive central platform where the stairs split to rise in two directions.

Her palms stung from slapping the stone, but Marra thought she was otherwise unhurt. Gathering her wits, she slowed her breathing. Be calm, she told herself. Slip out of this place as any messenger would after doing her duty.

And as she told herself this, kneeling on the floor with servants passing by, two things occurred. One was a pair of leather boots stopping beside her – expensive boots with a fox etched on the left inside ankle.

"Are you all right?" a familiar voice asked. The hair on the back of her neck tingled.

Not trusting herself to speak, Marra nodded. And kept her head lowered.

The boots turned and mounted the steps.

She looked up then, and it was a very good thing she was still on her knees, for surely she'd have fallen the rest of the way and broken her foolish neck.

A giant portrait dominated the huge entryway. The heavy gold frame was as thick as the length of her arm, and its subject's face hung above her head. Marra honestly didn't know if she'd entered the Palace a different way or had been looking down and missed seeing it the first time.

For she knew the man in the painting. His eyes, his mouth. More than anything, she knew that expression. And even telling herself that she must be mistaken, that it wasn't possible, the printed words on the gold plaque blazed before her eyes. 'Tryst, Prince and Heir to the Skullan Empire'.

"If it isn't the desert Brista."

Fox Boots stood at the top of the stairs. His hand grasped the rail as his boot stepped down.

She scrambled to her feet and fled.

In his best 'minion waiting' stance, Tryst now

hovered in the outside courtyard. He had turned his cloak inside out and wore a new hat he'd bought down the street, suspecting these foolish guards wouldn't recognize him.

She'd dismissed him. After all he'd done to gain entrance, after he'd stood in the inner courtyard, a hair's breadth from entering his home, she'd dismissed him. What had possessed her to do such a thing?

There was still no sign of Marra, and he kicked himself as all kinds a fool. The two worlds had been separate to him – his old life, the need to get into the Palace and see his father. And the surprisingly pleasant life he'd found with a band of gamesmen and a Trumen girl.

Now he'd mixed those two worlds with no thought to the consequences. Marra's face was not unknown to some of the conspirators and she had walked unknowingly into their den because he'd asked her to.

He heard a faint scramble. And looked up as she flew out the door.

A guard stopped her, staring down. She could only stare back.

"Did your mistress not like the message?" Tryst called out.

The other guards laughed.

Marra broke free, ran across the inner courtyard. She darted through the gate as Fox Boots burst through the Palace doors.

"Stop her!" the Trumen yelled. Hesitating to exchange looks, the guards surged after her.

Marra sprinted for the street, but one of the outside guards caught her wrist.

Tryst was there. In a spinning move he slammed the guard's arm, freeing her. Continuing the motion he drew his sword, whirling to face the gathering guards with blade at the ready.

Fox Boots locked eyes with him, and then glanced at the shattered bowl.

Tryst hurled himself at the closest guard, a big and clumsy fellow. The Skullan fell back, knocking two others down to effectively block the gate entrance.

Very poor guards, Tryst realized. Just bodies with no training. Things had really changed.

He wheeled about and raced after Marra.

Drail made his way to a table and fell onto a seat.

He was very late this morning. The tavern was almost empty and he realized he hadn't the slightest idea if there would still be food in the kitchen to serve.

He didn't really care.

Last night he had given up comet. He had let go – released the goal that had driven him since he was six years old. Now he was free to choose his new path. To sit back, consider, and decide the right course for his life.

And hunched over the table, staring at the grained wood, he realized there was only one thing he wanted to do.

Play comet.

He was a gamesman, he knew it in the core of his being. You don't choose it, Raston had once declared. It chooses you. There was nothing else Drail wanted to do.

How could he find the strength to go on, knowing now how bad he truly was? A single Skullan had utterly destroyed his whole team. They'd been used as a worn strap is used to sharpen a razor. By the Great Desert Crane, was there any chance they could even defeat a proper Trumen team in this city?

Did he truly want to find out?

The wench plunked down a bowl of oatmeal and a tankard of ale. It was the latter that caught his eye.

For the very first time, he understood his father. His father who'd discovered that he was nothing like his own sire, Raston. A father who'd never won the big games, never made it off the continent.

A father who drank a lot of ale.

Drail shoved the stein far across the rough timber surface. Whatever his future, he'd face it sober.

"I see there's some sense in you this morning."

Drail peered up, to discover Old Merle clasping his own tankard. "Couldn't get any sense out of you last night."

Merle sat as Drail forced himself to ply his spoon.

"Rough game, I'll grant you."

"No game at all." Drail wanted to slam his fist,

strike the table. And only that haunting familiarity with his father stayed his hand. "We were children playing against grown men."

"Not children," Merle shook his head. "Dust-dogs playing against a champion Skullan team."

Drail's fist did slam the table.

"Do not pretend we will play better next week. There is no training session, no drill or new technique that will vault us ahead of that team. Or that lone, grinning Skullan."

Old Merle leaned back, drawing a fair throat-full from his tankard, then wiping his mouth on the back of his sleeve.

"So if not training, what will you be doing today, young Drail? Seeking apprenticeship from a blacksmith? Hauling crates on the docks?"

"I'll be finding new accommodations. Seeing as how there won't be any more prize purses."

And he waited, his gut yearning for miracles, to hear some magic words from Old Merle. Some desperately needed reassurance.

Instead his grandsire's best friend rose and walked away.

Tryst spotted Marra as she hesitated at the spiral ramp. He caught up to her, grabbing her arms to thrust her past it, diving around the corner.

Feet pounded behind them, closing in.

Nearby pedestrians froze, and then evaporated at

the sight of the guards. Trumen pedestrians scared of the guards, Tryst thought in surprise. He raced on as fast as he could while dragging Marra with him. Briefly he thought of lifting her to run, but doubted it'd be any faster.

To the southwest was Gold Harbor, while due west was the Central Gate, and farther on the Old Gate and the Land Market. Those were the three possible escape routes from Missea, with the Central Gate the closest and therefore most likely destination. The guards had already seen them heading that way.

Taking one more corner, he veered south. This street was wider than most, yet empty. Ahead was a sort of carriage yard, filled with the horse-drawn carts that citizens with coin used to move about the city. There were two handfuls of the carts, a few drivers relaxing on a bench, and several wagons full of hay.

Tryst halted, then ushered Marra forward silently, avoiding the view of the drivers. He swung her up onto one of the wagons and covered her with hay – and hesitated a moment, in case she protested. Despite her stiffness, however, she obviously knew better.

Tryst shimmied in beside her.

Marra looked at him, her lips parting, but before she could speak, pounding footsteps drew close and stopped.

Tryst held his breath.

"You there! Which way did they go?"

Silence. Tryst heard his own heart drumming in his ears.

"Which way did who go, sir?"

The straw encasing them lurched and Marra gasped.

Tryst shoved his hand over her lips – and was startled at her glare.

As he drew his hand away, the wagon rolled.

"You telling me you saw no one running?" a rough voice growled.

"No sir. Running would have disturbed the horses."

The voices grew fainter as the wagon rumbled off.

He felt Marra sag in relief even as he tensed beside her. All it took was one guard noticing a wagon full of hay *leaving* the stables...

But it seemed the guards were as stupid as he'd first thought. No one noticed; no one tried to stop them. Just who had chosen these guards? Was the intention merely to get rid of the old ones, the ones who might have recognized the Prince? Or was the plot deeper – to leave the Palace and the King himself vulnerable?

The wagon turned a corner and rolled on.

"They helped us," he whispered, surprised at the risk they took for unknown fugitives. And he wondered what sort of past experiences led to their doing so without question.

"Trumen help each other."

She emphasized that first word and he peered at

her face. She wasn't frightened – she was furious.

"Marra what happened?"

As he studied her expression, a spot in his stomach chilled.

She knew.

The hardest part about being Prince was never seeing their eyes, he remembered. Normal people, good people, would stare at the ground, showing no glimpse of what was in their eyes. His father called it respect. Tryst had always found it lonely.

Marra did not hide her eyes, nor all the emotions raging within. Anger, wonder. Even disdain.

He tried to speak first, just to make it easier for her – but his tongue felt awkward and dry.

"Skullan," she spoke. "You're Skullan."

He nodded. Somewhere amusement welled that her concern was his race and not his station. There were several very smooth lies he could use now. She might even believe them, although the desert herb girl had a gift for sensing truth. But looking at her face, at her honest reaction, he knew he was through with lies. Because there was no other way to honor her for all she'd done for him.

And she'd done it for him, a mere man. Not out of duty owed to a prince.

"I woke up far from home," he said. "Marra, I woke up surrounded by strangers. How could I just blurt out who I was? You'd either have killed me – or thought me mad. And in all truth, it was not safe for you to know."

She cocked her eyebrow ironically – and he wondered where she'd learned the gesture.

"Remember the men chasing me in Port Leet. What do you think they'd have done had you already known my identity?"

He saw her face change. "Fox Boots," she whispered. "He's here. In the Palace."

"I saw." Somehow he'd gotten the impression that the only Trumen walking the royal corridors these days were servants and messengers. Yet it seemed the one who had tried to capture him on the Flats now roamed the Palace freely. Could Trumen have been so clever as to work within the Palace walls? Could this all indeed be a purely Trumen plot?

No. Tryst couldn't believe that. There had to be Skullan influence behind it. And trusted Skullan at that.

As his mind flew to possible suspects with possible motives, he caught Marra's narrowed gaze. She hadn't fully forgiven him.

"Marra, I woke to a nightmare. Bewildered and betrayed, my closest friends either dead or guilty of treason. You're revolted at the thought I'm Skullan. I was no less revolted finding myself surrounded by Trumen and thought to *be* one."

He touched her hand – and was relieved she didn't pull away.

"I ask your forgiveness, little one. But in all

honesty, knowing everything I now know, I must tell you I'd still act exactly the same."

He saw the change in her eyes, heard the long sigh of capitulation. "You ought to have told us later."

The wagon rattled over a large stone, bouncing them hard against the wood boards beneath.

"A lovely campfire conversation," Tryst grinned. "'By the way, I'm Skullan royalty'. Can you just see Olver's face?"

Drail had asked at the Blue Bone Anchor and found the accommodations half the price of their current lodgings. He intended to check farther, to find a better situation.

But his feet led him back to the Black Arena.

Oddly enough, the sentries let him in without hesitation because someone recognized him from last night. The one time he'd rather no one knew his face.

Even in bright morning light, the poured shadowy stone gave an odd feel to the place. So very different from anything on the Flats. And Grandsire had belonged here.

If only Drail belonged here.

With a sigh, he leaned over the railing and watched two Skullan teams drilling on the sand below. One of the Skullan bore the wave tattoo on his cheek.

The one who'd proven Drail had no place as a gamesman.

He watched the man hurl a ball, or a comet, as it

was called in Missea. The sphere slammed into the arena floor purposely, with that odd spin he recognized from last night. A sand wave crashed upwards in an arc, showering the Skullan on the other side.

Why, Drail wondered. To blind your opponent? Surely they grew accustomed to the movement. So why keep doing it – let alone waste valuable drill time practicing the move?

Two giant hands grasped the rail beside him.

"He concentrates on the wrong things." It was a guttural voice, so deep and scratchy Drail might have thought it an animal growl, if he hadn't seen the man's flesh.

His instinct was to walk away. Instead he forced himself to stay. "Why the spinning move into the sand?"

Silence followed.

Drail looked up – way up – to see a profile carved of granite, with the rough edges unpolished. The skin was mottled tan and white, and the naked skull had an odd pink patch above one ear.

Truly an ugly Skullan. And so large no one would ever tell him so.

"Spinning clears the dirt cover to reveal the dots. This one likes to make a showpiece of it."

Drail nodded. "To match the wave on his face."

"It does please the crowd. And marks the Black Tide, lifting them above the other teams." The Skullan spat and Drail was startled to see a blackish gunk fall from his lips. "But it helps his game not a wit, and prevents his practicing more useful technique."

Drail found himself nodding again – seeing the truth in the stranger's observations. "Who are you?"

"Wolfbur," the Skullan said. "I practice here at night, when no games are scheduled."

Wolfbur pushed away from the rail, and turned his back to walk away. His final words were tossed over his shoulder.

"Be here tonight and I will show you a thing. If you can muster the guts to face a Skullan again."

Kratchett marched into Rain's chamber without as much as a knock. "What was she doing here?"

Resetting the combs to secure her hair, Rain lifted an eyebrow. "I may favor you upon occasion," she spoke in her haughtiest tone. "But you will seek permission before invading my privacy."

Annoyance flared, but he controlled it. He knew this mood too well.

"Your pardon, milady," he bowed deeply, eyes lowered. He watched her foot tap, skirts bunched slightly from her clenched fists pulling the material on her hips.

He curbed his impatience.

The skirts dropped again, foot disappearing beneath. The storm had passed, but he knew better than to move before given permission.

"Kratchett," she murmured, her hand reaching out. He straightened and ignored it, reaching instead for her. Taking her into his arms, kissing those smiling lips passionately.

A passion that, frankly, he no longer felt.

"I've missed you," she crooned, stroking the side of his face. More like a caress for a beloved pet than an equal, he thought.

There were many Skullan males who played with Trumen women, finding some odd delight in the daintier petite frame. Rain was the only Skullan female he'd ever known to toy outside her own race.

He nibbled her ear, after pushing the heavy hair out of the way. "There was a Trumen girl in here."

Rain pouted and shoved, but not hard enough to really stop him. "A message from Catrona. That bitch dares tell me she failed."

Kratchett rolled his eyes. "Catrona was never worthy of your trust."

"She writes that I failed."

He suppressed a smile. The truth was he'd already told Rain of the failure. She'd brushed it aside, awaiting her messenger box.

"The Trumen girl who brought the message?"

She looked at him blankly, and he realized she'd never notice a mere servant. Rain was a powerful Woman of Agben, but like many Missean Skullan, very blind in some areas.

Her lips now formed a familiar pout.

Whoever was behind her – whoever had launched a plot to bring down a monarchy – must surely be blind themselves to have chosen this woman. She was very skilled in the Agben disciplines, perhaps even brilliant. But on other levels she could be a hindrance. A serious hindrance.

At one point he'd thought to discover who pulled her strings, mostly out of greed, but out of curiosity as well. Now, however, he wasn't so sure deeper involvement was a wise thing. They poised atop a high mountain, in a steep boulder field. Failure would yield a disastrous avalanche, and there might be no escape from the aftermath.

Suppressing a sigh, Kratchett set about soothing her.

The cart had slowed for pedestrians.

Tryst managed to dig a hole through the hay, but their tiny view of passing people and buildings wasn't nearly enough to show where they were.

"Let's get out of here," he told Marra.

He crawled towards the back and jumped off. The wagon was moving so slowly that he easily walked beside it, plucking Marra free when her head emerged through the straw.

They sped away.

"Won't they wonder where we went?" she asked. He already explained about the oddness of a wagon burdened with hay leaving the horse area before unloading.

"They wanted to help and did just that. Telling them our whole story would only put them in further danger."

He'd half expected the wagon to have carried them closer to the Land Market and the Old Gate out of the city. It hadn't, though he wasn't certain till he spotted a familiar tobacco store on the third tier above them.

The store reminded him of Jason. Whoever had done this would pay double for Jason.

He pulled Marra up one tier and strode purposefully toward the arena.

They kept a good pace, passing pedestrians without seemingly in any more hurry than anyone else. He was weighing his options when Marra spoke.

"We won't be so hard to find."

"They want me," he told her. And suddenly checked. "They'll want you, too."

"They'll want us all."

"No. Not if Drail knows nothing of value -- and they'll believe he's ignorant. Because they'll believe I kept him so." He slanted her a look. "I shouldn't have used you to try to get inside."

He watched the emotions cross her face, her lips purse. "You're planning to leave, aren't you?"

"I'm going to stop them."

She nodded. If she had any doubts, she didn't betray them.

"Marra, you're going to have to hide. I'll find

someplace for you..."

"I can't leave Drail."

He shook his head. "The first thing they'll do is hunt Drail down and he's not going to be difficult to find. If he obviously knows nothing, he's safe. They'll ask him two questions: where I am, and where you are."

"You wouldn't confide in me, either."

He looked at her a long moment. "You were in the Palace. Stars, Marra, they know you woke me. They'll want to squeeze you dry of everything you've done, or heard, or guessed."

They walked on. He watched her regretfully – and thus saw when her pace changed. Not faster, not slower. But different. Because, he realized, she wasn't hurrying to anything now, at least nothing she considered good. She was just fleeing from something bad.

And he felt a pang, like he'd accidently bruised a kitten.

"I can't just leave Drail."

"I'll send him word that you're safe. That something came up. Later, when they've questioned him, and watched him for a time, they'll move on. Then you can contact him."

She wasn't convinced.

"Marra, I don't think he's going to need a Brista for a while." And Tryst strongly suspected that after last night, Drail could use some time to himself.

"I have to get my things."

"It might be better -"

"I have to get my things."

Marra finally convinced Tryst to take her back to the inn.

Along the way the man – the Skullan, she reminded herself – had shown her how to escape a wrist grab, by circling her hand around the clasping fingers until she slipped free. It had been an impulse on his part – but she learned it because it could be useful.

And because she doubted she'd ever have his lessons again.

Now Marra breathed relief in placing Britta's book inside her single bag. The potions book – and not her clothes – was the true reason she'd had to collect her things.

She packed her sashes, her Trevor seed. The two glass vials she'd picked up along the way. Then she searched the room for paper and quill, to leave a message for Drail so he wouldn't think he'd been abandoned after losing last night. But there was nothing to help her, so she left the room.

Tryst waited down in the tavern. She was supposed to go to him directly.

Instead she knocked at Drail's door. No response.

Biting her lip, Marra slipped inside.

She plucked out the message box, now unlocked,

and placed inside it a glass vial she used for the Birr Elixir. And then pushed it under his pillow. A corner peeped out, such that he'd only notice it if he went to the window. He might not even notice it until tonight.

But Drail would find it, sooner or later. And he'd know that whatever had happened, she'd thought of him. That she was safe. That she vowed to return.

It felt so wrong, leaving.

Downstairs she scanned the faces in the tavern, longing to see him look up with his lazy grin. She hoped he'd already recovered from last night, was perhaps even now grilling Tryst about how to play better next game.

But the room was bare. No Drail, no Old Merle or Manten or Olver.

It felt wrong putting her future in Tryst's hands. In a Skullan's hands, she reminded herself. She couldn't help but notice he seemed to have no idea what to do with her.

Reluctantly she followed him out of the inn, onto a street where the mist had cleared. They strode on for blocks, Tryst carefully watching the passing faces and she sneaking looks over her shoulder. Neither saw what they sought.

When they rounded a corner, she spotted the bright colored shop with the vivid cloaks.

And stopped.

"It may not be the time for a scarlet cloth on your back," Tryst whispered from behind her. His hand touched her shoulder, urging her on.

But Marra turned, striding off in a new direction. This shop she had seen before. Leah had passed it on the way to the Land Market.

And nearby, just around a corner, was something much more important.

Tryst had to catch up. "Where are you going?" His eyes continued the study of approaching pedestrians.

That would be his life, she realized. Always on the lookout. She could choose a different path, right here and now.

The Agben School was halfway up the block.

Unlike the fancy building in Port Leet, this place had a simple gate. Beyond that, a path lead a few steps to a narrow door with a blue archway. It looked so small.

As is a key, she told herself.

When Tryst noted the gate, he stopped in surprise. He spoke as her hand reached for the iron handle.

"Are you sure?"

Marra found herself nodding without thought. "I can cling to your coat tails, or cling to Drail's. But maybe, just maybe, I can forge my own path."

She hadn't considered the words – they just sprang from deep inside her. And hearing them for the first time as she spoke, she knew them for truth.

Her fingers grasped the gate latch. It opened easily.

"All the best, little Marra." Tryst smiled a warm smile, and she responded with one of her own. She didn't know if she'd ever see him again.

The gate swung open on well-oiled hinges. The Prince stepped back, hesitated. And then strode away.

Marra watched him go. She saw his long stride, the way he seemed perfectly at ease. The manner his head moved – studying, she had no doubt, the area and the people around him.

A wave of sheer fear washed over her. Drail, Tryst, the two people she'd come to rely on to protect her. Two familiar faces in a very strange land, a whole continent away from the desert. She'd left them, and now her whole world had been pared down to this single entrance. She had no idea what may lie on the other side.

Well, she told herself, straightening her shoulders. That's easily solved.

Crossing the short walk, Marra opened the door.

5.

THE HOUSE OF AGBEN in Port Leet had been very large and very beautiful. Its rooms had seemed greedy in their sheer waste of space, made even more noticeable by the lack of people within.

This Agben door led to a tiny vestibule. There was a door to the left, a bell-pull to the right, and an enormous canvas painting of a lady seeming to eye Marra with distain.

Marra's first impulse was to flee back to Tryst.

Gathering her courage, she stepped up to the bell-pull. And despite the foreboding look from the haughty woman in the frame, she tugged.

There was no answering sound.

Did a loud clamoring alert a whole school of people

that she was here? Or was the pull disconnected from any bell, only there to appease the unwary and unwanted?

Biting her lip, Marra jumped when the door opened. And a gray-haired woman in a thick linen dress surveyed her with exactly the same expression as the portrait-lady.

"Classes start on the first day of the full moon. Come back the day before." The woman turned away.

"But – please! I was told..." Exactly what had she been told? "I need a place to stay."

"There are inns for the likes of you."

Mentally counting her remaining coins, Marra regretted her recent purchases. Having finally relaxed, having finally allowed herself to feel safe, she'd spent coin on clothes when Drail and the Hand had practiced, so she'd look more Missean and less desert dog. Pure vanity, she realized. Now she hadn't enough coin for a handful of days at an inn – and the full moon was twice that far away.

"May I work?" she asked. "For a bed and a meal, I mean?"

Half out the door, the woman shook her head. "Students perform all the work we require."

"I am a student."

The woman laughed. To Marra, it sounded cruel.

"Go away, or I'll have you tossed out on the street."

Marra fell back a step. She turned to the door as much to hide her despair as anything else.

Her fingers grasped the knob.

"Marra! Welcome, my friend!" a familiar voice said.

She whirled to find Leah, peeking out from the doorway. "Come in, come in."

Marra glanced at the woman, who pursed her lips but said no more.

And feeling her disapproval combine with the lady in the painting, Marra hurried past them both before they could change Leah's mind.

Stepping out of the tiny vestibule was like stepping into a new world.

Leah led Marra down an outdoor corridor beneath a sheltering overhang, with a stone wall on one side and a brilliantly-hued garden on the other. A garden that stretched a full city block, packed to the brim with vibrant life.

Clusters of white flower stalks burst through grass next to her, the tiny blooms stacked upon each other, seeming to scramble up toward the sky. Above them giant scarlet blossoms hung on dark green vines draped from the overhang. Deep purple, vivid blue, pale yellow, delicate pinks. She'd never seen such colors, such beauty.

"There are very few plants we cannot cultivate here," Leah grinned, turning to stroll through the center. The path had many tiny arched bridges to allow even more room for the flora beneath. Trees, bushes, grasses. And all so very healthy. Marra had been taught to collect only the most vibrant herbs from the heartiest plants, and scanning the entire garden she couldn't spot a single leaf she wouldn't want to collect.

They approached a small pool tucked between three bushy trees, where a very old woman worked on her knees. She was plucking baby leaves from a floating plant.

"Kirth," Leah stopped beside her. "May I introduce Marra? She's from the Desert Flats."

The old woman carefully placed her bounty in an ancient leather herb sash. Marra found herself staring at it.

And then Kirth extended a gnarled hand for Leah to help her up. When she struggled, Marra caught her other elbow. The elder rose slowly to full height – and towered over them both.

"Skullan," Marra breathed. For though the woman wore her hair in Trumen fashion, her sheer size declared her true race.

Kirth slanted her a look. "The Brista."

Marra knew she'd never mentioned that word to Leah.

"What do I hold in my hand, Brista?"

Panic flared, as Marra didn't recognize many plants here. "I do not know, Mistress."

"Hmm." Marra glanced worriedly at Leah, but saw only a friendly grin.

"Fetch me the three best leaves from that tree

there."

Scanning the tree, Marra saw large broad leaves on all the branches, with pale blue blossoms scattered among them. She hurried to pluck them.

And noticed tiny leaves on the bark itself. They were a deep, deep green, almost black, and radiated potency. She leaned in to select three and brought them back.

She laid them in Kirth's outstretched palm.

Kirth bent over to inspect them, bringing her face level with the two Trumen.

"Do you know what that tree 'tis?"

Marra shook her head.

Studying Marra over the leaves, Kirth finally turned to Leah.

"She may stay."

Drail took a very long walk around Gold Harbor. He told himself he wished to look at ships – but his eyes scanned the dock where the Trafalcon had been moored. Maybe, just maybe, he'd inquire on passage home.

Home, where he had been a champion. Home where he was loved, admired, talked about.

Home, where no one expected to see him for many years. Questions would be raised, and eventually tales would seep through of his single night at the Black Arena. His grandsire would be disappointed.

He'd be very disappointed, Drail realized. In his

mind he heard the conversation, pouring the whole story into Raston's ears. Raston would be furious. Not at how he failed, but at how he quit. "A single sorry showing, and you never took the field again?"

As the words echoed in his mind, the Trafalcon slipped past. So close – the second sail was just unfurling, billowing wildly in the breeze – that he saw the Captain standing on the bridge.

The Captain waved. Drail nodded.

Pausing on the wood planks of the dock, listening to the sea lapping at the support posts, Drail knew he couldn't run. Friends awaited him back at the inn, friends who'd given up as much as he had to be here. Whatever happened tomorrow and the day after, he'd face it with them.

Heading back felt good somehow. The mists were clearing, the sun shrugging off a heavy cloud. For an instant he could imagine he was back in the desert.

And thinking of the desert made him think of his desert Brista. Maybe Marra could find something useful in that book of hers. Maybe, just maybe, there was some special potion that would give them an edge in Missea. There had been one on the Flats, after all.

He was striding more purposefully by the time he reached the Arc Banner Inn. He marched past the tavern, up the staircase, and down the hallway to her door.

There was no answer to his knock.

Drail moved on to his own room, to remedy the

mud on his feet. Somehow the Misseans seemed to keep themselves neater, and he thought it might be wise to follow their lead. He was in the grand city on the Great Continent now, and by the Desert Crane he would fit in.

It was when he sat on the bed that he saw it. The messenger box that Marra had been given.

It opened easily.

He leapt up and strode to the tavern, still clutching the contents. Hoping she was still there, that she hadn't gotten far. He found Manten and Olver instead, licking the last crumbs from their plates.

"Did you see Marra?" he asked. Their expressions said they hadn't. Marra tended to stay in the background and his friends often missed the subtle.

Manten pushed back from the table, draining a mug and wiping his mouth on his sleeve. "Probably out collecting herbs."

Drail scanned the room. "Have you seen Tryst?"

Manten shook his head. And then grinned at something beyond him.

Drail turned to find Old Merle at his shoulder.

"You wanted a new place," the old gamesman smiled. "I've found it."

"Down market?" Olver wanted to know.

"Down Hay Street," Old Merle replied. And his wry look unsettled Drail all the more. "Let's collect our things and go."

In the end they left word with the innkeeper as to

their new lodgings. Because, cradling the empty vial used for the Birr Elixir, Drail knew in his gut that Marra would not return any time soon.

Hours later, Kratchett nosed around.

The innkeeper knew exactly who he sought and exactly where they'd gone. In another inn, Kratchett may have been looked at askance for his curiosity, but the Arc Banner was accustomed to hosting gamesmen in demand, and knew these customers wished to be found.

The innkeeper also passed on the knowledge that the petite Brista had disappeared, and he had a message for her as to their whereabouts.

A small dilemma, that. Kratchett would have preferred to question Drail, to discover everything he could about their journey and their time in Missea. But if Marra was no longer with them, they couldn't be part of whatever she was doing. Otherwise Drail and his men would not have left such telling tidings behind for her – and anyone else – to find.

In the end he decided not to pursue Drail. Instead he set a sentry on the inn.

It took almost three hours to reach Hay Street.

And when they did, Drail realized it was no inn at all. It was called the Muck Barn, and that was exactly what it was.

A muck barn was a place men could find room and

board in exchange for the sweat off their backs. The word muck hinted at the level of labor, and barn hinted at the level of room and board. There were two muck barns on the Flats, and the term had become synonymous for being totally defeated – sent to the muck barn.

And now here he was.

Its center was an arena, although after standing in the Gold Harbor Arena, this one hardly merited the name. A mere pit of sand, it felt small and lacked the surrounding platforms. Spectators – if anyone bothered to watch games in this place – were reduced to crowding around on the same level as the field.

The stare he gave Old Merle betrayed all his feelings.

"You said it yourself," Old Merle responded. "No money coming in. We need to earn our keep, you said. At least here we can study the Missean game."

"Comet is comet," Olver burst out. "The Missean game is with real Skullan playing at true Skullan level. We can't turn ourselves into Skullan."

"So you think 'twas Skullan skill alone that defeated you?"

Drail heard Raston's words in his mind – 'Know every win has a trace of luck in it. And every loss has roots within yourself.' But he was in no humor to give Old Merle any support.

And so they stayed.

If three walls could be called a room, then the Hand

of Victory had a room. The straw scattered on the floor constituted the bedding, and the eight pegs hammered into the old timber warned there'd be company if more labor arrived at the Muck Barn. The rooms, such as they were, stretched out in a loft over the arena, and it was clear little sleep would be found when the games went long into the night. Drail could see the whole arena through the holes in the floor.

From below wafted the smell of a stew – not exactly enticing, but not horrible – telling them what the meals would be like. But they were not allowed to eat until after a work shift. Brok, the owner, had a firm set of rules.

"Fresh straw on the floors every five days," he began, when they came down the ladder to find a cart loaded with hay just pulling up. "Rake the arena every morning, check the comet tail to be sure she's still centered. Clean up all spills and litter."

Brok led them around the arena, which was enclosed by a wooden building. On the outside it looked like a regular warehouse, blending in with the district in the city. But the inside showed it was old, semi-finished, and needing strong work to keep it upright.

"Any of you guys builders?" Brok asked.

Drail shook his head. The owner shrugged, and kept moving. "You, old man," he nodded at Merle, "will manage the players when they show. We play three games daily, with a break on the seventh day. Except for special games. We got one of those tonight."

Spotting a gamesman in full leather, Brok started away – and paused. "Work four hours," he told them. "And you'll get supper."

And watching the deference Brok then showed to the gamesman, Drail realized just how far he'd sunk.

Old Merle thrust a rake in his chest.

"This is all we're good for?" The words burst from Drail's mouth before he could stop them.

"You want to feel sorry for yourself," Merle told him. "Have at it."

Oddly enough, Drail found a comfort in the physical work.

Practicing involved the mind as well as the body. Concentration, mental review. One always had to be alert and ready. Raking the arena required no thought at all. It was almost relaxing.

Relaxing, that is, until another comet team showed. Old Merle greeted them, and they laughed at some sally that Drail couldn't hear. Their leathers were new, and more elaborate than the ones he'd bought in Port Leet.

And they were Trumen. How dare Trumen sport such nice leathers, here in Missea where obviously Skullan owned the game!

Drail ate his supper with his head down that night, avoiding eye contact with Olver and Manten. Those two, he knew, exchanged long looks, and a longer talk later when the first of the Trumen games began.

Brok's structure of three games nightly worked by allowing the first eight teams to present themselves to play, unless Brok believed a late team would draw a bigger crowd. Four played the first game, four the second, and the top two winners of each played the third game.

Unlike the big arenas, there was no cost to watch. Brok made his profit by selling ale and meat pies to the spectators.

And what should have been over in an hour took more than two, because Brok buffered long breaks between games to better sell ale. And because, as Drail discovered, comet games in Missea lasted longer than games in the desert.

When the ref yelled "COMET!" Drail watched, despite his avowal not to do so.

The very first move from the Trumen team in the fancy leathers was to hurl the spinning ball into the sand at a competitor's foot. Drail stared at the spot long after the ball was retrieved.

And turned on his heel. And left.

He was bone-tired from the physical labor. The sounds of the game sapped his will as he climbed the odd ladder to the loft. Cheers from the crowd, balls smacking dirt. Players smacking players. All the noise so familiar to him was suddenly so distant.

Mercifully, Drail tumbled into the straw and slept.

It was amazing to Marra how life could change on an instant.

She slept in a very comfortable bed – better than the one she'd had as a child. The mattress was stuffed with straw and herbs, special flowers and a weed that seemed to wrap one in warmth and calm, luring sleep easily. She woke each morning refreshed.

It was a large room as well. The bed had two drawers beneath for storing her things, and wall pegs nearby.

But the large room was not hers alone.

She valued her privacy, and had managed to claim it in some manner even as an apprentice at Britta's shop. Yet now she found herself sharing with three other women. One girl, Clara, was only a year older, but Sherry and Tinn were grown women, and Sherry spoke of grandchildren. Marra soon learned that to be alone she had to find quiet corners in the vast garden.

Clara and Tinn seemed annoyed with her, though she couldn't figure out why. They moved her things to the far corner bed, telling her they had seniority. Marra waited until the room was empty before slipping Britta's book out from beneath the old mattress and under her new one.

Sherry was very kind, saying Marra reminded her of her own daughter. When they moved her bed, Sherry merely smiled. "Well now, that puts you close to me. We can talk without shouting to one another."

Perhaps the oddest part for Marra was no men

inside the walls. In truth, Marra had only known two men in her life before Drail took her out of San Cris. One had been her father, who died when she was five. The other was Snark, Mistress Britta's brother. Escaping Snark was the reason she'd jumped at the chance to go with Drail.

But she missed the male energy, the feeling that Drail and Tryst, and Olver and Manten and even Old Merle, could handle whatever dangers loomed. To suddenly be without them felt vulnerable, like she had felt after Mistress Britta had died.

But I'm not vulnerable, she told herself. At least no more than any woman. Agben was a safe place, with a soft bed and good food. Stars, what more did she want?

Her biggest worry was for Drail and Tryst themselves. Tryst was in a bad situation, but by the Great Desert Crane he was Skullan royalty, after all. He did not need the likes of her to help him.

Drail, on the other hand, had just played the most humiliating game of his life. She could still see his face, feel the utter shock he felt. It was like finding yourself a kitten in a room of guard dogs, a feeling she knew well. How much more horrible must it be when you always believed yourself one of the guard dogs.

And she'd abandoned him.

If only she could see Drail, talk to him. Help him, as he had helped her. But Tryst had warned it would place Drail in jeopardy.

Well, perhaps if she waited a few weeks. And then was very careful.

For now, her days were heavily occupied.

Kirth placed her under Leah's care, which meant studying healing herbs. To her surprise, Leah actually taught a beginner's class at the school. She was only a few years older than Marra, but had grown up in a family of herb woman. Leah, she told Marra proudly, was the third to become a true Woman of Agben.

Marra sat quietly as Leah talked to ten women about basic healing methods. Internal cures, external cures. Hot teas to add warmth as well as herbs, syrups to coat parts of the insides so ingredients clung and soaked in where needed. And reaction potions, that forced a body to expel poisons.

There was much more to it than Marra had dreamed, but it was not what she wanted to know. And when Leah was done for the day, Marra told her so.

"What about the special elixirs? Things to enhance you, make you run faster, think better? For people who are not ill."

Leah sat on a large rock, one of the many conveniently placed for teachers to teach. "Marra, there are two accepted disciplines in Agben. One is the art of healing the body. The second is the art of enhancing it."

Something about her phrasing bothered Marra, but she had no time to dwell on it.

"Enhancing is a very sophisticated thing and few

women study it. Some say it's not truly natural. Healing, after all, balances a body as it is supposed to be. Enhancing takes it beyond that line. And whatever your own thoughts on the subject, you must grasp the rudiments of healing before you can grasp those of enhancing."

Abashed, Marra nodded. She owed Leah so much and didn't want to displease her in any way.

"I'll see you here tomorrow, after the noon meal." And grinning her old grin, Leah strolled up the path.

Watching her go, Marra heard the words echo: 'two accepted disciplines.' Had there been a strange emphasis on the word 'two'?

She remembered the odd pink gruel in the bowl at the Palace, the liquid churning blood red.

Could there be a discipline that was *not* accepted?

Drail found himself working harder and longer each day.

Brok was delighted and promoted him to Work Captain, which seemed to mean only that he could yell at the others to work harder. He never did.

The grueling labor was a way to lose himself. It yielded an exhausted sleep, which made it easier to ignore the games and the gamesmen. To ignore his own failure.

On the third week Olver and Manten cornered him. They had a night off, and dragged him to a nearby tavern. To spend money from their old prize winnings was not something he wanted to do, but Olver merely stared him down.

They found a table in a dark corner. The seats were benches with no backs, so they leaned against the wall and spoke not a single word until the first round of mugs stood drained dry.

Drail made no protest when Manten went for a pitcher.

"Is this it?" Olver demanded.

Drail gazed back, too tired to fully comprehend.

"Is this it?" Olver held his mug out as Manten filled it. "Are we done? Do you now intend to be the captain of a muck barn instead of leader of the Hand of Victory?"

"We can't be gamesmen," he sighed.

"We *are* gamesmen. Maybe we're not the top of the rankings in Missea. Maybe we never will be. But by the Desert Crane, we are gamesmen."

Drail shook his head. And was startled to see Manten agree with Olver. He realized he was quite used to Manten's support in all things.

Manten sensed his surprise. "I don't like muck barns," he grinned. "I'm a gamesman."

"I'd rather lose nine out of ten games," Olver eyed him over the rim of his mug, "than live out my days raking muck. Better still, return to the Flats and win nine out of ten."

"But we're awful. Stars, they *owned* us." Drail spluttered.

Manten – Manten, for heaven's sake – cut him off.

"First lesson Old Merle ever taught me: anyone can have a bad game. Play ten games and then see where you are."

"We know where we are." Drail drained his mug.

Manten refilled it, poured the remainder into Olver's mug, and then stood to retrieve more.

Drail caught his sleeve. "We really shouldn't spend money when we're not earning any."

Olver plucked a coin from his pocket and tossed it on the table. Manten took it and left.

"We'll not stay long," Olver swirled his drink, "slaving to put coin in Brok's purse. If you choose to remain, so be it."

Drail gaped at him.

But Olver's face was dead serious. "I don't know what the future holds," he told him. "But I'm damned if I'm going to cower from it here."

The next day Drail worked harder than ever.

His mind now teemed with doubts and concerns, and his body was desperate to outrun them all. But as evening approached, and gamesmen began to show, he found himself looking them over instead of avoiding their eyes. Trying to measure them against himself. Were Missean Trumen really any bigger? Any stronger?

After a somewhat watery stew and stale bread supper – Drail hadn't realized how stale the bread was here – he went to find Olver and Manten. The two had just claimed their one free ale Brok allowed them. Drail snagged his as well.

And then dragged his friends over to watch the first match.

The instant the Judge yelled "Comet!" a ball hurled across the sand to strike at a man's feet. The wave of grit made the crowd behind him duck, but the Trumen immediately kicked the ball. To dislodge it, Drail reflected. Easier than trying to pick it up, as he had done in the Black Arena.

These gamesmen did indeed block the comet tail, although no one seemed to be aiming for it. Instead the showy sand-wave hits continued. Spectators laughed when a ball hit a player, or the sand rose particularly high.

And then, blinks into the game, the strategy shifted. One Trumen dove at another, tearing the ball from his hands. Whirling, he hurled it to a teammate, who raced to center pit. To the tail.

But the other teams also sped to block him. The three other balls lay in the sand, completely ignored.

How odd, Drail thought.

The battle to sink that single ball raged fiercely. The match was already longer than any Drail had played, and he could see the players tiring.

The biggest man among them finally smashed two opponents flat, knocking the wind from their lungs. His teammate held the ball, and instantly leapt over the prone gamesman to reach the boundary line.

And toss the ball.

It bounced off the rim.

Astonishing, Drail thought. Any boy on the Flats could have sunk that.

A different team grabbed the ball, sprinted to the line. The others fought hard, all concentrating on the one man, the one ball.

But this time the gamesman dodged, and then knocked another from his path.

And sunk the ball.

Immediately, the others scrambled for the remaining balls. Focusing on one, they repeated the same crazy battle. The second comet sank, with the third on top of it.

The last team trotted the final ball to the cone – heads down, defeated.

"CEASE!" cried the Judge. And he lined them up, then pulled the balls out. There was no wiping the dirt from them.

Suddenly Drail understood.

The dirt was already gone. The gamesmen knew which ball was which – which had five spots, which had none. That was why they fought so hard for one ball over the others.

Scoring in comet was twofold – the value of the ball sunk, and the order in which it entered the tail. Sinking the five-spot first earned eight points total – and no one could score higher.

A team could only score once. They might sink a second ball to stop others from scoring with that one, but then would be retired to watch the remaining game.

Skullan, he recalled, did not trust their luck. On the Flats the Skullan teams had been startled at his sinking balls early in the game.

The Missean game was a totally different strategy. No wonder he'd been so confused.

Now this did not mean – he told himself firmly – that the Misseans weren't much better than him. Much better than the teams he'd faced in Port Leet. In truth, this may not mean anything at all.

But he watched the next match, and the one after that.

Tryst alternately rode fast, with the dark horse's hooves pounding the dirt road, or walked slowly through the shadows of night. There seemed no middle ground.

He was in the Draylin Provence, approaching a place he'd heard about through his friend's stories: Mauric's family manor.

It was a risk, but a small one. If Mauric had been in on the plot, surely he would not have remained behind with an illness. Besides, he and Mauric had been great friends, as great as a prince can be with handpicked boys ordered to serve as companions.

Still, and despite himself, Tryst would exercise a

sharp eye on the family holdings. Would there be any sign of newly acquired wealth? An infusion into the land, or fancy upgrades to the manor?

Now he passed a young woman on the road, a basket of fruit in her hands. Green applies, he saw. Mauric had often spoke of wandering through the apple trees, picking fruit to munch as he sat on a stone wall and watched the sea. And, if Tryst's memory served him well, to watch three young maidens who liked to bask in the sun on a warm day.

The girl carrying the fruit had long hair curling down her back, and he thought briefly of Marra. She'd been unhappy leaving Drail and the Hand of Victory – and he suddenly appreciated how cruel it had been to separate her. From all he could gather, she'd been a lonely girl, frightened before Drail had entered her shop. Drail had been her savior and now she was cut off from him.

But that was a sound decision, he told himself firmly. She'd be safe at the Agben School, and Drail safer in her absence. Tryst had been taught never to waste time second guessing decisions, and he would not do so now.

There were many decisions in a king's life. Each must be approached properly, all information gathered, sifted and weighed. All skills employed to reach the best choice. And once made, move on. It only wasted time to ponder a decision past.

Now the road crested at a sharp hill, and he found

himself galloping down the slope. With a jerk on the reigns, Tryst slowed the pace. He couldn't keep a horse racing the entire day, no matter his hurry. The animal simply couldn't handle it.

Below was the manor home, in a valley of green foliage and brown rock. Hard and soft, Mauric had called it. The sea should be farther on, less than a quarter day's march on foot.

Emotion rose in Tryst's throat. He realized he really wanted to see Mauric, not just to learn what he knew, but to be with a friend. Someone who'd shared his old life, knew him as Prince and wouldn't see him different because of it.

Someone who *liked* him.

The horse broke into a gallop again, reacting to his own desire to hurry.

He leaned forward and rode.

The manor seemed rather quiet.

No doors opened, no one rushed to take his steed. Of course, dawn was barely past and Mauric had never been an early riser. Perhaps it ran in his family.

Tryst threw his leg over the mare's back and slid down to the ground. With no hitching post, he wrapped the reigns over a low hanging tree branch and strode up the steps.

He knocked.

No faces appeared at the windows, no shouts came from within. Tryst watched a puff of breeze stir dead leaves, tickling his nose with a salt tang. The sea was close, it seemed to whisper.

The door cracked open. A young girl, perhaps eight-years-old, peeped out. Her velvet dress proclaimed her a daughter of the house, even if her hair was escaping its ribbons.

"Are you Gabby?" he asked.

The girl glared.

"I am Gabriella, of Canton House."

Despite himself, Tryst grinned.

"Who are you?" she scowled.

"A friend of your brother. May I see Mauric?"

She shook her head. "He's in Missea – at the Palace itself. I was going to marry him, you know."

Tryst felt a cold spot in the pit of his stomach. "I was told he was here."

Gabby shook her head. "Mauric came home when the Prince died. When they found out – not when it happened. But the King summoned him back."

The cold spot grew. Mauric was a minor companion, a very minor figure at the court serving no useful purpose without the Prince. Why would a grieving King send for him?

"I was going to marry him," Gabby demanded his attention. "I would have been a princess."

"How long has Mauric been gone?"

"Long time," she responded. "Since harvest. Would you bow to me? I'm pretending I am a princess."

"Gabby!" a voice in the manor called. The girl threw

an anxious look over her shoulder.

"Quick!" she whispered. "Bow to me now!"

Tryst did so. Before he'd straightened, the door slammed in his face.

Hours later, the manor door opened again.

This time Jason stood back watching, as a servant surveyed the new arrivals. "Master Mauric!" he cried.

Mauric grinned. "Hello, Shelby. This is the – this is my friend, Jason."

As Shelby bowed, Jason sent Mauric a wry look.

"Is my family at dinner?"

"About to sit down," Shelby stepped back, gesturing them inside. "I'll have two more places set."

Jason followed Mauric within.

Having discovered all they could, Jason had suggested the stop.

Mauric demurred, but really needed little persuasion. They must stop somewhere, and the promise of a nice meal and a warm bed far outweighed any reluctance he felt.

Jason did wonder if the manor would prove in disrepair, reflecting a lack of family wealth that Mauric wished to hide. But he soon realized Mauric's reluctance was for Jason to observe the family's treating him like a ten-year-old.

Mauric's father was obviously proud, but afraid to voice it in any way.

His mother kept a continuous scold flowing from

her tongue as she hugged her son three times.

And his sister, Gabby, eyed Jason up and down before demanding if he was a prince.

"I am not," he answered, pulling her chair out from the mahogany table. "Will you be seated, milady?"

Nose in the air, Gabby sat.

Jason eased her seat close to the table.

"I'm a princess," she informed him. He bowed, then took his seat.

"Father, what's with all the activity at Borden?" Mauric sipped his wine.

His jovial father frowned. "No one seems to know. So many things arrive, but the Great Goose guide me if I know where they go. Word is nothing ships out."

"Someone must be getting rich," Jason spoke casually.

"Not," Mauric's father raised his fork, "that anyone can tell."

Gabby cleared her plate, then eyed Jason.

He winked at her, and she turned to her father. "He doesn't bow as nice as that other man."

"What other man, sweetling?" Mauric smiled.

Jason remembered his complaints that everyone else indulged Gabby far too much.

"Dark man on the big horse." She studied the tiered cake setting on the massive buffet cabinet. "He bowed very nice."

"And when did he do this?" her mother asked, nodding at her empty glass. A servant refilled it.

"This morning. Before anyone else got out of bed. I was first up," she told Jason.

Jason studied her face, and then glanced at the others. They were all assuming it was some sort of game. "A big man on a big horse?"

"No." Gabby had difficulty speaking with her mouth full of milk. "He was just a Trumen. It was the horse that was big."

Mauric's knife clattered against his plate. He met Jason's eyes, who shook his head slightly.

They continued dining as if merely amused by Gabby's imagination, but Jason's skin prickled on the back of his neck. In his gut he knew this Trumen was anything but imaginary.

Tryst guided his tired stallion off the road. He'd spotted a footpath between two cairns, and as it led up a steep hill to a tangle of trees, it seemed a good possibility for the night.

Odd how the journey with Drail and the Hand of Victory had taught him more practical things for traveling than all the months of preparation for his princely epourney. He'd learned how to choose a secure camp spot, far enough away to remain undetected by other travelers, but with a line of sight to watch the road. Olver had shown him how to cook with low smoke fires at dusk, or else eat cold that evening.

Of course in all fairness, a prince traveling with

Elite Guards had no concern for his safety. But then, that one assumption had proved fatal.

It was cold tonight, and the thought of a warm fire was very appealing. He'd seen few travelers since reaching the Draylin Provence, and even telling himself the risk was not worth it, Tryst longed for the comfort of flames.

When he saw the fungus-like bark, he gathered it. The texture was very similar to the bark used on the Flats, bark that kept a fire from smoking. He found a cozy spot behind a large boulder, a barrier of trees and brush adding to the stone to hide any trace of smoke.

The small fire warmed him through to his soul. He took out his bag of tea, a last remnant of Marra's handiwork. She had a trick of adding a touch of cinnamon to spice the brew.

He was lonely, he realized. For so long no one had shared his burdens, had understood his situation. And that after having people surrounding him his whole life whose single purpose it was to clear the way for him.

When finally someone had learned the truth, he'd found no sympathy. Marra had been angry.

Seeing things from her view, he could understand that anger. Women, he knew, tended to feel with the heart in their decisions. Men thought with their head.

A king seeks council with his head and follows his heart, his father told him. Precisely how did you accomplish that?

The water boiled.

Tryst wrapped his coat sleeve around the handle, and poured himself a steaming cup. And then leaned back against the stone, holding the drink in both hands for warmth.

It wasn't so much a noise he heard as a change in atmosphere. Suddenly he knew wasn't alone.

His rapier lay beside him; his back protected by the high boulder he propped against. Someone could drop from the top of it, but they had a fair chance of injuring themselves.

"I have no coin," Tryst announced to the night. "Just tea."

Utter quiet followed those words.

And then two men emerged from the dark behind the fire. Both had drawn swords.

"You also have information," said a hauntingly familiar voice. "For what purpose did you seek Mauric of Canton?"

The sword point moved steadily towards his throat. Tryst rose to his feet. And hurled the cup, and launched himself at the speaker.

The two rolled in the flickering firelight, Tryst pummeling the intruder, while the other sought only to avoid injury. "Betrayer. Betrayer. Betrayer." Tryst spat through a clenched jaw.

The second man grabbed Tryst's shoulders, in a fleeting attempt to pry him off.

"Tryst!" he cried, laughing. And fell to his knees

beside the combatants. "Tryst."

Tryst slowed the assault. "Mauric..." And then, peering down at Jason's face, he saw tears.

He released the Defense Master's throat.

The three remained unmoving, staring across a gap wider than the space between them. Jason never touched his tears, while Mauric managed to laugh and cry at the same time.

"I thought you were dead," Tryst stared at his old mentor.

"I *knew* you were," Jason replied.

6.

TRYST SHARED THE LAST of Marra's tea.
"You shouldn't have a fire," Jason shook his
head. "Anyone might come along."

"Very little smoke," Tryst pointed out, and grinned
at his friend's startled face. How strange to tell his
mentor something he didn't know. "How did you find
me, by the way?"

"Not from smoke," Jason acknowledged. "We've
been tracking you since your visit to Canton House."

Tryst cocked an eyebrow – and saw Jason's dimple
appear. A rather unnerving sight, to the uninitiated.
Truth was, that lopsided dimple was the only physical
manifestation of Jason's humor.

"Mostly traveling the road in the same direction. I
– guessed – when I saw the cairns. Seemed a good

time to camp for the night. I just didn't know who we were following."

Tryst gazed back a long moment. "I thought you were dead."

Jason blew into his mug, seeming to appreciate the warm mist that billowed from it.

"For six months I was." He set the mug aside, then pulled free his coat and lifted his shirt. The scar there was the size of a broad sword. If it hadn't severed a rib he'd been very lucky.

Mauric gasped. Tryst merely nodded, though his eyes misted.

"I berated myself a long time for missing the signs." Jason smoothed his clothing back into place. "Days before, Baldar had commented on Mauric's feeling ill. And being too foolish to own up to it. I said something about speaking to him, but he didn't want me to do that. Baldar was afraid, so he said, of Mauric thinking he'd betrayed a confidence."

From Mauric's reaction, Tryst knew this was the first he'd heard of the tale.

Jason lifted his cup again. "I'd been told by the Elite Guard that we needed to pass through a certain town quickly. There was to be some sort of Trumen festival, and the guard captain felt it prudent to be gone by then. Thus, when Baldar and Kellan strode into the courtyard that morning, I was annoyed at Mauric, but anxious for no delays."

"Problems with Trumen? I never heard of such a

thing," Even with the fire, Tryst suddenly felt cold.

The Defense Master nodded. "That was the second intelligence they'd passed to me. Nothing serious, just a tiny bit worrying. I'd even been asked if I felt I could protect the Prince. Naturally it would have galled me to say no. So we climbed through the mountain pass in back of the Palace, and were eight days on the road. Our pace had been better than average, and the guard called an early halt. I was told Tryst was tired."

Tryst shook his head.

"I know, my Prince," Jason spoke softly, but there was much emotion suppressed in his words. "Three simple lies carefully fed to me, all leading to that one night. The cook prepared a special stew, smelling of heavy spices, but I never cared for such. I took a bowl, ate my share of bread, and then tossed it in the woods. I honestly didn't want to upset the cook, and we weren't exactly starving."

Tryst froze, suddenly remembering. "I disliked it. Kellan kept commenting on how great it was – and I agreed. Pretended to eat, and poured it out later."

"Because you knew!" Mauric's eyes shown in the firelight.

Tryst closed his eyes, a wave of fury washing over him. At the conspirators, at the ease with which they'd taken him. At their ease in manipulating him. "I never liked disagreeing with Kellan. Truth was he annoyed me, and so I took pains not to show it."

Jason tossed the dregs of his mug into the fire. "I

awoke after midnight to see two guards moving swiftly through the sleeping men. They'd reach a body, pause, and then hurry past. I didn't know what they were doing – but it couldn't have been good.

"I was next. As one approached, I saw the blade flash in his hand – and leapt up. He cried out – young fool. He had no idea what to do, and I didn't leave him long in his ignorance. Then I raced to you."

Tryst nodded. "I woke to chaos. Men yelling, running towards us. You yanking me away. I tried to grab my sword."

"Eight men," Jason told him. "There were eight men, and I think most of them were strangers, waiting for us on the road. But there were at least two Elite Guards in on the plot – that I'm sure of. And Kellan, I know because I saw his face. I didn't see Baldar's – but I'm very sure of him as well."

Jason grimaced. "The last I knew, we were running through the woods. Couldn't even get to the damned horses. Moon flashed out from a cloud, and we saw that cave.

"I left you climbing towards it, and ran back to delay them. To prevent them from seeing your path."

Tryst saw the despair of that moment reflected in Jason's eyes. "I couldn't hold them long. Someone threw rocks..."

Tryst had to clear his throat before he could speak. "It wasn't a cave. Just a pockmark on the face. I ran on – but they got me a few blinks later."

"They caught you?"

Tryst nodded. "Forced some sort of liquid down my throat. The next thing I knew..."

He shrugged. There were some things he didn't really want to share. "I woke up on the Flats of Beard."

"You *what*?"

"I wasn't supposed to wake at all. An herb girl woke me."

Tryst would have liked to leave it at that, but Jason would not allow it. The Defense Master prodded and poked, and Tryst realized he'd been so determined to reach home, reach his father, that he never truly thought through why he'd been taken to the desert continent. "The shopkeeper was a greedy Trumen," he said slowly.

"And this greedy Flats Trumen orchestrated the most daring plot against Skullan royalty in our thousand year history? All to have you brought to his little desert store?" Jason's tone brought home just how ridiculous the whole thing was. Why hadn't they just killed him? Why go to so much trouble, take him so far away?

"It was an herb shop," Tryst frowned. "The mistress was dead, but I think that had been recent. She was supposed to be very good."

"The House of Agben is in Missea. Some of those mistresses are very good."

Tryst met Jason's hard look across the flames. "I can only tell you that's where I was. It took me almost a year to get home."

Jason folded his hands – a gesture so familiar it warmed Tryst's heart. "Mauric tells me they thought you were on the epourney for over a year. Suddenly, three months ago, the Palace announces you've been kidnapped by Trumen. It sent Warships to the Flats to retrieve you.

"And then two months ago, they announce those same Trumen had murdered you."

Tryst nodded ruefully. "They chased us across the Wavering Continent." Thinking about it, the timing made sense. "They thought they had me in Port Leet. They failed. If someone sent a message that day, on a swift ship in the harbor, it could have been delivered around that time."

Jason nodded. "Apparently they didn't want the King to miss you – until there was a danger of you showing up at the Palace."

"But why the word I was dead?"

Jason mulled it over. "Well, it makes it harder for you to get near the King. Alive, he'd have sent the entire army to scour the continent for you. Believing you dead, those same men surround him, protect him. As he hides in grief."

"It also ramps up emotions." Tryst spoke slowly, his anger simmering. "If someone wished to stir things up against the Trumen, I can think of no better way."

"You must tell the King," Mauric told him earnestly.

"I did try," Tryst sighed. "I'm barred from my own home."

The sun danced on the mountain horizon, as if reluctant to yield to the approaching night. Drail snatched a few copper from his pocket and hurried up the street to find a passenger wagon. It cost him three copper when he demanded speed.

Even so, the sun had set when he leapt off in front of the Black Arena.

At the conclusion of the matches two nights ago, Drail had walked all the way here merely to check schedules. Tonight, he knew, there were no games.

Somehow without the buzz of spectators, the poured walls seemed even blacker. He felt a chill as he trotted inside, worried in case he'd misunderstood. Or in case that offer had been limited, and he was already too late.

Sounds rose from the arena floor. Drail crept up to the railing, almost afraid to peer down.

There, in the sand below him, one Skullan raced with a ball. Three more steps, and he hurled it at the comet tail.

It went in. Drail realized it was the farthest distance he'd ever seen a Skullan sink a ball.

He stepped to the ramp, feet moving faster by the time he reached the arena floor. The Skullan was running again, repeating the drill.

The ball arced through the air in a perfect shot.

"I'd almost given you up," Wolfbur said, and turned.

Drail faced him man to man, which he realized he hadn't done before. He didn't allow his shoulders to hunch, nor let his eyes avoid the Skullan's.

"Comet in Missea is a very different game now," Drail spoke quietly, watching Wolfbur's face.

"Yes," the old Skullan nodded.

"Raston didn't know."

"Raston changed the game."

Wolfbur launched the ball at Drail's feet, creating the sandy wave. "Raston's team, of the Red Storm Banner, beat Missean Trumen teams. The best Trumen teams defeated by upstarts from the Flats. Skullan thought their Trumen counterparts too arrogant, and so delighted in this. The Red Storm even played in a Skullan game – and came in third. Not last."

Third sounded poor to Drail, but he felt Wolfbur's undertone of respect.

"So the Prince of the time, now King Bactor, offered them an opportunity never before granted. To play in a big game in this arena. Just two teams: the best Skullan had to offer, and Raston's band."

Drail felt his throat tightening, though he knew not why.

"Raston tied the game. That wasn't supposed to be possible. It sent a shudder through all Skullan society – we took it very personally. It was as if females had suddenly stormed the arena and defeated our mightiest heroes."

Suddenly, Drail saw it through different eyes. The Skullan had always been a mighty race, roughly a third bigger than and, so some claimed, twice as tough as any Trumen alive. And comet, especially the way they played, was a power game. It must have felt like four little Marras had strolled into the ring and thumped them.

They wouldn't have celebrated Raston and his men – not with the core of their confidence rocked. And they'd have blamed themselves.

"The prevailing belief was that Raston was lucky. That Trumen are lucky. The balls they sunk were always the high ones. And Skullan as a race never trust their luck.

"Over the years, the strategy developed to play until the balls reveal their worth. And then fight to sink the winning one. Takes more stamina – and that's an edge we have over your race."

Drail nodded. "We're not as bad as I thought. Just – ignorant."

He tried to lift the ball at his feet – and realized just how deep it was. Straightening, he kicked at it under and up. And neatly caught it.

Wolfbur grinned. "A little understanding is required. A little change in tactics."

"But can we win?"

The answering roar of laughter startled Drail –

because it reminded him so much of his grandsire.

"Can anyone win, on any particular day? The answer lies in the match itself."

Drail hurled the ball, spinning, into the dirt. No sand-wave, but at least it buried in well. He looked up, studying the Skullan's face. "Will you teach us?"

Somehow, with the ugly mottled skin, Wolfbur's grin was more frightening then his frown. "I will teach Raston's cub," he said.

Drail found himself strangely reluctant to leave the Muck Barn. It offered security, food and a place to sleep in an unfriendly city. And while his heart wanted back in the game, his mind was a little dubious of success.

They also had a problem – still no sign of Marra or Tryst. No Brista was troubling, for she'd become a luck charm to him. But no Tryst meant they were a man short.

Fortunately, the games at the Muck Barn offered plenty of opportunity to measure various gamesmen. Most, frankly, were raw. Few had any real ability, which Drail supposed was only to be expected. The pit at the Muck Barn was not exactly the pinnacle of comet competition.

"I liked you better when you were just my work captain," Olver told him. They had continued their labor in the day, and hurried across town to train with Wolfbur three nights in five. And when they didn't train with Wolfbur, they drilled.

Drail had worried that the day's labor would diminish their capacity at night. Instead their muscles grew even stronger and their stamina better still.

The little leisure time remaining was oft spent watching comet games. Partly to observe how the Skullan strategy affected play, and partly to find a fourth man.

Old Merle, who'd disappeared for several weeks, suddenly returned. "Visiting old friends," he said. Drail couldn't help but notice he seemed very informed on their situation. "Let's find our new gamesman."

There were a few candidates, yet no one that Drail felt comfortable admitting to the Hand of Victory. One man caught Drail's eye, as he could make great shots from long distances. But he was the captain of his team, and disdainful of Drail and his 'desert dogs'.

When this candidate took a hard knock, Old Merle pointed out, he was very slow to get up again. Drail thought the shot had rattled him – but in watching other matches he realized the man did not like to get hit. He tended to back off afterwards.

Another gamesman was very physical, seeming to feed off the heavy hits, playing even harder after each one. Drail noted that he was a showman, wanting to do it all himself. Never once did he pass off the ball when a teammate had a better chance.

Yet Old Merle watched the showman's team

carefully, prodding Drail. "That's our man."

"He's a ball hawk," Drail shook his head.

"Not him. The youngster he plays with."

Following Old Merle's nod, Drail spied what looked like a rookie on the other side of the cone. The boy managed to streak past two defenders, positioning himself for the ball.

The Showman ignored him, trying to sink it himself. In the end the ball was stolen, and another team won.

The rookie sent a hard frown at the Showman before walking away.

"He seems too young," Drail said.

Old Merle slanted him a look. "As opposed to the great age of twenty-four?"

Drail nodded. "Having spent fifteen of those under the influence of Raston."

"Oh yes," Old Merle nodded thoughtfully. "All that great experience leading up to a Muck Barn."

The next morning, as Drail raked the straw surrounding the sand pit, Old Merle led the youngster to him.

"This is Fallon. And this, my boy, is Drail."

The young man nodded once.

Drail realized he was skeptically eyeing the rake in his hand.

"You guys any good?" the kid asked.

"Can you learn?" Drail replied.

Old Merle grinned. "Be here tonight, my boy. And

you may each judge the other."

Marra balanced on a small ladder, arms high over her head. She was hanging Dru Weed in the drying shed, and it had to be hung exactly perpendicular. Dru Weed had a thick stalk with feather-light leaves growing upwards toward the sun. By drying it upside down, the sap in the stalk trickled back into the foliage, which in turn could be crushed and used to stimulate the heart and blood.

Tying off the last piece, Marra hopped down.

And hurried out the door. Kirth's class would begin soon.

Racing through the lilacs, she jumped over the small pond with the frog and the wood moss, and dove behind the Beetlebush. The latter was tall and very thick. It hid her quite well.

She forced her breath to slow.

The hardest part for her was learning the names. Everything had a name, and sometimes the name of a flower didn't match the name of the root or the leaf. Worse, she didn't really need names because she never forgot the look of a plant.

But names were how everyone referred to them. Leah spoke of using the flower bulb of a Twilly to calm a patient – not the big white flower with the crooked pointy leaves. Or how a paste of wood moss – not the greenish mold on trees – would cling to the skin and linger for days. Adding almost any herb to that paste would mean the herb effects lasted twice as long.

And of course, the names of the plants were what Mistress Britta had written in her book.

Noticing the grass at her feet, Marra realized it had a yellow tinge to it. A sort of vibrant yellow. Surely it had some calming property?

Various footsteps approached.

"Did you meet Sten last night?" a girlish voice giggled.

"Hush! No, it's tonight at the comet game." Marra recognized this voice, belonging to the very pretty older Skullan girl with black curly hair. Skullan had incredibly long hair – it staggered Marra to see it.

Then came the slower tread, and silence settled on the group behind the bush. "Did you succeed with the hair balm?" Kirth's voice demanded. "I can see that Rima did."

More laughter.

Marra sighed.

Kirth's class was on herbs to enhance the body. Marra had been very disappointed to discover that students were required to spend three years studying the healing herbs before moving on to the other discipline. Three whole years.

She hadn't meant to break any rules. But she'd gone to every class she ever saw; sitting quietly by herself, absorbing every word. Naturally when she'd spotted Kirth on the far side of the garden, talking to a handful of girls, she'd rushed over to hear her talk.

Kirth had sent her off to scrape wood moss.

So the next week, when Kirth gathered the same girls in the same area, Marra made special note of the day and time. And the week after that, she hid behind the bush.

Not that it had been worth the risk yet. So far Kirth's class explored external enhancement – hair balm and skin softeners. Things the Skullan girls all seemed to love. Marra wanted internal enhancements, like energy potions.

But the class today droned on about the mortar and pestle and the need to grind Dru Weed to a fine powder. "Very fine," Kirth warned. "It will have no effect unless it is so fine you can't see the individual bits in the lotion."

When Kirth dismissed the students, Marra tossed aside the yellow grass she hadn't realized she'd picked. She heard the students walk away – but not the old Skullan.

"Marra," Kirth said.

Marra froze. And then pushed up off the ground, and rounded the bush.

"Are you learning what 'tis you seek? To make yourself more alluring?"

Startled, Marra shook her head.

Kirth's stern face reminded her of Mistress Britta, back in San Cris.

"I'm sorry, Mistress," Marra told her. "I was curious."

"Curiosity is a dangerous hunt, my girl. For in beating the bushes for the rabbit, one may well disturb the wolf."

Marra stared back, wishing she'd never been so foolish. What would her punishment be? Would they ban her from the school?

Kirth heaved a heavy sigh and gestured Marra to sit on the grass.

"The discipline of healing herbs grounds you in the basics of the art. You learn an appreciation for the body balance, and the very real danger of upsetting that. All healing 'tis directed at that simple principle – restoring balance."

Biting her lip, Marra nodded. "I won't do it again, Mistress."

Kirth peered into her face for a long moment and then cocked a wry eyebrow. "I'm told you're like a sponge in learning – sucking every last bit of knowledge up before the teacher has fully laid it out. They say your memory 'tis quite good."

Marra started breathing again. Maybe they wouldn't expel her.

Kirth pushed herself up off the rock.

"I've got rheumatism, girl. In the fingers 'tis mostly, but my back gets twinges as well. Make me a proper potion."

Marra blinked at her, puzzled. And then hastily nodded.

The next day Marra found Kirth scraping bark from the tall red tree in the center of the garden.

"Well, girl?" She placed a hand to the small of her back as she straightened.

In response, Marra lifted a tiny vial.

Kirth eyed her a long moment, and then nodded.

"It's -"

Kirth held up a hand. "Tis for drinking?"

"It's rubbed on the fingers." Marra proffered the oil, waiting for questions.

None came. Instead, Kirth held out her hands palm downwards. Marra plucked the stopper from the vial and poured a small amount on each.

As Kirth slowly rubbed, a tiny smile appeared. She said nothing.

"Massage for a full blink of the sun," Marra told her.

"Thank you, girl."

"And – your back."

When Kirth raised her brow, Marra added, "It will really help."

Kirth slowly turned, lifting her blouse. Marra poured more oil into her own hand, and briskly rubbed her palms together before applying to the elder's skin. She started tentatively, but soon found herself digging into the muscles, kneading the oil.

When she was done, Kirth gave her a very strange look and then, picking up her knife and bowl, the old woman went back to work.

A day later, Marra found the elder at breakfast, and applied more oil.

When she was done, Kirth held her fingers to her nose, drawing a long sniff.

"Tis different. What did you change?"

"Lemon Balm," Marra answered. And, reading the question in the woman's face, "to cool. Your muscles felt – hot, yesterday."

Kirth made no reply, but Marra knew the old Skullan watched her as she left.

On the third day, Marra brought her a hot tea as well as the ointment.

Kirth shut her eyes, inhaling the aroma.

"Red bark, grape root. And hot desert pepper."

Marra nodded. "You should drink it four times a day until no more twinges, and then three times a day for three days more."

Kirth chuckled.

As Marra started to leave, Kirth waved at the bench beside her.

Marra sat.

"Tell me, little Marra. Why did you not ask any of your teachers for advice?"

Marra stared. "I didn't know that was allowed."

Kirth shook her head, reaching for her tea. "Make friends here, child. Real friends."

Marra wasn't sure how to do that. "Yes, Mistress."

Kirth shot her a look and shook her head. "A friend 'tis someone you trust and who can trust you. There will be times when you love them for who they are, and times when you do not quite do so, but always there must be trust.

"It's like the plants, herb girl. You have a feeling about which are the best, the most potent. You have that feeling about people as well. Trust is a thing that must also be offered to be received. Find a good person, trust her to do right, and forgive her mistakes. 'Tis then she'll do the same for you."

"What about men?"

Kirth chuckled. "You can trust men as well," she told her. "But only so far."

Marra nodded as if she understood, and rose to her feet.

Kirth tapped her cup. "What else is in this tea?"

"Trevor seed, Mistress."

The old woman's face changed dramatically.

"Where did you get that Trevor seed?"

There were bags of Trevor seed in the storage cellars, available freely for all students. But Marra hadn't used that – she'd used one of her own seeds from Britta's stock. And Gran, a woman in an herb shop in Port Leet, had warned her that Britta's Trevor seeds were special.

"I have a supply," Marra told her.

"Show me," Kirth said.

So Marra took Kirth to her fist sack of Trevor seeds. The old woman sniffed the small bag, and stood stock still.

Marra reached beneath her mattress and slid Britta's book free to set it before her. Trust, Kirth had said. Well, there was nothing more trusting than revealing this book.

The elder stared at the old tome for several blinks of the sun. Just as Marra's stomach began to churn, she spoke.

"You've read this book? You've tried the recipes?"

Marra nodded. "Some, Mistress."

Kirth reached out to touch it, and then let her hand fall. "Get your things, and follow me."

The pit of Marra's being went cold. Hastily she grabbed all she had, tossing it in the bag she bought in Port Leet. Squaring her shoulders, she followed Kirth.

But when Kirth reached the stairs, she led Marra not down to the entrance, but up. All the way to the top tier. And along the hallway, to a small room with only one bed, and a table with a shelf above it and a chair tucked beneath.

"Tis your new room," Kirth told her. And then settling her rump on the mattress, the old woman nodded at the chair. "Now sit and tell me about Britta."

Marra had to gasp aloud before she could find enough breath to speak.

"Mistress Britta took me as apprentice. She died ten months later."

"Britta was on the Wavering Continent?"

Marra nodded. "San Cris."

"How did she die?"

"She – I found her on the floor in the back room one morning. Snark said her heart was never too good."

Kirth's eyes grew hard. "The only thing in Britta's life that wasn't good was her brother."

Marra nodded.

Kirth eyed her thoughtfully. "'Tis true you didn't like Snark."

"No, Mistress."

"How did Britta meet you?"

"San Cris – is small. We know everyone there."

"You lived on the Flats your whole life?"

"Yes – no." Marra shrugged. "Mother came from Missea, I think. I know my father did. I believe I was born there – here, I mean. But San Cris is the only place I remember."

"How did Britta find you?"

"In her shop one day. We wanted something for Mother's headaches, and the boy there pulled down a jar of Cris bark. He poured a bit on the paper – and I asked for fresh bark."

"How old were you?"

Marra shook her head. "It was five – six years before I became her apprentice. Mistress Britta came out of the back, shoed the boy away, and made me look at several herbs." Marra smiled softly at the memory. "I got to hold them in my hand."

"You've a special knack, child. We can teach anyone

the basics of herbs, anyone who cares to learn, that is, but ability to see the energy within can't be taught. Oh, you can memorize rules, remember the best colors. But to know the potency of the thing itself goes beyond that."

Marra looked at Kirth in wonder. "I – sort of have that. Maybe."

Kirth shook her head. "What you have, little Marra, goes well beyond that. You seem to see what that potency is. Somehow you knew which plant would do what. Hot desert pepper," Kirth suddenly laughed. "No one here has ever used that, ever even thought of that. Yet it worked. Did Britta tell you about it?"

Marra shook her head. "It just – felt better with it added."

Kirth rose to her feet. "I've got students to teach," she walked to the door and then looked over her shoulder.

"Marra, you will tell no one else what you just told me. You will show no one that book or the Trevor seed. 'Tis understood?"

She nodded.

Once the door was closed, Marra hopped up to roam the room, touching the table, and gazing out the window to the garden below.

She couldn't believe her luck. A place to live, people who could teach her. Friends.

Friends. Marra suddenly knew she had to find Drail, and let him know where she was. And if he needed her, well then. She'd just have to give all this up.

It was another Muck Barn match. But this one, Brok worried, pitted his work captain against a brutal team.

Brok had set two idiots to watching the doors because the more reliable Drail and his men were warming up. He'd needed to sort the teams himself because Old Merle – who wasn't that old, Brok muttered angrily – was giving last minute advice.

Brok wouldn't allow them to play at all if he didn't suspect they'd play anyway, at another sand pit. And that the other owner would boast of their traveling all the way from the Wavering Continent. Port Leet champions.

That other owner would snatch a good portion of Brok's customers for the night.

Drail and his men were in the pit now, stretching muscles, talking low amongst themselves.

Brok strode over to them. "The Barking Dogs Team plays tonight," he warned.

The Barking Dogs were undefeated at the Muck Barn, and Brok knew Drail was aware of their skill. "You would be wise to debut another night." Brok's eyes shifted to Old Merle, hoping to see a nod of agreement. Old Merle was often in agreement with him.

But not tonight. Instead the gray-haired man suppressed a smile, as if he saw through Brok's ploy.

"Their time is now," Merle clapped a hand on young Fallon's shoulder. "Their place is here. Their opponents are for the stars to decide."

And that idiot kid Fallon, who should be looking very nervous, merely grinned at the older man.

So Brok left to spread the word. If he couldn't stop them, he'd make as much coin as possible.

Drail stood in the sand, facing a barn full of Trumen flushed with ale and grinning in anticipation. The Barking Dogs had become local favorites, although Drail thought there were better teams. The Dogs liked to live up to their name, barking and growling before the match – and at strategic points during it.

Drail had been nervous this morning. Tiny fears had nagged, although he'd done his best to ignore them. He'd even raked the sand pit himself, just to suppress their voices. But now, feet firmly planted, friends at his side and Old Merle at his back, he found that serenity he'd been missing since defeat in the Black Arena.

The crowd swelled, the noise volume grew. This was where he lived, he realized. Here, in the sand. Playing comet, competing against all who would challenge him.

This was where he belonged. Not because he was the best, but because he would do his best. Yesterday was gone and unmourned; tomorrow an unknown road. Today was the game. Let the future judge him as it saw fit – he had no control of that. All he could do was play.

"Gamesmen!" called the Judge.

Drail marched to the line around the comet tail, waiting for permission to cross. The other team captains eyed each other, hurling a few, good-natured insults. Ignoring Drail altogether.

Brok had announced the Hand of Victory hailed from the desert – and that put them on the level of children in the eyes of these gamesmen.

We shall see, Drail smiled.

Choosing a ball was not important, as no comet would score before the values were revealed. He took the ball near him, and strode towards his team.

"They don't even take the trouble to insult us," he told Olver.

Manten grinned. "They will next game."

"COMET!" shouted the Judge.

A ball hurled at his feet, but this time Drail saw it coming. The Barking Dogs loved to open with a howl and a shot at the team they judged the least threat. He was already moving, launching his own ball.

It landed at the moving feet of the Dog's leader, causing him to stumble. The leader always opened the same way – fast throw, and run to the right. Drail had been ready.

As the game progressed, the hardest part was waiting to sink the comet. He did have a shot, but the ball was still dust-covered. So Drail threw it down instead, spinning into the sand at Olver's feet. Not a move done by the other teams, he grinned.

But in doing so, spots appeared beneath the covering, positioned such that there had to be five of them. Olver kick-lifted the five-spot and sent it to Manten.

Manten caught it and whirled, seeming to aim it at the Dog's leader. The leader ducked – and the ball arced over his head to drop perfectly into the comet Tail.

Longer than most games, Drail thought, but in other ways, very easy.

The crowd had quieted as much in shock by the long shot as by their favorite team losing. In Missean games, Old Merle would point out later, it becomes very clear when the five-spot has revealed itself. The battle changes and the spectators see that change.

With everyone else frozen, Drail found he was tired of playing by Skullan custom. He dove at a second ball – one that had not revealed its spots – and sent it hurtling at the tail.

It, too, sank.

The Judge needed several heartbeats to shout "CEASE!" Apparently this was not a situation he handled often.

Once Drail and the Hand retired from the field, the other teams continued foolishly in Drail's opinion. They played until they knew the point values of both remaining balls and then fought like the animals that they called themselves to finish the game.

The crowd's shouting had diminished with Drail's play and he wondered what the reaction would be when the winners were declared. They had, after all, upset the local favorites.

As the Judge lined them up, setting the five-point ball at their feet, Brok cried out, "The Desert Dogs have defeated the Barking Dogs!"

From the resulting wild cheers, Drail guessed the spectators had enjoyed the game after all.

It was after Marra decided to see Drail that she remembered the boy. He worked in the kitchen, where his mom served as cook.

His clothes were a little small, but not so small as to hinder her. He was the one who suggested the fireplace ash, which when brushed through her hair turned the dark red to a gray-brown. She gathered it into a ponytail, and donned the boyish boots and loose vest. It was difficult to judge with only a small mirror, but she thought no one would recognize her as female, let alone as Marra.

Thus dressed, she made her way to the Arc Banner Inn.

Mindful that Kratchett might be watching for her, she scanned the tavern twice before crossing the threshold. There was a man at a table, despite the early hour. He drank his ale with only a glance her way, so she kept her feet moving.

Up the back stairs and to the left, she went to their old rooms and knocked on Drail's door. There was no answer.

After a moment, she turned the latch and peeped in to see a woman's blue cape on the peg that should have held Drail's leathers. Marra wondered if he'd found a lady friend.

But the few other items in the room were all feminine. Nothing of Drail remained.

She ran lightly down the stairs and stumbled upon the innkeeper in the hall.

"I have a message for Drail of the Hand of Victory," she told him softly. That man in the tavern may well be just thirsty, but there was no need to let him overhear.

The innkeeper shook his head. "He's moved on – to Hay Street."

Something in the way he spat out those words worried her. His accompanying look seemed to share the disgust, as if she would know all about the place.

Her lips parted to ask as the patron stepped out of the doorway. "Any of last night's stew still in the pot?"

She left.

Hay Street was not easy to find.

The street itself was off-tier, meaning there were no levels above it. Only two areas of Missea were like that: the one surrounding the Palace; and the

Warehouse District just south of the Old Gate. The Palace area was the grandest in the city. Hay Street, in the Warehouse District, was its very opposite.

Rumors whirling around the school said Trumen should avoid the third tier these days, something about rising emotions in the death of the Prince. But when she found herself on a wrong path for the second time, and the rising mist shrouding the lower level, Marra needed to climb higher to find a familiar landmark.

She set foot on the ramp and glanced around. No one seemed concerned, so she sped up the spiral.

Almost immediately she saw a Palace turret far in the distance. That had to be east. Hay Street was supposed to be in the opposite quarter, so she turned in that direction.

Marra hadn't gone far before realizing all the other pedestrians were Skullan. Suddenly nervous, she spotted the nearest ramp and took a last look to get her bearings.

Nearby was a Cigar Shop, draped in black. Mourning a prince who wasn't dead, she thought. The shopkeeper stepped out, stretched, and eyed her. "Trumen filth belong on the lowest level. Lower – they belong in tunnels. Like rats."

With her eyes dropped respectfully, she sped past him towards the spiral – but was blocked by three men striding up. Three large Trumen. One of them gazed at her.

And turned that gaze on the shopkeeper. "Zag, I've bought cigars in your shop. I've leaned on this rail with you, listened to your complaints of your wife. Now you threaten a mere girl for trying to avoid the mist?"

The shopkeeper wavered. He even sent Marra a look of regret.

Then two more Skullan appeared.

"You dare criticize a Skullan? One in mourning for the Prince that your kind murdered?"

One of the three Trumen thrust Marra aside, moving to meet the newcomers. When a Skullan pushed him back a step, another Trumen quickly joined his friend.

"We've murdered no Skullan. But we're happy to break a jaw or two."

The third Trumen hissed in Marra's ear, "Go, girl. Get out of here before this gets worse."

He strode out to join the others.

Marra hesitated – she hated to run like a frightened desert hare. Yet she could serve no useful purpose. And in truth, her presence might well make things worse. A logical decision, surely, to leave.

Speeding down the spiral ramp, however, she still felt a coward.

7.

WHEN MARRA SAW the Muck Barn, she almost passed it by.

As luck would have it, however, she spotted Drail with a hay bale on his back, unloading a cart such as she'd hidden in several moons ago.

The sight made her heart freeze.

Drail looked up at that moment. The frown on his face slowly seeped into a smile. Dropping the hay, he strode up to her.

"You are alive. I've been worried, little Marra." His eyes took in her disguise and he cocked an eyebrow. "If strangely dressed."

Marra smiled her first true smile in many a day. "I'm at the Agben School," she told him. "That man with the Fox Boots saw me with Tryst. And he's still looking for me. Tryst said he won't bother you if he thinks you're not involved."

Drail's eyes took on a hard glint. "Let him bother me."

It warmed her heart to hear him say so – but he had no idea just how high placed and dangerous this man was.

"Are you..." she looked at the hay, at the Muck Barn. "Are you..."

Drail grinned. "The Hand of Victory has played three Trumen games in this pit. We've come in second the last two matches, but we did win the first." He winked at her. "We're gamesmen, Marra. Maybe not up to Gold Harbor play, but we can give some of these city-Trumen a challenge."

"You will win Gold Harbor someday." Marra felt sure of it. "When do you play your next game?"

"Tonight."

"I'll bring the elixir."

Drail flicked her ashen locks. "Can you bring it with red hair?"

Answering his grin with one of her own, she left.

As Drail and the others warmed up, Fallon described their competitors.

"Two of the teams tonight are put-togethers. Four men who wish to be gamesmen are trying out for all the other gamesmen to see. They hope to get picked up to play with a real team."

"Like you," Olver shrugged.

Fallon's eyes flashed. "I was with a real team – a good one. Put-togethers play with a few great moves and a lot of miscues. They'll look like guys who've never played together."

"And the Street Rats?" Manten asked.

"Rats usually play in the better arenas. They may not be the best Trumen team in Missea, but they're good and they got fans. They're here tonight because they heard about a lucky team from the desert."

Old Merle leaned on Fallon, pushing him into a deep hamstring stretch. "Any useful observations?"

Fallon nodded. "They like to position themselves surrounding the comet tail. Once the five-spot is revealed, they're in place to intercept and sink. They've played together for more than a year."

"What about..." Old Merle looked up in surprise. "Well, I'll be a desert hare."

Drail followed his gaze – to see Marra approach, her red hair newly washed and glistening in the torchlight.

She unwrapped a crystal vial and offered it to him.

Drail grasped it. Feeling the familiar glass in his hand, he knew the Street Rats were going to lose tonight. He drank his portion and passed it on to Manten.

Fallon eyed the vial dubiously.

"Fallon," Drail placed a hand on Marra's shoulder. "Meet Marra, Brista to the Hand of Victory."

She sank into a small courtesy, a new trick for her, he realized. "Marra, if I send Fallon to you for the elixir, how long does it take you to make it?"

Her brow furrowed. "The elixir itself, about thirty blinks of the sun. But I might be in a class."

Drail nodded. "If we sent you word in the morning? And then picked it up around quitting time?"

She gave him a peculiar look, but nodded. "The Birr itself will be potent for at least a few days. But I should come to you."

"Didn't you say you had need to be cautious?"

She looked in his eyes, thinking rapidly, and then nodded. "Will you at least tell me where you play that evening? So I can watch if possible?"

"Absolutely."

That night the Street Rats proved their level, both in soundly thrashing the two put-together teams and in the sheer number of fans who invaded the Muck Barn to watch. They did indeed surround the comet tail and defend it well, for no one could get past them to sink the ball.

But they'd never encountered a team like the Hand of Victory, where three of their gamesmen could shoot from long distances. Drail dove to wrest the comet from the ground, rolling to his feet again to sprint towards the tail.

The leader of the Street Rats blocked him with a shoulder shot designed to dislodge his reason as well as the ball.

But Drail saw it coming, and in spinning to take the shot on his arm, hurled the ball to Manten, who also raced towards the center.

Two of the Street Rats closed ranks to stop him. Manten faked to one direction, leapt to the other, and threw.

It wasn't the longest shot the Hand of Victory had ever made. It was, however, the longest shot ever seen in the Muck Barn – long enough that most thought it pure luck.

But in comet, luck counted.

So three things happened that night. The Street Rats found themselves a rival worth the name. A multitude of comet fans came to know a new team to follow.

And Fallon became a firm believer in the value of their Brista.

Lump watched the little herb girl leave. And followed.

He'd worked for Kratchett for a handful of seasons. His boss was a sharp one in many ways, but oddly blind in others. Such as choosing the point to watch for her at the Arc Banner Inn – popular, crowded, and a place where men like Lump stood out like a black gosling in a brace of white geese. It was too expensive, brimming with young Skullan celebrating victories. It was also too hard to observe all the entrances, let alone the windows.

But here at this Muck hole, no one could approach Drail without being seen.

So after a week of drinking at the Arc Banner, Lump had simply followed his gut and shifted focus to Drail. Either Kratchett was dense or he didn't understand women.

And thinking about that Agben female his boss was caught up with, Lump figured it might be the latter.

The little herb girl had dutifully delivered her potion, watched the match, and then left before the next game started. That was Lump's only regret – he'd have liked to have seen the rest of the games.

When he followed her to her new home, he could have kicked himself. Where else would a little herb girl go but the great herb school?

The next day he found Kratchett at his favorite morning table – at an odd inn near the Palace. It was a Trumen kitchen with a specialty of freshly-baked sweet bread, and Kratchett was always one to pander to his tastes.

"Got her," Lump told him as he sat down.

He watched the man's eyes light up – and wondered again just what Kratchett thought little Marra could tell him. Only a fool would expect Skullan royalty to confide in a Trumen waif.

"Afore you go off running," he added, "she's at that Agben place."

Lump felt a satisfaction in seeing Kratchett's face fall. It might be time, he mused, to look for better work.

The next morning Marra began creating her first tincture.

There were various workrooms in the school, but Marra chose one of the lean-tos outside. She could see the sun there, and smell the heady perfumes wafting in from the garden.

She was especially excited about tinctures. The key with enhancing mixtures was exotic ingredients – herbs from far away, some of them very far. To be truly effective, they had to still have their potency, which was difficult months after they were cut.

Some could be properly dried, such as was done in the drying shed. But others stored their value in the juice or the sap of the plant. Drying them out made them lose potency.

Tinctures were the answer. The most vibrant parts of the plant were put in a bottle of vinegar and then shook twice a day for two handfuls of days. At the end of that time, the essence was preserved in the liquid itself, which could last a full three years. But as glass bottles did not travel as well as the plants themselves, the expense was naturally higher.

Kirth had given her a handful of fresh Snow Daisy, a plant that grew high on an artic mountain. Marra used the flat glass top of her bottle to bruise the leaves – pressing them to break the veins and release the essence – before sliding them into the wide opening of the jar, pouring in the vinegar, and sealing the bottle. The key with Snow Juice – which was what this tincture was called – was never touching the leaves after the bruising. Oils on the fingers that handled them would render the juice ineffective.

Kirth watched her work with a sharp eye.

It made Marra nervous, but she soon lost herself in the wonder of creating it. She'd encountered the name in several recipes in Britta's book, and to be actually making it now gave her a thrill-spike in her gut.

"Where did you get the Snow Daisy?" Marra suddenly asked.

Kirth smiled broadly. "Leave your jar on the shelf there, child. And follow me."

She was led to the stairs, where Kirth pulled a small handle that was hard to see in the dim light. A door Marra would have never have known existed swung open, and they traveled down the steps.

There were three sub levels. Kirth skipped the first two, taking Marra all the way to the bottom and through another small door.

They entered a room that was more cave than construction. The floor and walls were dirt, illuminated by the low light of rag-oil, a diluted oil that lasted much longer, though providing a fainter light. Rag-oil was oft used for passageways where one needed to walk without lingering.

This cave was chock full of plant life.

A fire pit lay ready to light in the center. Kirth

struck a fire-steel with a flint piece and set the pit to blazing.

Startled, Marra looked at her.

"This one we warm up for a few hours a day. For the plants."

Marra looked around, spotting a lot of curious grasses, a few stubby trees. Kirth strode through the cave and out under an arch, so Marra followed.

The floor sloped down a long narrow passage before opening again to a second cave. This one had moss of odd hues and a single gnarly shrub that both drew and repelled Marra.

But the Skullan woman kept moving.

Another long narrow path, stretching twice as long as the first, led to a final cave. This one had a heavy door protecting it, and when Kirth swung the portal wide, a frigid blast struck them.

"Tis the truth, I keep forgetting my cloak," Kirth muttered. She waved Marra in and tugging the door shut, sealed them both in the cold.

In the dim light, Marra saw her breath puff in tiny clouds. The Snow Daisy must grow here, she thought. Stars! The Agben School was interesting for the teaching, but its true value might be the many ingredients so tenderly kept.

The wonder she felt must have shown on her face, for Kirth chuckled.

"Yes. It's taken centuries, but there are very few plants in the world we don't have here."

"Are there any at all?"

"Oh yes. Not many that we know of. But a few."

Later, as Marra strung more Dru Weed in the drying barn, she pondered Kirth's words.

Kirth had warned her she did not yet have cave access and was not to go down there. There were no locks on the doors, of course, as most of the school ran on an honor system, and except for Marra, no one below fourth year actually knew of the cave's existence.

As Marra would never violate that honor, she had asked Kirth how to gain access.

"Tis earned over time, child."

She was pondering this from atop the ladder, when she heard a familiar voice.

"Come down at once, girl."

Her eyes flew to a tall Skullan woman, all in pale blue. The Lady of Agben from the Palace.

Dru Weed slipped from her fingers to plop in the dust at the Lady's feet. Nervously, Marra glanced around, but she knew they were alone.

She climbed down.

"Come with me." The woman turned and strode out.

Marra followed her into the sunshine, crossing the garden rich with aromas and color. When the Lady marched beneath a seldom used archway, she hesitated.

The Lady turned, saw her standing in the sunlight. She sighed and nodded.

A Trumen male stepped out, clamping a hand across Marra's mouth. Recognizing his face, she struggled violently.

He had grabbed her once before, in a city a continent away. Many bad things had happened.

Frantic, she bit his hand. He grunted, but didn't release the grip. She kicked his shin, struggling to get an arm free – to punch his nether region. Both Drail and Tryst had assured her that was most effective.

But even as her hand escaped his grip, she was struck on the side of her head and knew no more.

The sensation was one of swaying. Gradually she grew aware of it.

Marra realized she was hanging upside down. Opening her eyes, she saw the wood planks of a tiered walk passing below her. She was draped over someone's shoulder, someone with a rough stride.

Her head throbbed.

Pale blue silk flitted into view and out again. Memory flared – the Lady of Agben. Marra had to force herself not to struggle. She remembered the archway, the man hidden there.

These people were after the Prince.

Well, she knew nothing more of his whereabouts than they did. She hadn't seen nor heard from him since the day they'd been chased from the Palace. Do what they would, Tryst was safe.

But was she? Surely Fox Boots must suspect she had little to tell.

She peeked to the sides without turning her head, seeking help. There were few people about and from her angle she couldn't tell if they were Trumen or Skullan. Skullan stood out from their height and their hair – but not their feet. Marra couldn't trust Skullan to rush to her aide.

Indeed, could she trust Trumen? They would see a true Lady of Agben and would probably think Marra some sort of recalcitrant servant. Flailing and screaming might only add to the illusion.

Panic rose, making her muscles twitch with the need to react. She even felt the change in the man carrying her, as if he sensed she might be waking. She forced herself to relax, to hang limp.

After several long steps, his own muscles slackened.

Tryst had once said that the mind was a more powerful weapon than any muscle in the body. She could only hope he was right.

The man walked on. At one point, he strode to the edge of the walkway, yielding a very dizzying view. They must be at least four tiers up, though Marra didn't try to count. The distant ground swayed below, as a horse drawn cart rolled beneath a flapping banner. Her stomach knotted.

And then came the ramp. The spiral downward was

hard to watch and her eyes clamped shut of their own accord.

When the stride leveled out, she peered cautiously between her lashes. The increasing number of large flower pots told her they were near the Palace.

She caught a glimpse of the stone wall and a trellis covered in spice-roses. Would they just stroll through the huge gates with their masses of guards, without anyone wondering about an unconscious girl over a man's shoulder?

Her captor veered, crossing the planted grass by the wall, stepping behind a trellis. Marra caught a glimpse of a doorway and a single guard in the hidden alcove.

"Halt," grumbled a hoarse voice.

"Give over, you dozy Churmen," the man carrying her retorted.

"Lump, you idiot. You startled me."

"And this here's Rain, the Agben Lady. Best make your apologies and open your door there."

Hearing the rustling, the door creaking, Marra panicked. Surely she'd fare better outside the Palace than within.

She burst into action, feet flailing as her body writhed. With a grunt of pain, the rough hands slackened.

She tumbled onto the flagstone.

Three faces stared down at her. The guard and the lady were frozen in surprise, but Marra knew that wouldn't last for long. Lump rubbed his bruised thigh, his eyes narrowing angrily. It was he that she feared most.

Scrambling to her feet, she dove for the path back, but Lump leapt to block her.

"Stop the girl!" cried Rain. Marra saw Lump's eyes roll in annoyance. She knew she'd never slip past him, which left but one option.

Whirling, Marra streaked through the open Palace door and ran.

The doorway led to a wide tunnel arch with a second door at the end. Marra burst through.

And found herself in the sunlight between a giant spice-rose hedge and the Palace wall. She spied another door, sprinted to it, and yanked it open.

Hearing a noise within, she didn't enter. Instead she dove under the nearby hedgerow.

Flattening herself between prickly branches and the ground, she tried to see the door she'd left open, but the foliage blocked her view.

Pounding steps approached, and just as quickly vanished. An instant later, she heard the slower steps of Rain pass.

And the quiet click of a door.

Immediately Marra was up again, racing back to the way out. She found the door by the spice-rose hedge and yanked with all her might.

It was now locked.

Whirling, she frantically looked about for an exit.

The Palace garden itself was large, although nothing compared to Agben. Delicate paths wound charmingly through neatly trimmed grass, flower beds, and carefully cultivated trees. Spice roses climbed the walls to disguise the stone with nature.

There was no place to hide.

Marra darted across the pathway to the far wall of the Palace itself. She found two doors, chose one, and breathed again when it swung open easily.

She dreaded running farther from the one exit she knew. But that one exit was locked – she had to find another way out.

So she slipped inside.

Within was a narrow hallway, lit by low-burning oil lamps. It was not as clean as the previous portions of the Palace she'd seen, and she guessed this was a servants' passage. Quickly she brushed herself off, then chose a direction and walked.

Rapid footsteps approached, and she looked up fearfully. A maid hurried towards her, offering a quick smile as she passed.

Marra adopted the same pace and kept moving.

The passage sloped up, curving. She saw light ahead, and heard voices.

She hesitated.

But the voices were female and without the refinement of Rain's. Marra drew near enough to make out the words.

"This bird's too tough."

"Ash said to make a fricassee."

"I want to roast a chicken."

Somewhere behind her a latch clicked open, making her decision for her. Marra stepped through the door before her.

She found herself in a large room, lit by cascading sunbeams from windows high up on one wall. A giant hearth commanded the center, with a small fire burning in just one corner. Ten such fires could easily be set beneath the cavernous chimney.

One cook pot dangled from a hook near the flame, ready to swing out over the blaze. Marra realized an entire system of iron hooks and grills clung to the chimney stones.

Beyond them stood a large table ladened with freshly-chopped vegetables, a pitcher, and a plucked fowl. A fat cook stuffed the bird as a young girl peeled an apple.

The girl spared her a glance. The cook did not.

"Ash is supposed to give us what we need. He don't set menus – and so I'll tell him," the cook growled and waddled away.

The young girl sighed and shrugged at Marra.

"I'd hide if I were you," she smiled. "Cook's battles with Ash get very loud." And then, looking Marra over more carefully, "who are you?"

"I'm lost," Marra answered. "Took a wrong turn somewhere. How do I get out of the Palace?"

The young girl grinned knowingly. "Looking for

Land Market Street? I'll show you."

Marra felt a huge wave of relief – until the girl stepped past her towards the door she'd just left.

"It's back that way?"

The girl nodded, and continued on. Reluctantly Marra followed.

"You ever been in a Palace kitchen before?" the girl chuckled at Marra's reaction. "New, ain't ya? That's the third biggest one."

"Third... what?"

"Kitchen, of course. East Kitchen. South's bigger, and the Central Kitchen's twice that big."

Bemused, Marra nodded. Her attention focused on the sounds ahead of them. She thought she caught whispers.

Footsteps approached, moving much faster than the usual servant trot.

Marra whirled. "Forgot something," she muttered, and sped back to the kitchen with only a glimpse of the girl's astonished face.

Getting out of the East Kitchen was easy – the problem was choosing which way. Three cavernous passageways beckoned, but their very size made her wary.

Many people must pass through them all at once or they wouldn't need to be so wide.

A scrape behind her spurred Marra on. She dove into the nearest passageway and ran.

The next room seemed filled with racks and shelves

above rough benches for servants to rest. Not that any servant did so – the place was empty.

An entire wall of bells dangled to the left.

This wasn't for rest, the thought flashed in her mind. It was a place to wait. Servants awaited summons by some noble in a room high above them.

She sprinted up a staircase – again there were three – and achieving what she guessed was ground level, ran on.

And what had worried her, the many choices that she'd been forced to make fast, suddenly seemed a good thing. For her pursuers would face the same choices, and surely must lose her.

Surely.

Racing on, she heard muffled voices ahead. Marra forced her feet to slow as she neared a corner. She again assumed a servant pace.

And stepped out.

Before her was the giant portrait of Tryst. She actually smiled in relief – then quickly schooled her features into those of a servant. Turn right, she thought. Keep looking down.

Marra watched the legs of people in the grand entrance, the clothes so much nicer than those of the servants. She kept her distance, gliding smoothing toward that large opening to the courtyard entrance, toward the sunshine and freedom.

A fist clamped her arm.

"Marra," said Fox Boots. "Why, Rain is looking

everywhere for you, little herb girl."

She jerked wildly, trying to free herself – but he lifted her up onto her toes, so she had no purchase. His eyes peered down into hers and she realized he had no intention of losing her. Thoughts flashed of tricks Tryst had shown her, of kicks to parts of the anatomy.

But guards passed them, and servants hurried on their business. If she tried such a thing, even if she succeeded, it would not go well for her. Frantically her mind whirled to seek a solution.

None occurred.

And as he dragged her up the familiar stairway, past the watching eyes of the portrait Tryst, she almost laughed aloud.

How peculiar it was that Tryst couldn't get into his Palace, and she couldn't get out.

Rain's chamber was very large.

Marra hadn't properly looked at it before because she'd been nervous. Now, when she ought to be scared out of her wits, she stood calmly surveying her surroundings. Maybe her mind was still working on getting her out of here.

"Go find Rain," Fox Boots told a servant. "Now." Then he entered the room and shut the door.

Marra stared at three glass bottles on the table, glistening in the sunlight streaming from the balcony. All three were filled with colored liquid. By the Agben

School standards, different bottle shapes denoted different categories of contents. She recognized the first shape indicated a strong enhancement, and the second some sort of poison – harmful, if not lethal.

The third bottle, a delicate pyramid shape, was one she'd never seen before.

A shiver ran down her spine.

"What do you want from me?" she turned to face her captor. "I don't know where he is, you know. I haven't seen nor heard from him since that day."

Fox Boots smiled. "I was reasonably sure that was the case. He's abandoned you, girl."

Her instinct was to deny that, but she held her tongue.

Fox Boots actually bowed to her, although it was more mocking than respect. "Marra, my name is Kratchett. And I'd like you to join with me."

She pressed her lips together.

"You know now who Tryst is. That he's off on his own business, with no thought to what dangers he's exposed you to. He's not even Trumen. He's an elitist Skullan, in truth the elitist of the elite. He used Drail and his men – and most particularly you – without any thought to the risk. And then, when you knew who he was, this disgraced prince disappeared to save his own skin and left you to your fate."

She frowned at the word 'disgraced'.

"Oh yes. Disgraced," he spoke softly. "His own father commissioned all of this rather than publicly denounce the royal heir."

He watched her very carefully, waiting for a sign of capitulation. A smart person would have given the sign and pretended to be won over.

Marra couldn't stomach it.

"Kratchett." she said.

And his eyes flared at the contempt in her voice.

"We've been calling you 'Fox Boots'."

He stared back at her, then slowly looked down at his boots, and smiled.

"I suppose dust-dogs know good leather when they see it," he murmured. Dust-dogs and leather – a mocking belief held here in Missea, and probably intended as an insult. It was true the finest cloth came from the Wavering Continent. But the joke was that they of the desert weren't able to keep any for themselves, as poor as they were.

Well, Marra knew nothing of leather, but she knew better than to react to that. "You're correct – I haven't seen him since that day. And he never told me at all – it was the portrait that gave him away."

She gave a mock curtsy. "There is nothing more I can tell, sir. But I'm glad to know Tryst eluded you."

Fox Boots – no, Kratchett – laughed. But she could see the anger he was trying to smother. He took a step closer, grabbed her by her shoulders, snatching her off her feet.

The door flung open and Rain checked on the threshold.

Kratchett stepped back, releasing Marra.

The Agben woman strode inside, hands on hips. Somehow, it was all the more frightening when Marra saw the haste with which Kratchett jumped to shut the door behind her.

"My, we are feisty, little Trumen." She stepped close, towering over Marra. "If I have to chase you again, you will deeply regret it."

All Kratchett's talk had simply made Marra angry. Somehow this woman's every word scared her to the core. Because she believed her, Marra realized. There was no hidden agenda, no attempt to manipulate. Subtlety was unknown to this lady.

And the Skullan was in charge. Marra wondered what would have happened if she'd agreed to Kratchett's proposal. Would he have told Rain? Or simply hidden her himself?

"Now tell me where that petty little princeling is."

"Lady," Marra realized she was trembling and quickly tucked her hands behind her. "By the Desert Crane, I swear to you I do not know. I haven't seen him since that day in the Palace."

Rain exchanged a long look with Kratchett.

Marra could see he'd already told her what he suspected. And the Skullan Lady hadn't believed him. Still didn't believe him.

Rain strode to the table.

Marra couldn't help but be fascinated at her mannish stride, her skirts swishing out with the long steps she took. She paused by the three bottles, a hand hovering between the poison and the unknown pyramid flask.

All of Kratchett's threats hadn't unnerved her the way this simple gesture did.

Long fingers wrapped around the pyramid shape, lifting it. Thumb and index plucked the stopper free.

And an aroma Marra had never experienced before wafted through the room. It smelled of a hearth, of a home fire, a teasing, welcoming scent that beckoned her in. Yet just beneath it lay the odor of something horrible – charred to death. It awoke a primal terror deep in her gut.

Kratchett was still behind her, blocking the door.

Circling the table, Rain came towards her.

Marra launched herself for the balcony.

The room was nearly a man's height above the private garden that Marra had first entered. Two men strolled along a pathway, conversing as they drew near.

Marra leapt over the rail.

She landed in a heap, feet tangling in her skirt. And when she tried to scramble up, her wrist gave out in searing pain.

The two men halted beside her. As she lifted her gaze, it dawned on her she was in the presence of royalty.

Both Skullan wore thick, luxurious robes of a cloth so fine she couldn't begin to guess its origin. She knew the one on the right was the King himself, although he wore no crown. She knew because his face was exactly that of Tryst with perhaps a little more meat and those tiny lines of wisdom at the corners of his eyes.

The other man was just as richly garbed, but without any trace of resemblance. It was he who extended a hand.

She took it because it never occurred to her not to obey the implied command.

For the second time, she caught the whiff of the pyramid bottle, the welcoming home fire, not quite masking the charring stench of – death. No. Something worse than death.

"Charis, I think she flees our Lady of Agben," the King said.

Charis nodded.

"And Rain looks most annoyed. If I were you," Charis's gaze dropped from Rain to Marra, "I would keep running."

She suddenly knew herself safe for the moment. Rain could not vault the railing in her skirts, nor screech commands at the King himself. And Kratchett, she noticed, was keeping well hid.

"Your Majesty," Marra curtseyed and rose at the smile in his eyes. A smile hauntingly familiar, she realized. "Your son lives," she whispered.

Then she raced for the spice-rose hedge, to the entrance she'd first come through.

The guard was still there, of course. Preoccupied, he had his hand on the chest of a young noble, stopping him from entering. He was guarding the way in, not the way out. Stepping past them both to gain the street, Marra ran.

She never slowed till she was safe inside the Agben School.

8.

SOMETHING ABOUT THE GIRL running away from the Palace seemed wrong. But Mauric had no time to dwell on it.

"I live here," he patiently explained for the third time. "I always use this entrance. It's never been guarded before – just kept locked. See? Here's my key."

The guard shook his head. "Tighter security now, since the Prince's murder. All visitors must enter the main gate."

"I'm not a visitor and I don't wish to go through the main gate. Just let me get my things. Please! My father is waiting and very annoyed with me."

The young guard wavered.

Mauric worked hard to keep the grin off his face.

And then a Trumen male ran up, his pace echoing that of the girl. He hesitated, scanning the street. Mauric was sure he was looking for her.

But she was gone. And the Trumen finally noticed the two of them.

"No one enters here," he snapped.

Mauric was startled to see the young Skullan guard straighten and nod, as if the instruction had come from his captain.

"He's just leaving," the guard said.

The Trumen turned on his heel. "You will lock up now," he tossed over his shoulder, and then disappeared.

The guard sighed.

"Who was that?" Mauric asked.

"He belongs to Rain," the guard replied. "If you really did use to live here, you should know things have changed in the last few weeks."

He retreated through the entrance. "Agben commands here now."

The door shut in Mauric's face.

As Mauric would later explain to Tryst, he waited a few blinks of the sun. And then inserted his key into the lock. He wasn't in the least surprised to find it no longer worked.

He was surprised at the reaction when he told the tale later, in a tavern with the Prince and Jason.

"Agben," Tryst echoed. "Then we go to Agben."

Mauric gaped. "My Prince, I do not believe..."

"Men are not allowed within the school walls," Jason told him. "And if you think to announce who you are..."

Tryst was already shaking his head. "I'll not declare myself in a place so obviously involved in my disappearance. But I have a friend there."

The comet ball flew at him. As he snatched it, Fallon whirled and sprinted for the goal line.

The dust had long come off, so he knew he clutched the five-spot. Twice had the Bone Crushers stolen the ball away; twice had they missed the tail.

Fallon also knew Drail was in a better position to make the shot, but he'd come to distrust the big man's ability to make clutch goals. He always sunk the second ball; rarely the first. So Fallon launched it from where he was.

It bounced off the rim.

And right into the hands of one of the Bone Crushers, who dashed away. Manten and a man from another team pursued, knocking him as he launched his shot.

He missed.

The five-spot now lay in the arena dust as Drail, Olver, and two Bone Crushers streaked towards it.

The Bone Crusher leader scooped it up, saw Drail coming towards him, and launched the ball not at the tail, but at Drail's feet.

It hit the dirt, spinning wildly. The sand flew up in

a great wave, and Drail flinched.

Fallon had tried to teach him the timing to look away to protect your eyes even as you dove for the ball. For some reason, Drail could never quite tear his gaze from it and thus was always blinded for a heartbeat or two. Just long enough for someone else to leap in, knock him down, and steal the ball. As the Bone Crusher now did.

With Drail sprawling in the dust, the Bone Crusher raced to the cone, stepping on the line as he sunk the ball.

The judge might have called that, Fallon thought. But he wasn't surprised when no such call was made. He also wasn't surprised when Drail suddenly came to life, sprinting for the three-spot half an arena away. By rights, he shouldn't have made it.

But he did.

And with two more amazing weaves through furious men, Drail ended with a dive roll of his own – and took a shot from far away.

And sank the ball.

Second place, again. With his old team, Fallon would have been thrilled to so consistently score in the top two spots game after game. But these Desert Dogs were better than that. He was tired of standing on the edge of victory, failing against teams that they should defeat.

'Stuttering', they called it in Missea. 'Spitting sand', they called it in the Flats. Both terms referred to letting fear seep into the nerves at a crucial moment, just enough to effect aim, or timing, or judgment.

Just enough to lose.

It would be foolish, Fallon told himself, to leave this desert team right now. He was learning so much, both from their unusual style and from the great Skullan gamesman, Wolfbur. At the moment, Fallon was the least skilled on the team.

At the moment.

Drail climbed over the railing to join Wolfbur and Old Merle. With a shrug, he waited until his teammates also stood near.

It seemed odd to see only the men with no little Marra between them. She had brought the elixir of course, although late enough that he'd begun to worry. She'd also been distracted, starting at noises, looking over her shoulder. He'd offered to walk her back to the school after the match, but she'd shook her head, returning a quick smile, and vanished.

She hadn't even waited for the glass vial, he realized.

"What happened?" Old Merle cut straight into his thoughts.

Drail looked at him in surprise. "The Bone Crushers are a good team. Even so, we finished second."

Old Merle stepped forward, ready to argue.

Drail sighed, not wanting to renew this discussion

again. They'd had it several times.

And then Wolfbur clasped the old man's arm, stopping it before it could begin.

"Best warm up for the third match," he said.

They all moved outside the Muck Barn to a work yard lit by a waning moon.

Manten and Olver stretched while Fallon hesitated before joining them. Drail watched him carefully, knowing the young man was growing disenchanted with their losses.

As he eased into a wide stance, Drail swung his arms in a gentle motion that released all the knots within.

"We may have a problem," Wolfbur casually spoke into the night air. "Brok has been chatting with the Bone Crushers."

Drail paused.

"Apparently, they want your spot in the Muck Barn. They're Missean, unlike you, and they win more games."

Out of the corner of Drail's eye, he saw Olver grin. Olver, he knew, thought it time they left the hayloft of the Muck Barn and find themselves proper quarters. Drail wanted to wait. Wait until they were more consistent, had more notches on their leathers. Wait until they again claimed the name of the Hand of Victory.

The Hand of Victory was still the name of their team, of course. But one did not display banners at the lowly level of Muck Barn play, and as most referred to them as desert dogs, it had somehow become their title. He kept meaning to change that, but hadn't yet.

He supposed he didn't feel quite worthy – yet – of the name bestowed by his Grandsire all those years ago.

"Are the Bone Crushers willing to work for their keep?" Drail asked.

Old Merle was staring at Wolfbur as the old Skullan spoke carefully. "Brok thinks he can bring in new workers to sleep down by the arena itself. This place has become more popular of late."

Drail straightened, thinking. "I suppose if we must, we can sleep on the straw at the arena edges. Will he allow us to...?"

But Wolfbur was shaking his head. "He only wants one team – not two. You and the Hand will be pushed out."

Drail leaned heavily against the Barn. "Is Brok just contemplating this? Or is it already decided?"

Wolfbur's look was steady. "If you lose to this team tonight, I fear you may be seeking new quarters tomorrow."

When it was time for the third match, Drail and the team entered the arena.

"We'll find new quarters soon enough," Manten told him.

Drail realized Manten expected to lose.

"New quarters with a better cook," Olver added. "And a pillow."

Fallon grinned. "Blanket for warmth instead of straw."

There was a time, Drail realized, when he would have been the first to speak of better things. But now he was anxious less they lose their home of more than three moons. "You're all expecting to lose?"

"We always lose to the circuit teams," Fallon told him.

The Judge beckoned.

Moments later, Drail chose a ball and strode towards his team. The best thing, he knew, would be to win tonight. The challenge was that the Bone Crushers were a circuit team, welcomed at any of the twelve Trumen arenas in Missea. That meant they were good.

"Better than us," he told himself aloud.

"COMET!"

The Bone Crusher leader snagged a second ball from another team and whirled to face Drail with a sphere in each hand.

He hurled them one after the other.

One ball spun at Drail's feet, blinding him in the wave of sand. The second slammed his face.

Drail kept his feet, shaking away the confusion and dust. He heard the laughter of the spectators, the other teams. Too much laughter at his expense, he realized. They knew the spinning balls never failed to slow him, just as they knew he couldn't beat a circuit team. Right behind that thought he heard Raston's voice. "You think you can't win? Then you've already lost. Why do you bother to play?"

The others were fighting each other now. Manten dove in to wrestle a ball free and sent it arcing over the arena to Olver.

Not to him, he realized. Because he was distracted and Manten knew it.

No one tried to block Olver. Instead a flurry of serious wrestling erupted for a different ball, which must mean it was the five-spot. He watched Fallon leap into the scuffle, peel the ball free, and hurl it at Manten. Drail shook himself, and sprinted for the center.

Manten snagged the ball and tried to keep running – but two defenders streaked to intercept.

Manten launched it at Drail.

Drail caught it, whirling, and felt that flash of hesitation. That flash of – doubt? Fear? And all the time Raston's words echoing: think you can't win? Think you can't win?

A defender leapt out between Drail and the comet tail. Drail stopped.

And took aim. And faked the toss.

The defender jumped to block it – as Drail knew he would. These gamesmen might be good, but they had very obvious habits. Very predictable.

He sunk the ball as the defender fell back to the

dirt.

Stunned silence held the crowd. And then roars erupted – not in disappointment, as he'd half feared, but in jubilation.

The other balls quickly followed the five-spot and the match was over in a few blinks. Brok strode out to the Judge, grinning from ear to ear as he lifted Drail's hand triumphantly.

"Hail, Desert Dogs!" Brok shouted.

Drail shook his head and bellowed, "Hail the HAND OF VICTORY."

It was much later, after many ales, when he asked if Brok still wished to give the Bone Crushers a bed at the Muck Barn.

The owner of the arena set his palm over Drail's mug in reply. "Man's had too much to drink!" Brok, Drail realized, had no idea what he was talking about.

And having overheard the exchange, Wolfbur threw back his head to vent a full belly laugh.

It was three weeks before Marra relaxed.

For days she'd kept a careful lookout for Rain. She took to carrying a grinding stone in her pocket, with a wild thought of hitting anyone who tried to snatch her away again. But she found it only made her feel more on edge, as if she were looking for trouble.

Her classes with Kirth were the only time she truly felt safe, and then only after the class was well underway.

In her fourth class after the incident, Kirth kept her behind when the other students left.

"Enough of this, child." The old Skullan woman peered down from her great height. "Marra, what has you as jumpy as a cat in Wild Dog Canyon?"

Marra could only stare back at the elder.

Kirth sighed and sat down again on her favorite rock. She always brought herself down to Trumen level when she wished to calm them, Marra realized.

"You do tend to keep all your thoughts penned up in your head," Kirth grasped her chin, reading her eyes. "Life 'tis much easier if you let them out for a run occasionally."

Marra released a breath that she hadn't known she'd been holding.

"You'll see them all much better in the light of day," Kirth smiled. "Sharing thoughts helps reveal the little flaws."

"Rain," Marra blurted out. "She – took me from here. I'm fearful she'll do it again."

Kirth slowly straightened, her fingers tightening into a fist. And Marra's concern that the Skullan women would protect each other faded.

"Why did she do that?"

Marra sighed. There were parts of the story that weren't hers. She couldn't betray Tryst, and the tale didn't make much sense without that piece of information.

Yet looking into Kirth's eyes, she saw the old

woman understood.

"Tell me what you can."

So Marra told her of being snatched, of Kratchett and Rain. And although she hesitated, Kirth guessed it was to the Palace she was whisked away. "I know whose bed Rain sleeps in these days," the old woman sighed.

When the tale was told, Marra watched Kirth's face, miserably aware of the story's gaps. But the elder accepted her words without comment.

And considered.

"I'll talk to Rain. Everyone will know I'm looking for her, so if she shows herself she won't be able to walk quite so freely. If she comes to you, refuse to go with her anywhere. Instead, tell her to wait while you fetch me."

It was later, when Marra was shaking her tinctures, that she saw Kirth again.

Once the herb to be tinctured was placed in the vinegar, it needed to be shaken at least twice a day for a week. Some tinctures only required three days, but Marra was trying more exotic ingredients, and curious if a full week's time would make them stronger.

The shed in the garden yard was normally used for such work, but there was a large worktable in the first of the underground caverns area where the temperature was cooler. Marra worked there, hoping the lack of sunlight would make the tincture better.

When the door behind her creaked open, she

realized how vulnerable she was.

She whirled to find Kirth regarding her with an amused expression. "You do seem to turn up in places no student ever finds."

"I – didn't know it was restricted."

The elder grinned and rustled over to a far table covered with glass containers. "The only restriction we use is ignorance, child. And that seems to be a quality you don't subscribe to."

Uncertain if that was a compliment, Marra finally smiled. It was true – she liked exploring the Agben School, discovering what everyone else was doing, and seeing how well it worked. After more than a year of no training at all, she was starved for knowledge. And fearful less it disappear again.

Kirth shook two bottles – tinctures, no doubt, and then hefted a large empty bowl. She opened a paper packet and dumped the white leaf contents into it.

Curious, Marra took her time shaking her tinctures. Kirth's lips twitched, but she uttered no word as she measured a small amount of cinnamon oil and poured it atop the leaves.

Marra was wondering if she dared step closer to watch when the elder uncorked a glass vial of powdered contents.

The scent was an earthy wild grass. Beneath it lingered...*charred death*. That same primal-terror aroma she'd caught in Rain's room.

"What is that?" Marra tried to keep her tone casual,

and knew she'd failed at Kirth's penetrating look.

"Kwitt. A rare plains grass from the Dim Continent. Newly arrived – Rain obtained it from one of her sources, I believe."

Marra stood rooted to the floor. "What are its properties?"

"Powerful relaxant. Very powerful."

"It smells horrible."

Kirth sealed the vial and then left her bowl to confront Marra, tilting her face up to the dim oil light.

"It smells of earth, Marra. Grass and earth. Why would that seem horrible to you?"

Marra shook her head. "Beneath that – it smells of charred flesh."

Kirth stepped back.

Worry touched Marra's spine – for the elder's eyes were greatly startled. Whirling, the old woman plucked a different bottle and uncorked it. And held it under Marra's nose.

"What do you smell?"

Marra swallowed, and obediently sniffed. "Sweet spice rose."

"And beneath that?"

"Old earth with salt."

Kirth flew to the shelves, snatching another flask. "What do you smell?"

"It's just honey."

"And beneath?"

"Animal fodder. Goat."

Kirth repeated the process three times more. After the last smell, she plunked down hard on a bench, her head thumping back against the wall. "Oh Britta!" she whispered.

She was staring at Marra as if she'd found a Flatmouth viper in her bedroll.

"Mistress?" Marra asked nervously.

"Tell me when Britta chose you for apprentice. It wasn't from picking out healthy plants."

Marra bit her lip. "We walked into her shop, my mother and I, for my birthday present. It was sweet oil, to rub in my hair. Mother loved sandalwood and held it out for me to sniff.

"I said it smelled like beetle dung. Mother rolled her eyes and laughed. The Mistress bade me inhale the scent of three different vials. And then she said she'd take me as her apprentice."

Kirth nodded, studying her face, seeing more than Marra wanted her to see. "You didn't want to go."

Marra grimaced. "I didn't want to leave home. Mother said..." she was startled to feel a tear slipping down her cheek and quickly scraped it off with the heel of her hand. "Mother said it was easier for two desert women to make it apart than together."

The gnarled fingers drifted over to pat Marra's arm. "It wasn't all bad. You like herbs."

"Oh yes. It was fun, actually. Just took too long to get really going. Mother remarried to a man in another town. And then Mistress Britta died."

"Smells have layers to you," Kirth said. It wasn't a question.

Marra blinked in confusion and the elder chuckled.

"Child, that is a rare gift indeed. Most mere mortals barely smell at all. They can tell a fish has been dead for a week or a cooking pot has a promising stew. Yet you noted the second layer of a spice rose..." Kirth shook her head. "I knew one other who claimed such a gift. To be honest, I was never sure she wasn't lying to us all."

It was Marra's turn to stare. "Mistress Britta."

Kirth nodded. "I would still have my doubts. But the very first scent she ever described for me was the layer beneath spice-rose. She named it earthy salt."

Marra sat down beside her teacher.

"So smells have layers. What actual use can that really be?"

Kirth patted her hand.

"Britta believed the true properties of an herb were tied to the smell." Kirth was shaking her head again, seeing things in the past that Marra couldn't begin to guess. "Those of us not so gifted classify them by taste – not smell. I don't know if they can be better defined by the aroma. Britta was very gifted – crafting more new and exciting concoctions than anyone had ever done before.

"You might can do that, little Marra. You might advance the art beyond...beyond what we less gifted folk can do."

Marra leaned away from the elder, shaking her head vehemently. "I'm barely a novice."

Kirth rose, moving back to her potion. "Then, little novice, I'd give a lot to know what Rain wants from you."

As she trudged up the steps, Marra felt more shaken than her tinctures.

And, she admitted, she felt excited. For the first time she wondered if she belonged exactly where she was – if it had been something more than luck that brought the apprenticeship into her life.

What if, she wondered, she tried combining the earthy smells with the –

"Marra, you have visitors in the vestibule." Leah stood before her, grinning and wiggling her eyebrows. She waved her down the stairs.

Marra froze. "Three men," Leah added. "Three such handsome men! If you decide to discard any one of them, let me know." Before Marra could question her, Leah trotted off in the opposite direction.

Surely Rain would have simply entered the school again. Kratchett and that Lump fellow could hardly expect to snatch her from the vestibule.

It might be Drail, she thought. She sped down the stairs and then hesitated at the door. Finally she cracked it open to peek.

The first thing she saw was the young Skullan, the one the Palace guard had stopped when she escaped.

As she gaped, unable to imagine how he could be looking for her, the two men next to him turned. One was a larger Skullan, a somewhat terrifying stranger.

The other was Tryst.

There was no noise when the door eased open. Tryst caught the movement out of the corner of his eye.

He turned as Marra stepped out, her eyes wide and staring. She hadn't expected to see him again, he gathered. Without conscious thought, he strode over to clasp her shoulders affectionately. She hesitated – Marra was never one to invite physical contact – but a welcoming smile spread across her face.

He realized he hadn't been entirely sure of that welcome.

"That girl," Mauric said. "She ran out when I was trying to get in."

Tryst peered down at her. "You went in the Palace again?"

"Not by choice," she answered, and recoiled at Jason's hard look.

"Shall we find a better place to talk?" Jason gave Tryst a significant jerk of his head.

Tryst noticed Marra's hesitation. He wondered if the additional Skullan males scared her – or if she was reluctant to leave the safety of the school grounds.

"Is there a place here we can be private?"

She looked over her shoulder, considering. And

shook her head. "Men aren't allowed in most areas."

They escorted her out through the single gate, and onto the street.

"We make an odd assembly," Jason said under his breath, his eyes scanning the pedestrians.

Tryst realized he was right. Two Skullan males with a Palace air about them, walking with two lowly Trumen posed a strange sight. Perhaps if Marra had looked like a Woman of Agben it might work – but nothing about the herb girl proclaimed her as such. The Agben Women he'd seen were easily spotted by their wealth in dress and arrogance in manner. Marra had neither.

Jason suddenly moved to slide an arm around Marra's shoulders, hugging her close. Now it looked for all the world as if they'd found some sport.

Tryst saw her stiffen and in startled amusement watched her little fist clench, her elbow touching Jason's rib. One of the moves Tryst had taught her was a groin strike.

She glanced at him; he gave her a wink. The fist slowly relaxed.

"Jason, we'll meet you down at the Gold Harbor docks."

Jason nodded and veered away. Mauric frowned, but reluctantly followed.

Tryst guided Marra in a more direct route.

He almost put an arm around her to take up the disguise Jason had created. But he knew she wouldn't like it, and there really wasn't a need now.

"You're still a Trumen." She slanted him a look, trying to match his stride.

He slowed his pace to accommodate her. "My apologies. Jason felt it was for the best." And he hated it, he almost told her.

To wake up in a foreign desert land, mistaken for a foreign race, had somehow seemed all of a piece. With everyone being Trumen, he'd never really felt a need to change.

But once he found Jason and Mauric, it was different. He resented the Trumen hair and the subtle style of clothes when striding between them. It made him feel less, somehow. Different. Jason, however, thought it much safer to remain hidden in plain view.

Now, walking beside little Marra, he did place an arm over her shoulders, in pure affection.

She peered up at him askance. But at least there was no fist clenching.

"Marra, we came because something odd happened when Mauric tried to enter the Palace. He's a resident there, one of my – one of the prince companions. He was barred from the grounds. The guard said something about Agben ruling there now."

Startled, she shook her head. "Agben is just a school. Brimful of teachers and students. Potion makers."

He frowned. "What about the higher echelons? The politics, the leaders?"

Her forehead puckered in confusion. "There's nothing like that. It's just women caught up in the art of herbs." She shook her head. "If it's the Palace, it's probably Rain."

"Rain?"

Marra told him an odd tale of being kidnapped by a Skullan Woman of Agben. Of Fox Boots – apparently his name was Kratchett – and of all their questions about Tryst.

"So you believe this Rain acted without the involvement or approval of Agben."

Marra nodded slowly. "I've not seen any hidden agendas. I've not seen anyone doing anything but work with herbs. Maybe Rain is doing this all alone."

"Not alone," he told her. "There is a deep laid plan here."

Entering the Sea Market, they barely rounded a corner of stalls before Jason and Mauric joined them.

"Do you know Rain?" Tryst asked them quietly, as they strolled on like interested shoppers. Jason shook his head.

But Mauric nodded. "Woman of Agben. She moved into the Palace a few months ago."

Tryst raised an eyebrow. It would not be unusual for the Palace to have a Woman of Agben or two, just as there were resident physicians and dancers for entertainment. While certainly not servants, they were not exactly royal guests. No one above stairs should be aware of them 'moving in.'

Jason tilted his head. "What do you mean, 'moved in?'"

"There was much ado of a courtyard chamber being specially furbished for her," Mauric grinned. "She rejected the color scheme. It had to be completely redone, and that in a matter of days."

Jason exchanged a long look with Tryst. Courtyard rooms were a premium in the Palace. Minister Charis himself had one.

"We need to place you before the King," Jason told Tryst firmly. "Now. Before it is too late."

Marra had stopped at a stall, holding a bowl of powder aloft.

Tryst caught the quick look of approval Jason sent her way and had to smother a laugh. Jason thought she was cleverly pretending to look at wares.

He knew she'd just seen something of interest.

She sniffed the bowl, then set it down far from her. "What is that?" she asked the peddler.

"Powdered Kwitt," he told her. "Rare and exotic, all the way from the Dim Continent. It is treasured highly by the House of Agben."

"But what is it for?" Marra asked.

"Very powerful," was his answer. He raised his voice to others passing by. "Rare and exotic powders from the Dim Continent itself!"

Jason led them firmly away.

They traveled down the main street of the Market and up the familiar ramp to the fourth level walk. The one they always took in better times.

Tryst realized it may not be prudent to take this particular path, as Trumen were no longer allowed to roam freely. But casting a glance at Jason's determined face, at Mauric's eager expression, he knew no one would attempt to stop them.

"We take Marra back to Agben first," he announced. "Then we go."

"But how do we get into the Palace?" Mauric demanded. "There's a dozen guards at every entrance!"

"Not every entrance," Marra said.

Marra didn't like walking on the fourth tier.

For one thing, there were too many Skullan, and no Trumen at all. The rising Missean mist swallowed the lower levels, making it seem they walked a bridge spanning great gorges instead of city streets. And while she didn't miss the desert heat, clear air was something different. One could always see on the Flats unless there was a rare storm. Mists rose so often in Missea that the citizens pretended they didn't exist.

She was used to traveling with large men of course, but not Skullan. Somehow the hairless-ness made them all the larger, scarier. Even Tryst, now that she knew his secret, seemed to belong with these men rather than with Drail and the Hand.

They strode past a shop offering Palace shards – colored glass pieces wrapped in velvet, supposedly from drinking vessels broken inside the Palace walls.

After celebrations of a certain order, the men would hurl their empty glasses at a wall, shattering them so the glass would never be used for lesser things. These were gathered by the servants and then sold to mere commoners who could never take part in such things.

They were nearing the Palace. And even surrounded by Palace men, she feared going in a third time.

Marra stopped.

Tryst stopped beside her.

"Just show us the entrance and go back," he told her quietly.

Her eyes swept the three powerful Skullan - and she found her backbone. If she had to represent the Trumen race, then she'd do it properly.

The entrance Rain had used was on the far side of the Palace, away from populated streets and prying eyes. They marched there now, determined, seemingly confident.

Marra didn't share that confidence.

Jason stepped out ahead of them, striding across the grass, disappearing behind the trellis.

He returned a moment later. "Bolted tight."

"Let's try the hidden gate to the back training area," Mauric said as he turned, but Jason stopped him.

"We tried that path before. It led nowhere."

"We're here now! He belongs here!" As Mauric's frustration poured forth, Marra heard a different sound.

"Sshh!" She hissed, and the others, startled, did indeed shush.

She slipped behind Tryst as footsteps rounded the spice-rose trellis.

"Seems to me a foolish plan," an ugly Trumen was speaking to Kratchett as the two men emerged. Marra had seen him before, and in Kratchett's company. He was Lump – the one who had kidnapped her twice.

Lump and Kratchett ignored them entirely as they strode toward the ramp.

"You never argue with Rain," Kratchett was saying bitterly. "Just nod your head and then come see me."

Jason watched them from over his shoulder, and nudged Mauric. "You ever seen those two before?"

"No. No Trumen at all above stairs."

They kept watch until the two reached the third tier and disappeared into the city.

"Let's try this again," Jason said.

Marra slipped behind the trellis, to find the door shut and the same guard from the other day blocking it. She nodded to him and waited.

He stared at her. Her eyes rolled in annoyance – and then she saw it. Nestled in the grass near his feet was a small bowl of the pink gruel.

The guard frowned. He made no move to open the door.

"Rain needs this," Marra shook her empty pocket at him and tried to assume some of the imperiousness of the Agben woman.

The guard peered into her face, and recognized her. "No one's supposed to come in this door who didn't go out through it." He rubbed his chin, considering.

He was still considering when Jason appeared and struck his jaw. The man crumbled to the ground.

Yanking the door open, Jason stepped over the guard and entered. Mauric followed.

"Thank you, Marra," Tryst smiled as he turned to the door. She saw the pink gruel rapidly bubbled into the blood red color, and made her decision.

She darted through ahead of him.

"Marra..." Tryst began, following her inside.

They found themselves behind the hedges, as Jason shut and bolted the door. "Let her stay," Jason said.

Mauric sprinted away; Jason called him back. "We're the King's men on importance business," he told them. "Stride with purpose. Marra, you follow behind, head down. Keep close, but let us lead the way."

They marched through a courtyard entrance, down a long hall, and ascended the spiraling stairs. The guards they passed not only allowed it, but often stood to attention when Jason gave a quick nod of his head.

It wasn't until they reached the second floor that two soldiers barred their path. "State your business," one of them ordered.

Jason gave a level look. "King's errand," he announced, and stood proudly, never doubting his entrance.

One soldier would have argued, but his companion touched his arm. They stepped aside.

This was a very different part of the Palace than Marra had seen. Soldiers roamed this area, which made her nervous, but her companions marched on as if indifferent. No one challenged them.

Striding down a long corridor, they then climbed a smaller staircase to reach the fourth level – where they finally slipped inside a room.

Marra started breathing again.

This was a sleeping chamber, she realized. Not nearly as nice as the one Rain had occupied.

Mauric tugged open a drawer. "My razor is here."

"I can't believe you have your own razor," Tryst slanted him an amused look.

"Those of us not of royal blood actually groom ourselves," Mauric grinned.

Tryst dragged a chair close to a wall mirror and sat. Mauric plucked out scissors and – to Marra's horrified surprise - snipped Tryst's beautiful hair.

Watching her expression, Jason chuckled. "Of all the differences in our two races, I think the fact that Trumen prefer longer hair on their males than their females to be the strangest."

Jason poured water into a bowl and laid the razor beside it. Tryst smiled reassuringly at Marra.

"This would work best if we had your court robe." Mauric finished the rapid cutting, and reached for a bottle on the table. Unplucking the cork released a scent of rosewood oil, which he poured into his hand and then rubbed on Tryst's skull.

Marra gasped, causing Mauric to glance at her. "Would you like to do this?" he asked. "Females are so much better..."

"No," Tryst shook his head, and sent her a swift smile. "She'd never have done this before."

Mauric seemed surprised, but offered no further comment.

"Perhaps," Jason said slowly, "Marra could get your robes."

Jason led her back to the stairs, up another flight and down a wide corridor. There were no guards on this floor and Marra almost relaxed as they turned a corner and reached a double door entrance. The doors were locked.

"Couldn't be that easy," Jason sighed.

He took her back down the stairs and into a different room. Crossing the thick rug, he yanked back a curtain to reveal a small door.

Jason eased it open, and stuck his head in. "If there's one thing you can count on, we Skullan tend to forget the existence of servants." He beckoned and disappeared through it; she followed.

She found herself, she realized, on the servants' stairway. Jason mounted the steps, and she lifted her skirts to keep from treading on them as she hurried after him.

The entrance at the top opened silently – to a suite such as she'd never imagined.

They emerged into a normal-sized room, except that it consisted of nothing but drawers and hanging rods of clothing. Such material – silks and velvets and fabric so fine that she couldn't guess what threads wove it. Her own mother had earned a living making garments – and Marra had no idea what these were.

Tryst's, she realized. All of this belonged to Tryst.

Turning, she saw a single painted screen shielding the doorway. As Jason searched the hanging garments, she slipped past the barrier to find a room larger than anything she'd ever imagined. A giant bed, surely larger than some inn rooms, stood near one wall; a row of balconies adorned the other. The limestone floor was hidden beneath thick, vibrant carpeting, protecting bare feet from the chill. She had a fleeting impression of mirrors, giant basins set in wooden furniture, and endless cushions and couches and velvet bell pulls.

"Marra!" Jason hissed.

She darted back into the clothing room.

The Skullan shoved an armful of garments at her. And then dropped a necklace with a deep red jewel atop the pile.

She staggered as if the weight was too much, although it barely weighed anything at all.

Jason grabbed a heavy violet robe – dyed fur, she

recognized in awe – and nudged her back toward the stairs.

Her instinct was to flee like a desert hare. Instead she forced herself to walk with a servant's pace.

It was on their landing, the level where the Prince waited, that it happened. Shifting her burden to reach for the door latch, the stack of clothes tipped. The necklace fell, clattering across the landing.

Jason dove for it – but the jewel tumbled over the edge to strike the stones a story below.

They both froze.

The Skullan moved first, but she shoved her bundle at him, and hurried down the steps.

"Marra!"

"I'll get it," she tossed over her shoulder. It was her mistake, after all.

Somewhere below a door opened and she sped to reach the jewel before it was seen. Jason hissed something, but she couldn't quite make out his words.

The brilliant red gem sparkled against the limestone. Pottery crashed somewhere as she stooped to pick it up, and then a man appeared below – an angry Trumen in servant's garb. He looked up as she tucked the necklace into her pocket.

"Well don't just stand there girl," he rasped out. "Come clean this mess."

She hurried down to join the man.

The crash had been a pitcher of water, now just broken shards and a wet patch spread across the limestone.

The man beckoned at the mess, his face an angry red. "Quickly now! Clear it before the housekeeper sees."

The door opened again to a tall Trumen female. She took in the mess, the man and Marra in one sweep of her stern eyes, and set her foot to tapping the floor.

"Your mess, Burns. You clean it up," she told the male servant. "And you, girl," she directed at Marra, "come with me."

"Oh no. I've got to..."

"Leave it. I need this dining room spotless before someone demands tea."

Marra sent a swift glance up, where Jason peeked over the edge. His eyes were wide, but when they locked onto hers, he jerked his head. Indicating she was to go with the housekeeper.

So she went.

And trailing the woman down the busy hallway, it dawned on Marra that Jason would always do what was best for Tryst. Sacrificing her was a simple matter of choice.

9.

JASON NUDGED THE DOOR SHUT with his heel as he dropped the clothes on the bed.

Tryst's chin tilted while Mauric shaved him. With his head now bare, skin gleaming healthily, he looked very much like his prince again. Jason felt his dimple puckering in a smile, and suppressed it.

Mauric set the razor down as Tryst looked at him – noting the clothes, and the empty space behind him. When Tryst met his eyes again there was no trace of the boy. "Where is Marra?"

"A housekeeper nabbed her to clean a dining room."

He rose, seemingly taller now as a Skullan. "And you just left her?"

"Risk all to rescue her from a dust cloth? My Prince," Jason waved at the royal robe on the bed. "Her best chance is your taking your rightful place."

The boy he'd known would have apologized, abashed. He'd have hurriedly donned the clothes.

This man, however, gave him a long level look. "Marra came because we asked and she did whatever she could to help. You really couldn't have ordered her away from a servant in a larger apron?"

Jason lifted an undergarment. "You may berate me royally in the Room of Reception."

Marra stood on a wooden ladder, polishing one of a pair of gold sconces illuminating the doorway.

She'd been annoyed at Jason, but working here now, she understood his reasoning. The most important thing was Tryst reclaiming his throne. If she had to shine a few Palace valuables in the meantime, it was not exactly a huge price to pay.

Even as she smiled at the thought, footsteps pounded the stone hallway outside. Marra couldn't see who approached, but a chill raced down the chord of her spine when she heard them speak.

"He's here," Kratchett's voice hissed. "Your fools left him roaming around unchecked."

"The princeling?" Less refined in speech, this sounded like the man who had kidnapped her twice. "Be you sure? How, with all the entrances covered..."

The tapping tread silenced the others. A hollow tap

Marra had heard before – from the high heels of the female Skullan.

"It's taken care of," Rain said.

Marra desperately scanned the room for a hiding place, but saw no option.

"Taken care of? And just how do it be taken care of?"

"You let him address me like that?" Rain screeched.

Marra couldn't make out the hushed response, but Rain's next words were in a lower tone.

"Charis and the King are safely ensconced in the Royal Room of Reception. I've set bowls on every entry to the floor with our men watching them."

"And if he waits? That setup won't work forever."

"He knows we're searching the Palace, Lump." Kratchett spoke slowly, considering. "He can't wait."

Silence.

And then the footsteps moved away.

Marra realized she wasn't breathing, and slowly released the air in her lungs.

The bowls, she thought. The pink mushy stuff by the gate, bubbling blood red when Tryst passed. She had to find Tryst and the others – warn them about the bowls.

If only she had a clue where she was.

Jason eyed the young man in the mirror.

It was his Tryst, and yet not quite. Looking truly Skullan and royal again, there was yet more to him.

The eyes had more depth – experience had removed some of the laughter and innocence. Instead there blazed a determination to succeed in his own Palace, a knowledge of what was at stake.

The boy really is a man, Jason thought. He comforted the pang of loss with the knowledge that it was the man they needed now.

"Let's go find my father," Tryst turned toward the door.

"They'll be looking for you," Jason warned.

"I've had enough of hiding in my own home."

Marra scrambled up the steps. Tryst was two flights above, she was sure.

On the next level stood two guards. Startled, she pivoted to continue up, and then froze.

A small bowl of pink goo lay on the floor beside them.

"Be off, girl," a guard said.

"Forgot something," she whispered, still staring at the goo. Yanking her eyes away, she whirled and ran back down the steps.

The courtyard worried her because she knew Rain's room looked out upon it. Head down, she crossed it with the servant pace, reached the hedges, and darted behind them.

And paused, her heart pounding in her ears. But there was no shout of discovery, no running footsteps.

I've sunk the first comet ball, she thought. Now for

the second.

A new Skullan stood guard at the rose trellis entrance, but the bowl was still there – and its contents still blood red.

Marra smiled at the guard as she stooped to retrieve the bowl.

"Hey," he frowned.

She looked up questioningly as she straightened with the vessel in her hands.

"What are you...?"

"Rain needs to reset this," she told him, turning back through the door. Don't run, she told herself. Keep that servant's pace.

It worked. He let her go. Although she was all the way across the courtyard and inside the Palace before she breathed again.

Now if only she could find Tryst before it was too late.

Kratchett followed Rain through the hallway, not even bothering to hide his frustration. "He's here, I tell you. He could well get through to them."

"You posted men at every door, every corner. Ten guard the Room of Reception."

"Not all are truly our men, Rain. If just one recognizes him... if just one *believes* him..."

"Don't doubt me!" Rain interrupted yet again.

Kratchett clenched his teeth. Agben or no, he'd love to break her of that habit.

"Your problem is you don't truly appreciate who I am. The power I wield. That petty princeling cannot step on this floor without my knowing exactly where he is."

They rounded the corner.

Before them the corridor intersected a main hallway, the stately approach to the Royal Room of Reception. The passage stretched thirty paces, flanked by potted trees and culminating in three marble steps up to huge oaken doors. The doors stood wide open, signaling the Royal presence within. An official sign of welcome – nullified by the guards standing on either side of the entrance and lining the passageway.

Kratchett had to clench his jaw to keep from ordering the doors shut.

Instead Rain glided into the room, while he remained by the guards. It was a cavernous chamber in red and purple – clashing oddly with Rain's orange skirt.

"Your Majesty," she said, curtseying very low to the ground. There was insolence even in this gesture, and Kratchett marveled that neither man struck her down.

The King had been conversing with Minister Charis, the First Minister. The only Minister, it was whispered in the Palace corridors. Both men turned to Rain now, gazing at her bowed form.

Neither spoke.

And she was forced to hold the position, Kratchett realized, until they released her. Perhaps they hadn't appreciated her interruption after all.

Minister Charis slanted a look at the King.

King Bactor sighed.

Charis had raised an eyebrow, a little surprise showing on his face. The First Minister expected him to act with proper protocol, always.

Very well, he decided. "You may rise."

And Rain did so, albeit a bit miffed. He kept a steady gaze upon her until she lowered her eyes again. One did not show displeasure to one's King.

"Your Majesty," Rain finally spoke. "We must close these doors to protect you. Someone is in the Palace who should not be."

She made to turn away and had to hesitate again because he hadn't dismissed her.

It was Charis who voiced the questions. "An intruder in the Palace? After all these precautions, Rain? After every entrance sealed, additional guards brought in?"

There it was again on her face – anger, barely suppressed. This woman should be embarrassed, not angry.

"We must be careful, I suppose." The King told his friend.

"I sometimes doubt that," Charis replied. Rain stared at them, eyes wide and almost – frightened.

The King sighed again. He seemed to be doing a lot of that lately.

"Very well. You've sealed us into our own Palace – why not wall us off in a single room?"

His dry tone must have gotten through. Nervously she bobbed another curtsy, this one much less proper, and backed out of the room.

The doors swung shut behind her.

"You don't find all this strange?" Charis asked. "That girl did tell us, clearly..."

"No." The King shook his head firmly. "Tryst is... he's gone. We mustn't allow ourselves to hope otherwise."

Charis touched his arm, a familiar gesture of friendship he'd come to appreciate over the last year. "Is hope such a terrible thing?"

"Without it there is no disappointment."

"Without it," Charis replied, "there is nothing,"

Tryst strode down the steps.

Somehow wearing his own clothes, he felt whole again. A true prince. More so now, because he thought he had a genuine grasp of what that actually meant.

It had nothing to do with parading around, of being seen or acting 'royal'. It was responsibility for an entire nation, for a population and their welfare. It was choosing each action for the good of Missea.

And he would not fail before ever ascending the throne.

"My Prince, let us go first," Jason cautioned in his ear. But now with his feet shod in his own boots, he had no intention of stopping until he reached his goal. Sheer force of will would clear his path.

In truth, Tryst had absolutely no intention of cravenly hiding again. By the Great Goose, not in his own damn home.

Jason and Mauric flanked him as he turned the corner. In a passing mirror he saw how they both took proper position, slightly behind and to either side of him. By design or habit, he could only wonder.

Two guards appeared.

"Halt!" One held out a hand, but the other peered into his face and fell back with mouth gaping.

The first tried to persist. "No one may..."

"Out of the Prince's way, fool." Jason's tone held the perfect blend of haughtiness and subtle softening for a student.

The second guard dropped to his knee, and as they passed he said, "Your Highness. The guards have been told an imposter roams the hallways, intent on murdering the King."

Tryst paused. "You do not believe I am this imposter?"

The man looked at Jason and shook his head. "Not with the Defense Master at your side."

As they marched by, Jason spoke softly. "I cannot help notice how many guards are new. Not many will question that order. Few will hesitate to draw blade."

Tryst strode on.

Marra raced up the steps.

She'd almost reached Tryst's floor when the door latch clicked open. Immediately she lowered her head, assuming her best servant mien.

"Marra," Jason said.

Beside him, Mauric gawked at the bowl she carried, the bubbling mass within turning red. "What in the name of the Great Goose is that?"

She moved it farther from her face – the smell was awful.

"It's an evil mixture," she sighed. "They're scouring the Palace for Tryst."

"I'm going to see my father now," she heard the Prince say, though she couldn't see him behind Jason. "No one is going to stop me."

"He's in the Room of Reception," she told them. "They have guards at every entrance to that floor."

Frowning, Jason pivoted.

"They can search us for weapons," Tryst's voice declared. "But I insist upon seeing the King."

Marra bit her lip. She didn't know if her idea would work – and she was scared he wouldn't wait to find out.

"Are you going through that door?" she pointed down the stairs.

She caught a swish of cloth behind the Defense Master, but it was Mauric who nodded.

"I think I can – though I really don't know..." She sighed. "Will you let me try something?"

"Marra, nothing may -"

"Just wait five blinks of the sun."

The following silence wasn't reassuring. Jason, however, reluctantly nodded. "Five blinks of the sun. And then we pass through that door."

She flashed him a grateful look before lifting the bowl, covering it as best she could with her arm, and whirling to race down the steps and through that very same door.

Beyond it stood three guards – with the small bowl of pink goo at their feet. She lowered her head to hurry past.

"Wait," called the largest man. With a quick turn, she bobbed a curtsy and scurried away.

They argued behind her, but no one pursued. Marra rounded the corner and ran as fast as she could without splashing the bowl's contents.

The problem, of course, was that she didn't know which room the King was in. But even as that thought occurred, she passed a wide hallway, at the end of which three steps lead up to imposing double doors. Fully ten guards stood at attention, positioned between huge pottery jars of actual trees.

It was all she could do not to gawk.

Forcing herself to slow down, she walked past the hallway, and sped on.

Two more turns, and she came upon more guards, yet another bowl at their feet. Even as she watched, the door they flanked opened, and a man and a woman appeared. Recognizing Kratchett and Rain, Marra ducked behind a tapestry.

"Halt," said a guard.

"Don't be an idiot," she heard Kratchett growl.

"Does that look red to you?" Rain hissed.

Marra listened to their footsteps as they drew near.

"The problem with your plan," Kratchett murmured, "is it depends on fools."

"Fools who follow orders," Rain replied.

They passed.

Marra peeped out. The two were striding away, and she dare not delay any longer. Slipping out, she sped towards the three guards. Time was almost gone; Tryst would move soon.

If she told them she'd found the bowl by an unconscious guard...

One of the men stepped forward to meet her. "Sir..." she began.

His hand grabbed her hair. "Here's a little diversion," he called over his shoulder. His companions laughed.

Marra instinctively ducked away. And tripped over his foot.

The bowl of red gunk flew out of her hands to shatter on the stone floor.

The guard hauled her up, grinning. "Are you hurt, sweetling?"

She was so angry she wanted to kick his shin. And when his hand lifted to cup her chin, she did.

His companions burst out laughing as he released her to grab his leg. She saw the broken shards sparkling on the floor.

Tryst's one chance for a diversion and she'd messed it up.

Fingers latched onto her upper arm, hauling her against the furious guard. But not before she spied the pink goo frantically bubbling around a sliver of glass.

"RED!" shouted one of the men.

Marra wrenched herself free, but didn't try to run. Better to wait, she thought.

The other guards stared at the bowl. "What do we do?"

"Go get the Agben woman," said the tallest one. And when neither of his compatriots moved, he sped down the hallway.

Marra dropped to her knees, gathering broken shards.

The one guard rubbed his shin where she'd kicked him. And seeing his glare, Marra knew she didn't want to be there when he fully recovered.

She leapt up with the broken glass in her hands. "I'll be back with the Mistress," she whispered, and fled.

As she rounded the corner, she saw Rain approaching with those long, mannish strides, the guard beside her barely able to keep up. Marra held to a steady pace and kept her head down. They passed without a glance.

As soon as they turned the corner, she sprinted.

Reaching the wide corridor with the double doors and the ten guards, a potted tree caught her eye. Impulsively she dropped the broken glass inside a pot.

One of the guards watched. And started towards her before Rain's shriek echoed through the halls. "Here! He's here!"

The guards exchanged looks. One gestured, and six raced to answer Rain's cry. The remaining four took firm stances outside the double doors.

Marra backed off, and turned to run.

And there, in the midst of the bedlam, of men racing and Rain's shouts, Tryst strode down the corridor.

Marra froze.

Because he didn't look like Tryst at all. He appeared to be – he *was* – the Skullan Prince, the portrait come to life. Fine clothes, head bare and skin glowing with that vibrant, Skullan radiance. His sleeveless robe hung to his knees, fashioned of a thick, heavy silk. Subtle red interwove with the blue, a sort of look she'd only seen one other place. On the King himself.

How had she ever thought this man Trumen?

Tryst strode confidently, as one used to having doors flung open before him. Marra turned her head to see his impact on the remaining guards.

Two were staggered, but two stepped determinedly to block his way.

Tryst winked at her, but otherwise kept moving. As

Jason passed, she pushed the necklace at his fist. He never looked down – even when his fingers grasped the gold chain.

Tryst, Jason, and Mauric strode straight up to the three steps. "Open the door for Prince Tryst," Jason ordered.

Kratchett, Rain, and a dozen guards appeared at the end of the corridor. "Imposter!" Kratchett yelled. Some of their guards hurried towards Tryst.

And then slowed, suddenly uncertain.

"Trumen are rumored to have taken me," Tryst's voice, both calm and commanding, broke the silence. "And now you take orders from one?"

One of the door guards reached for the handle – the other stopped him. "He'll kill his Majesty."

Marra watched the play of emotions on the faces. He'll lose, she thought. They won't let him pass.

And then the doors burst open from the inside. The King and his Minister stood on the threshold.

Father and son looked each other over.

"Dear me," said the Minister.

The King descended the steps – and embraced his son.

"Fools," Charis glared at the guards. "What goes on out here?"

Marra managed a single glance away from Tryst and his father, to see that Kratchett and Rain had vanished.

King Bactor nodded at Mauric, smiling. The smile

broadened at the sight of Jason.

"At the birth of my son I named you his champion. I knew no other could fill the position as you would."

And Marra saw, for the first and last time, Jason blush.

The King drew Tryst into the Room of Reception; Jason and Mauric and the Minister followed. Smiling to herself, she turned to leave.

"Marra."

She spun back to find Tryst at the door. "I want you to come meet my father." He stretched out a hand.

Thus she was formally introduced to the Skullan King.

Tryst pulled Marra with him, entering the Room of Reception. A place he hadn't seen in more than a year.

It wasn't the room, the familiar thick carpets, or the roses that grew out of giant urns which made him feel home. It was the presence of his father. The half smiles, the quizzical looks. The warmth.

Now he tugged Marra out from behind, presenting her to the King. To his surprise and amusement, she sunk into a curtsey, albeit too shallow.

The King took her hand to guide her upright. "You," he said. "You told me my son was alive. It seems that you spoke truth."

"You spoke to my father?" Tryst was stunned. "Why didn't you tell me?" He watched her face as she thought about it.

"It's not like we chatted over tea." Her shoulders lifted in a faint shrug. "I bumped into him."

Tryst found himself smiling at this funny girl. So small, he'd thought her, so fragile. Yet she'd proved to be everything but.

"Would you like to stay in the Palace?"

Now it was her turn to be surprised.

"We have these wonderful rooms facing the courtyard..."

Something flashed across her face and then she shook her head. "I'm at the Agben School. That's where I belong."

"Are you sure?"

Marra's eyes roamed the Room of Reception – the tapestries, the throne, the dais for advisors to flank the monarch.

"I'm sure," she said.

The King approached, setting a hand on her shoulder. Charis came up behind him. The First Minister was giving Tryst an odd look.

Kratchett and the Agben woman had escaped, Tryst realized. No chance of finding out who their master was. Because he was certain, absolutely certain, that this plot went much higher than either of those could lay claim to.

He found himself studying Charis.

"You, my dear, will always have a room here," his father smiled at Marra. "Use it anytime you wish, however you wish. It is your home."

Marra stared at the King, and then glanced at Tryst. He thought he spied a welling tear before she blinked it away.

"Thank you, sir," she said.

Marra borrowed a glass vial from the school for the Birr Elixir.

Now, standing at the worktable in her own room, she carefully sealed the stopper. Kirth had suggested she was far too much a novice to work in privacy – that she needed the guidance passing teachers could offer.

This, however, was not something she wished to share.

Once the stopper was sealed, she set it down to lift her new cloak off the door peg. Did she dare wear it?

Warm it was against the chill of the winter's evening. Tryst said it was a special wool, but she'd never felt any wool so soft you wanted to rub it against your face. It was dyed a vivid blue, and had the mark of the King on the back of the hood. The mark of favor.

It was a rare and valuable gift, one that Jason claimed had never before been bestowed on a Trumen female. She'd worried it might be stolen, but they told her that would never happen. To steal a mark of the King was one of the few crimes to carry a penalty of death.

She shook her head over that. Murder, treason, and the theft of a King's Mark item.

Truth was, Marra acknowledged to herself, she didn't fear theft. It was being noticed that worried her, standing out in a crowd.

Her fingers caressed it once more. Then, flinging the cloak over her shoulders, she grabbed the vial and left.

She paused for a moment, by a back door which led to the street. She really was safe, Marra reminded herself. Tryst was home, Rain and Kratchett on the run for their lives. She was quite safe.

Outside, Marra hurried up the ramp to the second tier.

It was dusk. Trumen lads ran with big torches to light the pole-braziers along the walkways. She'd been astonished when she first saw that, wasting so much oil just to have light on the streets. Then in an Agben class she'd discovered a powder mix that extended the oil tenfold. Lamps burned a little less brightly than with the pure oil, but they burned the whole night through.

The Ring of Men Arena was nearby, just a handful of blocks away from the Agben School. Drail and the Hand were playing there tonight, which was a victory in itself. The Ring of Men was a crossover arena, having both Trumen and Skullan games. A team had to be invited to play there.

Tonight was a Trumen night. And the Hand played in the second game.

Being a crossover arena meant that the spectators

were crossover as well. Skullan watched Trumen games, which was very unusual. Trumen, naturally, watched Skullan games regardless, except for the more prominent Skullan arenas where they were barred from entry.

With almost an hour until the first game, the arena was quiet. It was bigger than the Muck Barn, with a half wall surrounding the ring itself. Straw to cushion spectator's feet was spread around the half-wall, and upon a raised platform, yielding a second tier of viewing.

Better, she thought. The team had moved up to a better venue.

Drail and the Hand were in the ring, stretching. She was barred from reaching them by the half wall, with the only opening on the far side. Marra began edging her way toward it.

"Marra!" Drail beckoned. She moved to the half wall where he stood, holding out the vial.

Instead of taking it, he lifted her up and over the barrier. And then accepted the elixir, drinking his share before passing it on to Olver.

"Welcome," he smiled. "You're staying to watch, right?"

Ignoring the lingering fear of standing out in her cloak, she nodded. After all, she really did want to watch. To cheer Drail and the Hand on to victory.

He squeezed her arm. "Wolfbur, did you meet Marra?"

The giant Skullan turned. Marra stared.

Wolfbur stared back.

"Our Brista," Drail took the elixir vial from Manten, and handed it to the new member of the team. Fallon gawked at her a long moment before emptying the last quarter of the contents.

More spectators entered, swelling the crowd. It seemed an equal mixture of Skullan and Trumen tonight.

"There's a bit of a celebration," Drail explained. "It seems the missing Prince is found." He clapped Wolfbur on the back.

The ugly Skullan was eyeing her cloak. He walked around her and when he appeared again, his face set in an odd grimace. He knew, she realized.

"Drail, about that," Marra began. She tried to draw him away from the others, but he didn't get the hint. And the others were avidly listening now.

She sighed. "It was Tryst."

Drail frowned. "Tryst found the missing Prince?"

Marra shook her head, as several gasps spread through the crowd. Too intent on her words, she didn't turn to look when the others did.

Until she saw Olver's gawking face.

And when Marra glanced over her shoulder, she observed the Prince himself striding towards them. "Tryst *is* the Prince."

Spectators and gamesmen alike parted before him as the Prince marched through the gap, through the arena itself, and straight to the Hand of Victory.

Marra watched with empathy as recognition washed over Drail. Stunned, incredulous recognition.

And then Drail burst out laughing and pounded Tryst on the shoulder.

Jason and Mauric both jerked in reaction, the Defense Master even reaching for his sword. But Tryst embraced the leader of the Hand of Victory, sharing his laughter.

She noticed the surprise in his companions – although it was nothing to her own. Tryst had chortled with them before, but never with this unrestrained, full throated humor.

Drail and Tryst laughed a moment more while the rest of the arena gaped in wonder.

A hunched Trumen in an old cloak watched the two men. He watched as they split apart and took their places as spectator and gamesman.

And then he slowly, painfully made his way to the stands, limping with each step. Head bowed, he chose a spot near Tryst, perhaps twenty paces throwing distance. He claimed his space at the rail and firmly planted his feet, the limp momentarily absent.

Long ago, Kratchett had talked to several men to find the one he deemed most useful. That one had been Lump, due to his physical strength and some wit despite his profession. The deciding factor had been certain skills that came in handy, such as throwing an old cloak about himself and suddenly seeming a crippled old man.

Now that he was in place, Lump gradually straightened. There weren't enough people in the arena as yet. Too few, and the confusion afterward might not be enough to mask his escape.

It would take Drail some time before he accepted Tryst's new look.

As he waited for the arena to fill, for the last competitors to arrive, his eyes slipped to Tryst and his companions. A Skullan Prince.

By the Desert Crane.

Odd, how the lack of hair made such a difference. The man he knew seemed bigger somehow, more menacing, less friendly. Skullan, he supposed.

Yet when Tryst smiled, Drail saw the Trumen he'd called friend. The teammate who'd helped win Port Leet. Stars – the first Trumen to defeat a Skullan team and now it turns out one of their men had been Skullan. Did that win even count?

As he noticed the spectators filling the arena, Drail realized he wasn't the only one staring at Tryst. The Royal Prince, long thought dead, stood here in person to watch a Trumen comet match. No wonder they all gawked. Drail suspected there'd be a huge crowd by game time.

Drail's mind drifted, as his eyes drifted over the swelling crowd. And then, for no reason he could fathom, his gaze settled on one man.

He was out of place, Drail decided. Perhaps it was the voluminous cloak with the hood still up. It was a cool night, but as the arena barn filled the body heat naturally warmed the area. Not that many had worn cloaks at all, and those that had now draped them over an arm or a railing.

Even as Drail watched, the man carefully lifted the cloth, clearing the hood from his head though still wearing the cloak. Drail's eyes moved on – and then came back as he recognized what bothered him.

The man never looked anywhere but at Tryst.

Everyone else was fascinated by his presence, yet they also watched the warm-ups, the arrival of a new comet team, or a pretty lass making her way through the crowd. This man ignored all other activity.

The man reached into his cloak and slid one shoulder out, freeing his throwing arm.

"TRYST!"

Drail sprinted for a practice ball, certain he'd be too late. Launching himself, he dove at it, rolled with it, coming to his feet again.

He saw the cloaked-man's arm already arcing. Tossing.

Drail never actually thought. The ball left his hands, speeding through the air. The older of Tryst's companions leapt in front of him, though it might have been too late. Probably was too late.

But by the Desert Crane, they would never know.

In the dead silence that followed, the younger companion rushed to Drail's ball and lifted it in astonishment. A gleaming protrusion jutted out of the leather hide. Drail couldn't properly see – but he knew what it was.

An imbedded dagger, intended for Tryst.

When Drail looked back, the cloaked man was gone.

10.

TRYST STARED at the comet ball in Mauric's grasp. He felt no shock, though he recognized the significance – his own intended murder. Reaction would probably come later.

Drail was already sprinting for the stands, leaping the half wall. Tryst knew, however, that the culprit was long gone.

First they'd tried to start a race war by blaming his murder on the Trumen. Now this in a mixed audience, where both Trumen and Skullan would witness. Trumen could not have been implicated easily this time.

In truth, it didn't implicate anyone.

So was it an act of desperation? With the single goal to remove him?

Tryst moved toward Mauric even as Jason gestured for him to stay where he was. He knew himself safe – whoever had thrown the dagger was probably racing down the street even now.

Clasping the ball, Tryst thrust it high overhead, and slowly turned to show the spectators.

"Someone has tried to murder me. Again." his voice rang out in the silent arena. "Traitors to Missea. Traitors to the Skullan race – to murder the Prince. Traitors to the Trumen race – to cast the blame on an innocent people."

Tryst dropped the ball to point at the man who'd thwarted the attempt. "Drail, leader of the Hand of Victory, Trumen gamesman, has saved the life of the heir to the throne. Let it be known, this day forth, that no one may call Trumen betrayers. Instead they have the gratitude of King Bactor."

Silence. The Prince drew a long breath.

A few cheers finally broke the hush. Tryst was not a fool – he knew most of the crowd had no idea what to think, how to react. Yet word would spread. His father would honor Drail, issue a proclamation.

Finally, this race war would be stymied.

Marra appeared at his side, startling him. She patiently waited until he lowered the ball, and studied the dagger. Her eyes closed, her nostrils flared. And then she peered anxiously through the crowd.

Tryst remembered the pink goo – and Rain, the woman of Agben. And he wondered what else Marra might have noticed but not mentioned.

He had, of course, talked to his father. He'd told him everything from start to finish. But things had not changed nearly as much as they should have. There was no effort to reverse the bad feeling toward the Trumen. The Palace was addressing the concerns of the guard, but slowly, and without Jason's help, as the King insisted Jason needed to recuperate before taking on any onerous tasks. Even though the Defense Master seemed perfectly hale and whole to everyone else.

While his father understood Tryst's suspicions of Charis, he insisted the First Minister's hands were clean. Yes, the Minister had urged caution, taken steps to protect the King and the Skullan people. But he hadn't, the King pointed out, ordered the restrictions within the city itself. Those had come about from the sentiment of a people who believed their Prince murdered by Trumen.

Tryst had been certain that Charis was behind it all. He still held that certainty. And now, having seen a little of what Agben could do, it dawned on him that his own father might be compromised. Could they slip some sort of drink to the King, place a powder on his food which left him amenable to their plots? Could they make him more frightened of shadow, more nervous of Trumen?

He needed Marra, he realized. She had noticed the bowls of pink; there may well be other things she would find.

Despite Jason's urging, Tryst stayed for the comet games. He watched Drail play in his best form, winning his first match easily, and out-battling the other winners in the championship game. The gamesman had indeed come far from that first display in the Gold Harbor Arena; he could spin the ball with the best of them, defend effectively, and play the waiting game for the spots to reveal themselves.

Above all that, Drail also had his keen accuracy in shooting, to sink the comet from great distances, odd angles. A desert trait, that precision, and it left mouths gaping on spectators and opponents alike.

After the final ball had dropped into the cone that night, and the spectators had trickled away to celebrate, Tryst approached Marra.

She was beaming at the Hand like a proud mother. He shook his head. Did women take all their success in watching the men around them succeed? Or did it only feel that way to the men?

She smiled at him, too, but the smile faded as he stopped before her.

"Marra, I need your help."

Fallon waited at a discrete distance, until the Prince – by the Great Goose, the long lost Skullan Prince, no less – had left, and the herb girl stood on her own. Then he approached her, a little more nervously than he was used to.

"May I walk you home?" Fallon asked.

She stared at him as if he'd spoken a different language, and then her eyes swept past to Drail. Fallon suddenly wondered if he'd misunderstood her relationship with his leader.

But when she looked back, she nodded.

So he escorted her through the dark streets. And had to grin at the way she walked.

Most females moved with their heads down, eyes seemingly on the ground before them. He'd often wondered if that was to avoid tripping in their dainty dress and shoes. But Marra kept her head erect, not letting the world pass her without scrutiny.

"How long have you known Drail?" he asked.

"Since back in the desert. He needed an elixir – and I made it. I've been making it for him ever since."

Fallon smiled, and took her hand. She seemed surprised, but didn't pull away. "I've been a gamesman for five full seasons," he told her. "Someday, I will earn good prize purses."

"Of course you will," she nodded. "Drail is a good leader."

Did the girl like Drail more than he'd first thought? Fallon tried to read her face.

When they reached the Agben School, Marra thanked him and hurried inside. No lingering in the doorway, no chance to speak. No chance for anything else. Fallon couldn't decide if she deliberately avoided giving him that chance – or if she never thought of it.

After a long moment, he left.

He returned the next afternoon to invite Marra to a fair down at Gold Harbor docks. But she'd already left.

When he asked where, knowing that Drail was practicing with Wolfbur, another girl came out, not to answer his question but to see who he was. A pretty girl, with long brown hair.

Her name was Leah. Fallon told her about the fair and impulsively asked her to go.

Leah smiled in a way Marra had not, and ran to get her cloak.

Mid-morning, hours before Fallon would come, Marra stood at a work table.

She clasped a glass dropper – a long thin tube with etched marks in it – and inserted it into the bottle of Snow Daisy Tincture. With her mouth on the other end, she gently sucked the liquid up into the tube. Her tongue then covered the tube opening, holding the drawn tincture in place as she checked the amount. The Snow Daisy was halfway up to the mark she needed.

She drew more, checked, and then shook a tiny splash off the dropper. And then held it over the bowl.

None of the tincture came out.

"Blow into the end," Kirth said quietly behind Marra. "Gently, or you'll spatter it everywhere. Snow Daisy tincture has that oddness to it."

Marra blew – and the tincture rolled out of the dropper into her mixture.

Kirth gazed at it.

"I can't recall a healing tonic with Snow Juice in it," the old Skullan remarked.

Marra's cheeks flamed. "It's a Britta recipe. Called 'Faster'. It says it speeds you."

Kirth shook her head. "I think you misread Britta's writing. Snow juice makes hair grow faster."

Marra grimaced. "Sometimes her handwriting is difficult. I saw the fast part, and thought..."

Kirth moved around her, finding a stool across the room and dragging it close. Her attention seemed on her own bottles of herbs.

"Speed, Marra? For what purpose."

Marra sighed.

"Drail calls me Brista, Mistress. He brought me out of the desert and makes no demur when I come to the Agben School. I need to do more – much more – than provide him a simple elixir before his games."

Kirth hunched over the table – and Marra realized she was shaking with mirth. When she looked up again, her eyes were slightly wet.

"Only you could refer to a Birr potion as 'simple'. If you really wish to..."

The door creaked open, and Leah stepped into the room.

"Marra, a man has come – a young man – from the Palace itself. He says he is to escort you there."

Kirth's eyes narrowed; Leah's face was alight with excitement.

"Give me five blinks of the sun," Marra sighed, as she stirred her potion with the dropper.

Of course, the difference started when Marra rushed down the stairs with her large bag.

It was a bit heavy, with Britta's book inside, and she stumbled on the last step. Fortunately she didn't fall flat on her face.

'Mauric' – as he insisted she call him – took the bag from her. Hoisting it over his shoulder he offered his arm, just as she had seen Kratchett offer his to Rain.

After the briefest hesitation, Marra laid her hand on his elbow.

He slowed his pace to allow her shorter legs a comfortable stride. When a vendor approached them – and suddenly many vendors did approach – Mauric shielded her, laughingly turning them away without her needing to say anything at all.

She was led past the guards and the front gate without as much as a word to the formidable looking men. The guards actually bowed as they passed.

With her head held high, Marra saw the number of servants running the Palace hallways, bearing items or scurrying away on errands. All with heads down, avoiding eye contact as she had done in her previous visits. Mauric did quite the opposite, his chin held at a proud tilt. She realized how much the manner of a man identified him, more than apparel or positions.

Up the familiar flight of steps they went, past the huge portrait of Tryst. Marra did stare then, shaking herself afterwards and hoping Mauric hadn't noticed. If he did, he made no comment.

He escorted her along several hallways, and into her new room.

Not room – chamber, she corrected herself. For she had a cavernous space of stone softly padded with blue carpet and tapestry and drapes. It was furnished with a large bed and dresser, a table and chairs. All gleaming with polish, smelling faintly of lemon wax. The double doors leading outside were also polished wood – and beyond them a balcony every bit as nice as the one Rain had enjoyed. The one Marra had used to escape.

A second door led to a dressing area, larger than most of the inn rooms that she'd slept in. A third opened to a bathing room – an entire room with the sole purpose of performing her ablutions.

"I trust you'll be comfortable?" Mauric asked. Somehow she managed a nod. He bowed and left, pulling the door closed behind him.

Marra liked to unpack wherever she was because it made it feel more like a home than a temporary space. Manten had teased her once about time wasted in placing her clothes into a drawer occasionally allotted, or hanging a blouse neatly on a peg, only to carefully fold them all back into her bag when they moved on. Marra had never confessed that her purchasing of new clothes often correlated with unpacking in a new place, when she discovered more space provided than she had things to fill it.

In the Palace, however, she'd need to curb that tendency. If she tried to fill all the space in this grand chamber, she'd use every bit of copper she could earn in a lifetime.

Home, she thought. Marra remembered a small desert house with a treated cloth roof, a tiny bedroom with a blue privacy curtain where her parents slept, and the odd fireplace peculiar to the desert, set in a far corner so as not to overheat the place. She remembered the window with shutters instead of glass and a small garden in the back. Tending it had once been her main chore in life.

She hadn't thought of the Agben School as her home, but she certainly liked it there. She'd hoped to stay awhile. This huge suite inside the Palace, with its balcony and bathing room, didn't feel quite as comfortable. Quite as – well, hers. Instead, it somehow felt lonely.

Standing in the center, Marra sighed.

Tryst had waited in the garden for some time and still no Marra. So much for his notion of being seated below her when she slipped outside to explore her private balcony.

He rose and called, "Marra."

No rustling of the curtains, no red head peeping out. He was about to call again when she finally appeared.

She was frowning.

He jumped onto a large rock set by her railing – and suddenly wondered if that rock location was mere coincidence. It was odd how many things he noticed now that he'd never thought about before.

Perhaps an epourney – even one such as his – was a good experience after all.

He plucked her up over the railing, much to her surprise. Setting her feet to the grass, they strolled down the path.

"How do you like your room?"

"It's nice," she said, in a voice that said otherwise. Startled, he studied her face. Those garden suites were highly prized. Could the accommodations in Agben be even better than rumor claimed?

"Tryst," Marra sighed, "I'm not sure I understand what you want me to do."

He smiled ruefully. "I suppose perform magic."

Standing there in the warmth of the sun and the security of his home, he realized he felt neither. The Palace itself seemed wrong, almost alien to the place of his childhood. As, he felt with a growing certainty, his own father felt wrong.

"Marra, there's something not right here." He glanced around, making sure they were alone, while he searched for words. "My father spends more time with the First Minister than ever, and insists the Trumen are still a problem. That makes no sense now that Skullan hands have been exposed in the plot."

Marra looked at him. "Your father has been through a nightmare, believing you kidnapped, dead. Maybe he hasn't truly realized you're safe yet. I mean, his mind knows it, but his heart may not have caught up to this truth."

He pondered her words. "Before I left, he refused to fight a war, no matter how Charis pressed him. This morning, he spoke as if the third race war was already upon us. As if it was inevitable."

She made no comment.

He realized she didn't understand. "Zaria's prophecy – the three race wars. It's an old tale of conflicts between Trumen and Skullan. Two wars have already been fought. The third is supposed to wipe out your kind altogether."

Now she reacted. "Fight Trumen? But – why?"

If he'd never been to the desert, Tryst couldn't have comprehended her astonishment. On the Great Continent – at least, he assumed it was the same outside the city walls as within – there was always a divide between the two races. But with so few Skullan on the Wavering Continent, they'd become more of an oddity than a threat.

"I grew up Skullan, Marra," he said. "Taught that Trumen were inferior. Inferior physically, mentally. I was also taught they harbored resentment towards my race and yearned someday to remove the threat we posed.

"But those notions are old and vague, and frankly lessening with each generation. You see, after the last war, which was a long time ago now, the Trumen capital on the Great Continent was wiped out. The survivors somehow ended up merging into our cities and becoming part of our own population. Over the centuries, they've been accepted."

Her brow furrowed. "I've heard bits of it, of course," she said slowly. "But it just seemed like a fairy tale."

Tryst nodded. "Our size is different – but I can safely say Skullan and Trumen are mentally the same. At least, as far as a Palace-raised Skullan can tell after living with desert do – err, desert-born Trumen."

She grinned. "Desert dogs."

"Marra, I believe the intention of my kidnapping was to wake that old resentment. You see, Skullan mingle with Trumen now, in fact, there are marriages. The House of Agben openly accepts Trumen women – and when confronted about it, calmly told the King they had done so for centuries. Perhaps in another thousand years the two races will be just one."

"I'm not sure I like that idea."

They reached the banyon tree – a rare wonder from the Dim Continent. Looking up, Tryst remembered climbing its plentiful branches as a boy, to hide in the bushy top and watch adults roam below.

Now he leaned against the trunk. "Others don't like the idea either. But there's a difference in not liking something and committing treason to stop it."

Reaching to pluck a leaf, he then twirled it between his fingers.

"No matter how many Trumen we find involved, the heart of this plot must be Skullan."

Marra sat on the grass. "But what can I do that all your powerful friends cannot?"

"You're a student of Agben. You see things that elude most of us, such as discovering that pink liquid and its properties. You saved my life."

She shook her head, but made no other answer.

Tryst pushed away from the tree, and reached to help her up. She hesitated before accepting.

"Jason is investigating all of this," Tryst smiled. "And he's very good at investigation. He will find the culprits. I just thought if you noticed anything more, it might be useful. And in the meantime, you have a home right here."

He'd never known anyone to turn down a place in the Palace. Yet watching her face, it seemed there might be a first time. More arguments rose to his lips, but he held his peace. Let her choose as she would.

Finally she looked up at him. "I'll do all I can."

Drail found himself in a tempest of demand. It made him nervous.

After foiling the attempt on Tryst's life, the Hand

of Victory – and indeed, himself – were wildly popular. Everyone wanted to see them, so every arena invited them to play.

The Hand had previously achieved a level to where no Trumen arena turned them away, as long as they were one of the first to arrive that evening. Now arenas reached out to them, offering prime game spots, allowing them to choose when they'd play, opponents they'd face. And twice, when they had to turn an arena down, coin was offered to change his mind.

Drail wouldn't let the popularity go to his head because he knew it had little to do with their skill. He suspected the interest would wane soon enough.

His nervousness came when a Skullan arena invited him to play. It was to be an exhibition game, played with other Trumen before the Skullan main event. They would not be playing Skullan.

But he could suddenly see the road. A way to gain his boyhood dream, to actually play real Skullan in a Missean match. If he continued to ask, to push, and kept winning his games – he would eventually entice a Skullan team to face them.

His problem was Drail now feared such a match almost as much as he wanted it. If he had to face Skullan today – if they were crushed as thoroughly as before – he feared he'd never step on a comet field again. It had taken all he had to do so after the Black Arena loss.

Admitting that, he felt ashamed.

They continued to work with Wolfbur, learning new moves, perfecting old ones. Regaining confidence. They focused only on the next game – never beyond.

The Hand of Victory now lived in the Ship's Bell, a nice inn near the harbor. Drail didn't know if it was their rising popularity or Tryst's influence, but they had decent rooms and did not pay for them. The innkeeper insisted their presence sold the rest of his rooms at a premium.

No offer came to play in the Black Arena where it all began. At least not yet.

For Marra, life had veered in a wild direction.

The first time she left the Palace to attend class at Agben felt very odd. She tried to sneak through the back door – the one she'd used to enter the Palace when they placed Tryst on the throne. The door had been locked, but a guard had noticed her.

When she returned that evening, a funny stuffed toy lay on her bed, clutching an ornate key and a note: "The key gives you freedom to come and go as you please. The toy is a Terrin, a creature supposedly from the Dim Continent. He will keep you company."

The Terrin had a round belly and squashed head, with tiny eyes made from black seeds and a two protruding green teeth curling over the jaw. Covered in soft fur, the toy delighted her.

Oddly enough, the key did make a difference. Perhaps she was constantly waiting for someone to declare she couldn't pass, or to whisk her off to face Rain. The key meant there was no permission to seek, no guards to pass. Just the freedom to come and go as she chose.

Her new worry was finding something to justify Tryst's kindness. She saw no more bowls of pink goo, nor any sign of Rain. The Woman of Agben's room was vacant and stripped of personal items, as Marra knew from her foray inside. The only thing she had discovered was the lingering odor of Kwitt – the smell of home hearth with an underlying charred-death stench. Kirth used it, calling it a powerful relaxant. Rain had also used it.

Smells, however, were not things to be grabbed and displayed to a prince and his protectors. In fact, she'd been told others could not detect the underlying layer.

And it was just a trace, after all.

Besides, she reminded herself. It only implied Rain had worked with the powder, which meant nothing really.

It did remind her of another place where she had caught the Kwitt scent – clinging to the King and his First Minister.

It would be best to be sure of that before speaking to Tryst. But getting near the King was no easy task, even if she did have a room in the Palace. Twice she had heard him in the great wide hallways of the second floor, and twice she had tried to pass him.

Both times the Minister and King had veered in a different direction.

So today she hid in the garden where the two liked to stroll as they argued points of state.

She'd chosen the banyon tree, with its branches in easy reach. The leafy top hid her well.

An hour later, the King and First Minister strolled below her, continuing on up the path. They were long gone before she dared slip off the branch, lowering herself to hang a pace above the ground before dropping.

Marra then walked as casually as possible to her own suite.

She'd been prepared to report failure to Tryst. She knew his reaction – he'd be kind and unconcerned. She even had thoughts of moving back to Agben.

Marra had never considered what to do if she succeeded.

Because the Kwitt odor was fresh, strong, and clinging to the two men. She couldn't tell which one bore the aroma – or indeed if both wore it. But this was no fading scent, rapidly disappearing. A very strong dose of the powder had been recently and thoroughly used.

Stars, she still had no idea what the effect was.

After pondering several things to tell Tryst, she grabbed her key and cloak and headed for the Agben School. Where, for the first time ever, she discovered that Kirth was outside the city walls.

Cook had directed her, smiling as if traveling outside of Missea was as easy as strolling to Gold Harbor. And when Marra repeated everything back to be sure she wouldn't get lost, Cook gave a single nod before turning back to kneading her dough.

Marra walked to the Land Market by the Old Gate. The gate was open, which it apparently always was when the sun was up. The road through it, of firmly trampled dirt and half-buried stone, was set wide enough for four large wagons to pass abreast of each other.

She was nervous of what might lay beyond the city wall, of what she might find – or what might find her.

But striding down the road, beneath a bright sun, Marra relaxed. She even began to enjoy herself. Missea was so full of people and activity; this road felt peaceful in comparison. Travelers passed, of course, but not so many as one might expect. Each time the lane forked, fewer people stepped her way.

Hills puckered the land, some steep, some gentle, and her path wound its way higher. She saw more trees in the first half hour than she'd ever seen on all the Flats. With its thick grass and flittering birds, the Great Continent teemed with life. Once that thought had worried her, but Marra found the reality rather pleasant.

The wall of the city rapidly vanished in a climb up a slope and a twist in the path. The sounds of the city faded almost as fast.

After an hour, she came to the branch off the road Cook had described. A dirt trail veered left when the road wound right, to slant up toward a seeming cliff and disappear into a gap in the rock.

She followed the trail through the gap, taking the faint path amidst heavy forest, and then spied the small foot track heading straight up a rocky slope.

Steps were carved into this slope, not by man but by nature. Flat stones, boulders with worn earth bits between. It had the feel of being well-traveled, although Marra couldn't say why.

When the trees gave way, she emerged into a grassy clearing. The sun shone on a large house – not a square desert structure, but a rectangle with a curved room on the side. Bigger, she thought in astonishment, than the tavern back in San Cris.

A billow of smoke puffed from a stone funnel, although it was a warm afternoon. Laughter seeped out into the sunshine, and she hesitated to intrude.

But she'd come a long way to merely turn around again.

Marra approached the front door, which was wide open. And inside, bending over the fire as she stirred a large pot with a wooden spoon, was Kirth.

Kirth ceased stirring, and straightened. And grinned.

"So you finally ventured past the city walls." The old Skullan woman walked towards her with a welcoming arm flung out. "Welcome, Marra. Welcome to our family home."

The house had two small sleeping chambers off the main room, a luxury in Marra's mind. In the desert, homes were a single room, the bed tucked in a corner. Children's beds stayed rolled up and stored beneath the main bed during the day.

Kirth had a drying barn in the backyard, as well as a fire pit and outside table. Marra saw this from the large half-door, where the bottom piece was latched and the top piece wide open. Allowing the breeze without inviting the chickens.

She also saw Clarey, another Skullan teacher from the school, disappear into the barn. Leah sat at the table, across from a young man whose face was familiar. As she watched, the young man clasped Leah's fingers. They exchanged a warm look and he lifted her hand to his mouth.

Fallon, she realized. Drail's newest gamesman for the Hand of Victory.

Marra felt her cheeks flush and quickly turned away.

"Do you be needing something?" Kirth asked with a grin.

"I need to know more about the Kwitt powder."

Kirth's grin faded.

Marra wondered just how much she could tell her mentor. The elder's face seemed to wonder the same thing.

"You know 'tis a rare ingredient, child, from the Dim Continent. Shaved from a root, though the powder does seem to last well. My own stash is old, but still effective. I use it for health reasons."

Marra waited, but she said no more.

"May I ask what problem you seek to fix?" Kirth gave such a look.

Marra realized if she wanted candor, she'd have to give a little of her own.

"Something...I think something is odd at the Palace. Tryst – the Prince – worries."

Marra watched Kirth's face, trying to see her reaction. The old woman merely waited, giving nothing away.

"I smell Kwitt when the King passes." Upon thinking about it, she added, "Or it might be his minister."

Now Kirth reacted – with skepticism. "It is a health bulb, not some odd ingredient for enhancement. I've found it superior in treating poison sumac."

"But – that makes no sense!"

"Unless the King has poison sumac." Kirth smiled again, and gently prodded Marra to sit at the table by the fire. She spooned a generous portion from the pot she stirred. It turned out to be stew with subtle spices.

And Marra turned out to be hungry.

She finished the whole bowl and was licking the spoon, when she spoke again. "Mistress, how do I find a – a fix to an herb?"

"An antidote?"

Marra nodded.

"You find an antidote to a poison, child. Not a health tonic."

Kirth sat down with her own bowl and waved a spoon at Marra's empty one. "Tis plenty in the pot, Marra. Dip yourself more."

Marra started to refuse – but it was good, and she was hungry. The food at the Palace seemed more like artful displays than satisfying meals. Kirth's stew nourished.

"How do you find the antidote to a poison?" Marra asked as she ladled more stew into her bowl.

The old woman's lips thinned – and Marra worried until she realized Kirth was trying not to laugh aloud.

"All right, Marra. It depends on the poison. For some, we have proven treatments and for some we have options. And there are those, I fear, 'tis no cure at all. At least, no cure that works all the time."

Kirth cut herself a chunk of fresh bread and looked at her inquiringly. As the yeasty aroma wafted by Marra's nose, she grinned and nodded.

The warm slice proved useful in scooping up strew.

"What if..." Marra hastily swallowed. "What if you knew what poisoned someone? Maybe had the bottle or recognized the ingredient, but you didn't have a cure?"

Kirth sighed. "There's still a lot more to know in your situation, my girl. Old Abba, our best healer, would actually stick a bit of the poison on her tongue and tap it against the roof of her mouth. She'd spit it out afterwards, so don't go trying to ingest nasty bits. 'Tis often her cures had charcoal and sometimes a trace of the poison itself."

The elder chewed her bread as Marra considered her words.

"Marra, 'tis it true you cured a powerful sleeping potion all by yourself?"

Kirth watched her most carefully.

"I found several antidotes in Britta's book. I tried one, then another, and then all the strongest ingredients from each. When I added some Trevor seed, he woke. I honestly don't know if one simply worked or the continual flow of cures just accumulated."

Kirth licked the crumbs off her fingers.

"It's possible this Kwitt is affecting the King's mind." Marra leaned back from the table. "At least that's what Tryst – what the Prince believes."

The elder rose, taking her bowl and spoon to a bucket in the corner and setting them inside. "Tis several potions purported to effect the mind. The main one I know of is supposed to be a love potion."

Marra stared.

"Oh, many a young girl has played with it as one of her first complex elixirs. Rarely 'tis the effect what she hopes. While such a mixture may enhance an existing emotion, it can't create that sentiment from nothing.

Or, perhaps it fails because an inexperienced girl is not so clever at making elixirs."

Kirth hefted the spoon to stir the pot. "All the mind influencers tend to rely on emotion clouding reason."

Mind influencers. Marra had never heard the term before. "Are there antidotes?"

"We never needed one for the love potions," Kirth shrugged. "I suppose the place to start would be a reason restorer. Something to make one mentally sharp."

So Marra began her search to counter an unknown effect from a suspect powder.

In scouring Britta's book, she discovered several mental strengtheners and a 'powerful mind restorative.' But nothing contained – or even mentioned – Kwitt.

The real challenge was not having a test subject. The King and his minister proved very elusive quarry and it wasn't as if she could continually bring odd teas to the throne room, asking him to sample various blends. She discovered quickly enough that one did not slip things into the food of a monarch. There were those whose whole job was to guard against that exact possibility.

When she explained her challenge to Tryst, he asked how she'd tested on him. "I couldn't drink your offerings."

"But you were there, an unmoving test subject. I

poured a few drops down your throat, waved inhalants beneath your nose. You couldn't exactly refuse."

Tryst bit into his apple. They sat beneath the banyon tree, away from prying ears. "An inhalant. Might that not be the solution here?"

"Your father already eyes me with suspicion. I can only ask his opinion on a perfume so many times."

He finished his fruit with no comment. His demeanor appeared relaxed, but Marra could feel his tension. She'd always admired him for never reacting in fear or anger, no matter the provocation. Now she understood he did react – he just hid it well.

Tryst stood, reaching a hand down to pull her to her feet. "Marra, I am sorry. I've put far too much pressure on you. There may be nothing you can do for my father."

Somehow those words didn't release her obligation at all.

Mauric watched Tryst leave and then drew back from the window of the overlooking room. He went in search of Jason.

And finally found the Defense Master currying his new horse. His old one, the black with the white band on its forehead, had disappeared after the epourney.

"I did follow him," he began.

Jason continued the strokes, softly following the brush with the palm of his hand. Funny, Mauric thought, how the only real affection he ever saw from

Jason was in the treatment of his horse. Well, perhaps the passion with which he pursued the Prince's enemies told its own tale.

"I asked you not to do that," Jason murmured softly, so as not to disturb the horse.

"He's meeting with the little Brista."

Mauric jumped at a sharp rap from the next stall. A fidgeting hoof from an unhappy steed. That Brushfoot horse, he guessed, crammed as it was into a normal sized stall. Who had thought to board such a mammoth animal here?

"Tryst has a lot on his mind," Jason stroked his animal. "If he succumbs to a little dalliance, who can blame him?"

Mauric shook his head. "She didn't strike me as the dallying sort."

Jason set the brush on the old iron hook, and gave a last fond pat to his steed. "Mauric, we protect the Prince – we do not spy on the man. The little Trumen is not to my taste, but she has her own appeal and he's been with her for some time now. It's his affair and not to be judged by either of us."

"But -"

Jason snatched up the curry brush again and tossed it at him.

Mauric managed to catch it.

"Attend to your own horse," Jason said. "And let others attend to theirs."

11.

ATHAN ROARED HIS VICTORY beneath the arc banners. Black Tide had won again, and the Black Arena thundered with crowd approval.

With his head thrown back, he couldn't help but see the Red Storm Banner hanging in its honored place, seemingly mocking his triumph. He'd heard of Drail's successes and wasn't sure what gnawed at him more – the fact that the arrogant Trumen had somehow spun his utter failure around, or that Athan actually knew of his little triumphs.

Athan didn't follow him at first, of course. After the desert dogs had been chased from the Gold Harbor Arena with their tails between their legs, he never gave them another thought. Well, perhaps the occasional sneer when he saw the red banner.

One of his own men had stumbled across them in town and found out that they'd managed to eke out a win, which surprised him as one of their opponents was supposed to be a good Trumen team. He asked a few questions and discovered that the team most now called the Desert Dogs was a team on the rise.

Nowhere near his Black Tide team's skill, of course. Getting noticed in the Trumen back circuits was a flea to a wolf compared to a Skullan Gold Harbor favorite. Truth was, he couldn't have named a top Trumen team if he tried.

Apart, he realized, from the Red Storm. He found himself staring at the arc banner.

Here he stood, with the crowd screaming his name in victory, and that cursed banner mocked him.

The very next day, Athan stood in a different arena, one of mixed play near the Land Market. Quentis leaned on the rail beside him, pointing to a very wide Trumen whose idea of warm-up was pounding a wall with his fist.

"The Pounders," Quentis grinned. "I've made more money on those men than any team ever – Skullan or Trumen."

"They go the distance," Athan nodded.

Quentis grinned in reply. "There are several that can go the distance. These lads cross the line."

There was time to place wagers, but Athan did not. For one thing, he never liked to risk coin on anything but himself. Too, he didn't really trust Quentis on such matters. To Quentis, a willingness to break bone was all it took. Skilled himself, he yet had no appreciation for true game expertise or sheer athleticism.

The arena stands swelled as the four teams found their spots on the field.

Athan caught sight of the red-haired Brista striding beside Drail. Marra, he remembered. His own Brista was considered better than most, for Bristas were more affectation these days, but he had to go collect her brew before each game. He strongly suspected it did no good – but he hadn't quite found the resolve to forego it.

The Trumen girl, however, stood here now beside her team. To see the effects of her work for herself, in the face of Drail's loss or victory.

She was a pretty morsel.

There was, Athan mused, a long-standing belief that Trumen females were more giving little creatures. Skullan women were often proud and arrogant, rarely giving unless assured of payment – in all things. He'd been told by one he trusted that Trumen females were satisfyingly meek, and pleasant company for a night or two.

Marra, he realized, hadn't been meek at all. She'd actually stood toe-to-toe with him. He grinned at the memory.

And then shook himself. By the Great Goose, he

sounded as jealous of Drail's Brista as he was of his claim on the arc banner.

A Trumen judge appeared; the teams took their places. Marra stood beside the older man Drail traveled with, as Drail selected his ball.

"COMET!"

Trumen moves by their Missean teams always mimicked Skullan moves – they just lacked the sheer force of muscle a great Skullan could achieve. As Athan watched, he noted spins in the sand, the solid defense of the comet tail.

And the tricks the Desert Dogs used to defeat them.

It had been a few moons since that drubbing the Black Tide had bestowed in the Gold Harbor Arena – but surely not long enough to have improved this much. He doubted his own eyes until Quentis' team, the Pounders, positioned themselves with only Drail between them and the goal. The Pounders had the five-spot, and must surely win. Athan saw his own grin echoed on Quentis' face.

Drail made a seemingly bad move to the right, diving to block a fake attempt, and the Pounder Leader launched his ball to his left side. He should have scored easily.

Except Drail's foot kicked it even as he fell, knocking the ball upwards. The whole arena fell silent as the ball hovered high in the air, its five spots visible to those in the first row. And then it fell back down into the hands of Drail's blond teammate.

Who, despite being a fair distance away, launched it toward the tail.

And scored.

The crowd thundered approval, at odds with the scowl on Quentis' brow. Athan found himself both annoyed – and oddly impressed. The boy he'd humiliated should have crept back to the sands on the first ship out of port. Instead he'd found the mettle to actually stay and develop.

And he had most definitely developed.

Quentis slammed the rail and stood up. Athan studied his teammate before rising beside him, and decided to inquire into his gambling. If Quentis was going to be a problem, he wanted to know.

With a last look at the red-haired Brista, he left.

Marra found three mental enhancement recipes in Britta's book.

She also found the courage to approach a few teachers at the school, but discovered it difficult to get the information she needed without a full explanation. They all assumed she was trying to improve herself for her school work and assured her she was doing just fine.

Britta's recipes were a little vague. One said it increased the mind, another said it restored balance, and a third was merely called the Goth formula. It had a tiny 'head' shape on the page corner, which, when

Marra looked closely, she found on the other two as well. She had come to realize Britta used such symbols frequently, symbols that were not part of the Agben curriculum.

When she asked Kirth about the powder, the elder only shook her head. "Goth? Are you sure you have that right? Never heard the word before."

The recipe itself was a bit odd. Marra recognized most of the plants listed, but on two of them Britta indicated that the roots be used instead of the leaf, and in another case the actual bark of a tree. Dandelion weed was common in several recipes – it was a tonic for strengthening the organs and could aid in purifying the blood. But Britta called for the root of the plant.

Another ingredient was Trevor seed, which was in several potions. This Goth had a notation at the bottom about double potency, calling for a second seed just prior to administering. Gran, a wise woman in Port Leet, had warned her never to use more than one of Britta's Trevor seeds.

Confused, Marra noticed a few more symbols on the side of the page and spent an entire night combing through Britta's book in a quest to understand them. She did not succeed.

Somewhere in the early morning hours, she found herself studying counter potions – the potion to remove a condition imposed by a different potion. She tried to see if she could find a pattern, but pursuing that line of thought yielded nothing of value. Some counter potions did indeed employ a trace amount of the offending ingredient to fix it, but not all. Truthfully, she couldn't begin to figure out why one did and another did not.

As the sun rose, Marra returned to examining the three mental recipes. Thus she was tired when she finally went to meet the Prince.

Tryst had developed the habit of dwelling under the banyon tree for a short time in the afternoon, sometimes eating a snack, other times reading a book. This afternoon was no different.

He was munching an apple, a book open in his lap, when she approached.

"Marra," he smiled.

She only shook her head. "I have a starting place," she told him. "But no idea how far it is from an answer."

He nodded. "It's more than I hoped for."

She gave him a vial of the first of the mental enhancements.

A day later, he handed her back the empty glass and shook his head. "No reaction," he told her. "Nothing at all."

"How did you give it to him?"

Tryst gave her an odd look. "In his tea."

"How hot was the tea?"

"I just poured it. It was hot – but not as hot as I prefer. It cools a bit coming up from the kitchens. Is that really important?"

Lost in her thoughts, Marra suddenly saw how wide his eyes were – how startled he was. "Probably not," she belated told him. "It just helps to keep track of all the details."

They tried the second enhancement with no result, so Marra prepared the Goth Formula. "This one he didn't drink," Tryst told her. "Somehow the tea got spilt."

But at the next attempt with the Goth Formula the King felt queasy – and didn't drink his tea. He ate a few biscuits instead.

Marra tried all three formulas in her own chamomile tea. Two were difficult to notice – the tea tasted the same, and she frankly felt no difference in consuming it.

The Goth Formula did not affect the taste as far as she could discern – but it seemed to cool the tea and change the color slightly. She tried it with her evening tea – and found herself unable to sleep for hours.

As it turned out, the King had a fondness for a certain sweet biscuit with a sprinkling of cinnamon and sugar. Tryst brought him some with a bit of the formula powder sprinkled on top. Again, he didn't eat.

So Marra tried rubbing some of the powder into her hand and found again she couldn't sleep that night.

The next morning Tryst applied the Goth to his fingers.

"When he clasped my hand, Marra, he looked at me strangely. And then actually moved away. That powder – he instinctively knows when it's there. And he does not like it."

"Nothing happened after he touched your hand?"

Tryst shook his head. "Nothing I could see."

At least, she thought, it might be a good basis. Perhaps if they could induce him to ingest it. Or if she could make it stronger. She hadn't used the second Trevor seed yet, wanting to wait until she knew the effect of the first one.

Tryst managed to place the next batch of powder in his father's robe. The King removed it immediately, scratching his arms and saying it needed cleaning.

So she tried an even stronger formula, with a smattering of the Kwitt powder and the extra Trevor seed. This Tryst sprinkled on the throne itself.

But the King never sat in it. He approached it, gave Tryst a penetrating look, and declared he would not see any petitioners that day. Instead, he walked in the gardens with Charis.

Who then ordered the entire throne room scrubbed and polished.

The end result being Tryst was no longer welcome in his own father's presence.

He never again shared a room with King Bactor without Charis and two Elite Guard at hand, and he never had the opportunity to pour tea or offer cookies. When he tried to clasp hands with his father, he was told the King had a cold and did not wish to infect his son.

"At least we know," the Prince told her, "we've got a cure."

Marra only shook her head. "We know the King instinctively avoids this formula. He might be allergic or just suspicious of your recent behavior. Do you often pour him tea?"

Tryst slowly chewed his bite of apple.

"No," he said after his swallow. "I have never poured tea nor held a robe for him prior to this."

Marra sighed. "He might even be talking to the First Minister right now, asking how to determine if *you* are under some influence."

Tryst smiled in response. But the smile never reached his eyes.

When the Prince had gone, Marra lingered beneath the tree.

There had to be a way to try the formula on the King without involving Tryst. Because someone was protecting King Bactor, which made perfect sense if that same someone had bewitched him. And if not, then the King himself might be leery of his heir returned from the dead.

She leaned her back against the rough bark.

The contact felt good – a connection with nature. And relaxing here, she could view the sky through the banyon leaves. In the desert, the air was often bleached a sort of white-blue, and somehow looking at it added to the oppressive heat. Missean mists were as likely to hide the heavens altogether as not, but when skies were clear the sun shone proudly in a gorgeous blue setting. Clouds floated by, forming odd images that took on dramatic colors in the early morning and at sunset.

She could come to like the Great Continent.

And as these thoughts fluttered through her mind, Jason strode down the path. His face was grim, and when he dropped to his knee before her she shivered as if a lizard had scampered across her grave.

"You brought a small vial with you today," the Skullan Defense Master began.

Marra kept her face calm.

"May I see it?"

"No," she said.

Mauric approached from a different direction. Between the tree, the boy, and Jason, Marra felt hemmed in.

"Tryst seems to eat apples in your company," Mauric said accusingly, although for the life of her she couldn't see what the accusation was. "And the potion I saw you carry is now gone."

When the gist of this sunk in, she leapt to her feet in sheer anger. Jason had to step back to avoid getting bumped.

"If your curiosity must be appeased, make your demands of Tryst. I cannot answer you – and I will not be bullied."

As she started to leave, Mauric grabbed her wrist. "Hold on."

She used the release Tryst had shown her, spinning her hand around his instead of trying to yank free. It was far easier than she'd dreamed. Snatching her hand away, she gave the Skullan boy a long withering look.

She nearly trod on Jason as she marched off.

As he watched the little Brista go, Mauric knew she hadn't done anything wrong. It would have been far, far better to have listened to Jason in the first place and left the whole thing alone.

He looked at the Defense Master now and saw the lopsided dimple appear as Marra stalked up the path. Stars, Mauric thought. The man is actually amused.

"There's no need to tell the Prince about this," Mauric suggested.

Jason turned his gaze to him – and the dimple deepened.

"Oh there's every need," he told Mauric softly. "I suggest you do so before the little lady beats you to it. She may refuse to give us the time of day – but Tryst will know of this word for word as sure as the Great Goose flies in the sky."

"But what if she really is bewitching him?"

"I taught that wrist release to Tryst myself," Jason grinned. "He didn't teach her that under any herbal fog."

Mauric sighed.

The crowd roared.

As he stood beneath the fluttering scarlet cloth, Drail felt a wave of sheer joy. He knew that roar was for the District team, the Scrappers. They paraded into the arena, arriving late as always. Fists raised, acknowledging the milling spectators in their grand entrance.

A month ago, he'd have been nervous. The Scrappers were a very good team, perhaps the best Trumen team in all of Missea. Now Drail nodded to the new arrivals, winking at Manten. The Scrappers had not felt the need to warm up, to practice here in the Land Market Warehouse.

And the Hand would make them pay.

The Hand of Victory did not win all their games. But then, no team did. Their numbers were very good now, and while many Missean teams entered the arena with a sly grin, no one left still smiling. He knew at least two teams had tried to lure little Marra away from them.

She stood there now, watching their practice with that serious look on her face, and he smiled despite himself. A place at the Agben School no less and she still brought their elixir to them. A room – apparently a fabulous room – at the Palace itself, and she never missed a game. When others spoke of her to him, the word 'loyal' was often used.

Bristas were rare among Trumen teams, he'd discovered. In truth, few Skullan teams had one, and those that did used them more as another notch on their game leathers than a genuine advantage. One could purchase energy potions in a second or third tier store, or even seek a special brew from Agben, but employing a proper Brista was very difficult. The more available a potions mistress was, the less capable she seemed to be.

He was lucky to have Marra. Stars, she'd been offered a place with a great Skullan team in the Black Arena itself. She'd turned it down.

Watching her now, he saw the lifted face, the startled look. Drail followed her gaze to see Tryst and his friends striding through the spectators even as the crowd hushed, and then began the excited clamor that always seemed to follow the Skullan Prince.

Just as, inevitably, the younger man broke away to talk to Marra, and escort her to Tryst's side.

One of the Scrappers grinned as she passed, nudging his leader. Comments were exchanged, knowing looks shared.

Drail didn't like that. Marra was not the sort for intrigue. To refuse a prince was a delicate operation and he doubted his Brista would know just how to go about it. It was cruel of Tryst to lead her that road. Stars, Tryst was not alone in his pursuit. Fallon had taken to disappearing for long gaps, and rumors said he'd found a girl at the Agben School. Olver thought it was Marra – but Drail doubted that. She never so much as glanced the young man's way.

Wondrous things lived here in Missea. Drail enjoyed it now even more than he'd ever expected. But there were some desert things he preferred, and one of those was the women. The bold demeanor of the local girls was exciting in some ways and he'd enjoyed his share of the attention a gamesman garnered. Yet the companionship of a desert woman – soft to cuddle, yet with wit and warmth as well – was lacking in these city girls.

His eyes drifted towards Marra.

Someone yelled, "Comet! Comet!" The crowd took up the chant.

The Judge marched out to inspect the center cone and the ring drawn around it, although that was more for show than necessity.

Raising his hand, the Judge's fingers curled into a fist. The "Comet!" chant rose swiftly around the arena as the team captains strutted out to their places. Drail matched them stride for stride.

And snatched up the ball before the Scrapper leader. The Trumen frowned.

"COMET!" shouted the Judge.

Drail hurled his ball to spin in front of Manten, who was already sprinting his way. Timing it perfectly, the comet had barely settled in the sand before Manten's foot launched it up again. An instant later the sphere imbedded into the ground once more.

Their spins had grown very effective. It took few moves now before the spots began to reveal themselves beneath the dirt covering. When it came back to him, Drail grinned to see he gripped the five-spot ball.

He'd developed a pattern of holding the ball aloft, allowing the crowd to appreciate he had uncovered the winning sphere, while he set up his team for their run at the tail. It made for more exciting play, bigger screams, and happier arena owners.

It was a careful balance not to overdo, not to lose the match in stretching the game.

When he thrust the ball high, turning slowly, grinning at the spectators, he felt the anticipation swelling, the roaring encouragement. For these next minutes, the crowd and the Hand would be as one.

Assuming, he realized as he completed his turn, that they won. For three other teams were bearing down on him and the Scrappers were leading the way.

The Scrapper leader hurled a ball at his head.

Drail blocked with a forearm, but the movement dislodged the five-spot in his grasp. Both balls now lay at his feet – as three teams bore down upon him, cutting off Manten and Olver. No way to elude them, he saw. No way.

Near the tail, he spotted the Scrapper's best scoring man. They'd set up the winning move. Drail had no tactic to block or steal the ball. The leader was but a hair away.

When he was asked later, Drail said that he simply saw with a gamesman eye that he could not reach the first ball. So he reached for the second.

There was no conscious thought when he dove headlong for the farthest ball. The Scrapper leapt to stomp on his hand and at the last instance Drail curled protectively, away from the ball.

The Scrapper kicked it up and sprinted toward the tail. The others instantly veered to follow. Behind them, Olver sent him a worried look.

Drail answered with a grin, rolling upright with the first ball, the true five-spot.

Together they raced. The Scrapper's ball sailed in, the gamesman turning with arms thrust up in victory. He blinked in surprise as Drail launched his comet into the tail.

They still thought they'd won, Drail realized, but the Scrapper leader was startled at the ferocity with which they'd continued play.

By looking at Drail's face, at Olver's fist pump, at Manten's roar of laughter, he suddenly knew. His arms lowered slowly as Drail's raised high into the air.

"KYYYYRRRAAAA!" Drail shouted.

A hush blanketed the crowd.

Slowly, spectator noise rose again, a few suspected, many did not, yet when the last balls were sunk, and the Judge plucked each to set in its place, the truth was heard.

"Hand of Victory – seven points. FIRST PLACE."

Word spread, slowly at first, then tearing through the stands. A clever pretense some would call it, but in time the move would be christened 'the Desert Deception'.

And when Old Merle described it to Wolfbur the next day, the old Skullan gamesman laughed hard enough to pull a muscle.

Before the match began, Marra's mind kept slipping back to Tryst's problem.

Tryst couldn't administer the powder because the King wouldn't allow it. So perhaps the mixture was indeed a cure, the right combination to clear the King's mind of influence. Or, perhaps, suspicion had naturally arose with the attempts to administer it, and she was actually no closer to helping him than before.

Regardless, they needed a way to get the powder past Minister Charis to the King.

Tryst had forbidden her to try it herself. And, thinking about it all game, she honestly couldn't see how to do it even if he gave permission. If the monarch was wary of his own son, she doubted he'd accept tea from her hands.

Besides, the Kwitt aroma was very strong. That, above all else, must have tipped off the conspirators as surely as any action they might have noticed.

She watched the game anxiously – though she'd never have admitted it to anyone. When Drail had seemingly lost, she berated herself. Too much time spent on Princely concerns – on Skullan concerns – when she should be helping him.

And thus worrying, Marra was the first to see the mischief in his stance. The triumph shining in his eyes. As Drail and Olver raced to the cone she rose to her feet, clenching her hands.

She just knew.

Tryst patted her arm when the Scrapper sunk the ball. "Scrappers are a top Trumen team," he said. "Smart play."

"Not as smart as the Hand," she'd whispered back. And Tryst, watching Drail's face in confusion, had suddenly seen it as well.

He and Jason laughed for a long time.

Marra joined the laughter, though not at the cleverness of the move, nor the victory the Hand had snatched before an appreciative crowd. Although she did find herself smiling warmly at Drail.

She laughed because deception was a very good strategy.

Long ago, on the voyage to Missea, Tryst had taught defense principles. In particular the front door/back window idea. If one insisted upon leaving the house through a guarded front door, the game was set and defeat a strong possibility. Victory became a matter of sheer strength.

When that exit was difficult, Tryst had said, simply choose another direction. Make it a battle of mind over muscle.

It was foolish to keep bringing tea to a king who does not want it. Especially now that she saw an open window.

It was very late.

The three at the Old Barnacle Tavern huddled far from the fire, away from the small drinking crowd in the room. The Barnacle had a reputation for its clientele – and it wasn't good.

Her eyes flicking over the place, Rain noticed not the slovenly men who drained their mugs with too much enthusiasm, nor the single barkeep with beefy arms and no sense of humor.

What she noticed was cobwebs in the corner and dust on the floor. The cold knot of fury in her stomach tightened.

She deeply resented being here – being reduced to furtive meetings in dingy places. She hadn't forgiven the loss of the balcony chamber in the Palace, the loss of favor.

She blamed it all on Kratchett.

Now he intended to right all wrongs in one simple maneuver. He thought himself brilliant for the notion, although she'd bet anything it hadn't been his. Even now he looked to her for enthusiastic response.

And all she could think of was that he must have gotten access to her contact.

Her contact. Her man at the highest level in the

Palace, the one who protected Rain, promoted her. Who leaned on her to bring his schemes off successfully.

The one who no longer responded to her messages.

"She's the key to everything," Kratchett insisted in a low voice. "Without her, they cannot strike – or even know they need to strike. Her removal solves it all in a single blow."

"Ridiculous!" Rain was tired of hearing so much attributed to the little desert drudge. "She's no herbalist. No threat."

Kratchett gave that look again, the one where his eyes rolled before he blinked and produced a soothing smile.

She itched to claw those pupils out of her life.

"It will make certain people happy to see her gone. What matters if she truly is skilled or not?"

"You have blades. You have men positioned," Rain studied Kratchett carefully. "Why must it be my hand that does the deed?"

"You, Rain, have something to prove. If you think otherwise, walk out that door, but keep walking, my sweet. He'll not want to see you again."

Her fingernails dug into the flesh of her palms. She had to force herself to ease up, push the words through clenched teeth.

"I will deal with little Marra," she said.

The next morning Manten ran through the streets

of Missea.

He'd grown to love the run. In the desert he'd run every day, a route down a path to an old dried well, then through a grove of Cris trees, and finally back home. No one saw him run and he had liked it that way.

Then he had found himself in Missea, belonging to a losing team before the Hand found traction and changed that.

There was no privacy in the city. No matter how early he rose, citizens roamed the streets. Sometimes there were many, and sometimes only a handful, but his route was never empty. People thought him mad, running with no destination. They thought him mad anyway, he realized, belonging to a bad desert team.

So he ran.

And as the Hand of Victory won, as their reputation grew, Manten found an occasional greeting, a random cheer as he sprinted down the cobbled street.

Now as he rounded the last corner, he caught a warm smile on a serving maid's face. She cleaned their room, he realized. And could make a pleasant armful in a tavern tonight. He grinned back before mounting the outside steps to the second floor doorway of the Ship's Bell Inn.

The room was empty – but he heard Olver's voice, and found him next door with Drail and Old Merle. After Drail's famous deception maneuver, the Ship's

Bell had offered them a second room so they wouldn't leave.

"You are a good team," Old Merle was saying. "Very good. I'm proud at how hard you fought, how far you've come. But you're not ready to return to the Black Arena."

Manten leaned heavily against the wall. "Black Arena? As in the Gold Harbor Arena?"

Olver nodded.

Manten swallowed his protest – just. He still had nightmares of standing on that huge field, surrounded by a thousand jeering Skullan. Defeating a few clever Trumen did not give him confidence to stand there again.

"It's by royal decree," Drail said, in a tone that suggested it was not his first time saying this. "And not a full match. We play against one Skullan team as a demonstration of the King's gratitude."

"We took the field for one exhibition game already." Olver set a fist against the wall. "That did not go so well."

"This won't be anything like that," Drail sat on a bed, propping himself against the wall. "It's a special honor – we're to be awarded some sort of sash or such. For saving the Prince."

Manten watched Drail's hand flex and relax, flex and relax, and realized his leader's physical actions were completely at odds with his words.

"Must we do this thing?" Manten asked quietly.

The room fell silent.

Drail sighed, long and deep. And nodded. "To refuse is cowardice. It's a spectacle for Missea – they expect nothing more than a show."

"You would think Tryst would know better," Manten gave his lopsided grin.

Drail was not amused. "I wonder if we know Tryst at all."

Marra worked by the flickering candlelight in an outside shed. It was late, but then that meant more privacy. Few worked after dark.

So she was startled when a steaming mug appeared at her elbow, and the woman who set it faded back into shadow.

"What is that?" Marra asked.

The woman hesitated. "Kirth sent it. To keep you sharp."

Marra turned to look at the woman – but she had vanished.

Trust Kirth to know where she was. Well, whatever she'd brewed, Marra wanted to sample it. She quickly poured the measured Kwitt into the bottle.

One of her favorite aspects of the Agben School was the abundance of glass – glass bowls, bottles, and vials. Glass was expensive, but also the one container that would not react with potions. And when you worked with rare ingredients, hoping for peculiar results, it was best to avoid unexpected reactions.

Satisfied, her fingers reached for the cup as the door creaked open. She looked up into Kirth's face.

Marra lifted the mug. "I haven't tried it yet."

Kirth merely stepped aside.

Drail entered.

"Do you always work so late?" he smiled.

Recklessly dropping the mug, its contents splashed.

"Not always." Marra darted a look at Kirth, surprised the elder had led him to her.

Kirth cocked an eyebrow at him. "He urgently wants you to do something. I thought he should see how late you work now."

Drail grinned at the old woman.

"See that he finds his way out," she told Marra, and left.

He took his time to speak. And she was content to wait. Truth was, these days she supplied the Birr Elixir, but she didn't feel quite so much a part of Drail's team. And she missed that.

"More elixir?" Marra guessed.

He nodded. "For a special exhibition game – in the Gold Harbor Arena."

The light mood faded. Words tumbled through her mind, of caution, of doubt. But there was nothing she could voice.

Drail, however, seemed to understand. "So you did not know. It's by royal invitation, a reward for saving the Prince."

His fists pressed against the table. "Do you know why he does it, Marra?"

"Stars! I think he...Stars!"

Drail waited, watching her carefully.

"He needs a way..." she thought rapidly. And her anger grew with each new thought. "I won't do it unless he tells you. Unless he *asks* you. By the Desert Crane – not even then! It should be one of his own Skullan teams, one loyal to him!"

By the time she reached the end of her diatribe, he was actually chuckling. "Marra, Tryst is a friend, a gamesman, though he now chooses to call himself differently. I'll help him if I can."

He clasped her shoulders, smiling down at her. Her indignation melted.

Drail watched her a long moment before he spoke again. "It is rumored you have a special room at the Palace."

"I don't use it."

"Why not?"

She blinked at the question. "It's – empty. Cold and sterile. Here there are friends. The Trumen at Agben aren't servants."

"Better than traveling the desert with gamesmen."

"No," she said. "Not at all."

His smile was infectious. Her answering grin was hard to suppress.

"You'll probably have to show me the way out."

She nodded, moving reluctantly towards the door.

"I'll go talk to Tryst –"

"Let me speak to him," Drail told her. With a firmness that stopped her argument before her lips could part.

She led him out the door.

Kirth hurried back to the shed. Well, lumbered might be a more apt term. At her age, hurrying was not easily achieved.

The mug was still on the table. Raising it to her nose, she inhaled.

Licorice, she detected. Inviting and able to camouflage other smells. She was just reaching for a vinegar mixture when Marra returned.

"Mistress?"

Kirth waved at the cup with the vinegar jug. "Who brought you that?"

The girl stared. Kirth turned with a glass bowl and a tiny vial of Gajh. "Marra, who gave you that drink?"

Marra shook her head. "I thought you had."

Kirth broke the seal on the Gajh, spilling the contents into the bowl. She next tipped the vinegar jug, filling the vessel nearly halfway to the brim.

"What are you doing?" Marra drew close to peer into the container.

"Gajh is often a fair determinate of the health or harm in a substance. Not foolproof, of course."

Kirth tilted the cup Marra had been served to splash a few drops into the vinegar mixture. "'Tis a rare test these days. Perhaps unanticipated."

"But..."

The vinegar hissed. Bubbles danced across the surface, subsiding quickly. Kirth watched a moment longer, and then shook her head.

"Not a good sign," she frowned. "Did you see who brought this?"

"Smells sour," Marra screwed up her nose. "A woman about your size. I think. She tried to just leave it on the table and when I asked, said you sent it."

"Was her voice familiar?"

The girl shook her head.

Kirth dropped the vinegar mixture into an empty bucket. "When you finish, my child, please carry that bucket to the kitchens for cleansing. And Marra?"

Slowly the girl's eyes lifted from the mug. Kirth waited until she had her full attention.

"Don't be taking food or drink from strangers."

12.

TRYST STRODE into Gold Harbor Arena with Mauric on his left and Jason on his right. Stars, it hadn't taken long for old habits to fall back into place.

He rather preferred walking abreast, as he had with the Trumen. But that was not to be.

The sounds of practice – flesh on flesh, comets smacking sand, grunts forced out of bodies – led him to the rail.

Drail, Olver, Manten, and that Missean youth drilled on the field below.

The leader of the Hand balanced on the balls of his feet, waiting for Olver to run past with the comet. Olver faked right, dove left.

Not fooled, Drail struck his arm, dislodging the

sphere. He dove to recover – but Manten snatched it first and streaked off.

And slowed, and stopped. They reset to go again.

"Congratulations," Tryst called down. The Hand ceased, everyone looking up.

Manten frowned; Olver positively scowled. The young Missean gaped like a fawn staring at a bowman in the woods.

To all but Drail this should be an honor, a special privilege granted by royal decree. Not one of these men looked honored.

Tryst cast a glance at Jason – and saw the Defense Master's face wore that serene look that boded ill. Jason was never serene; the look meant he saw exactly what you hoped he did not. Jason didn't understand why Tryst had done this – and wouldn't tolerate insolence from the Trumen.

Drail strode across the arena, stopping at their feet. With the stands so high above the field Tryst was far above him.

"Prince," he said, in a tone Tryst had never heard from the desert gamesman.

Suddenly Tryst vaulted the rail, rolling in the sand to come upright. He clasped Drail's arm in the old gesture of friendship. He won no smile from the man, but when he tilted his head, indicating a walk, Drail nodded.

Striding away from the others, Tryst breathed in relief when Jason didn't follow.

"Is this not, in some part, your dream?" Tryst asked.

"My dream is to earn the right to play here by my own sweat."

Tryst nodded. "I am sorry for this."

"You stood here with us, played at our side that first game. Did you not guess our feelings to confront that same team, again and in this place?"

Having fallen back into the role of prince, Tryst was startled. Few took him to task for anything except Jason, and Jason did so with a careful approach. Drail voiced anger as one would to an equal.

Or as one would to a friend, he realized. And Tryst vowed then and there to keep these friends. To be worthy of their friendship.

"I am sorry," he said again, and meant it this time.

After several blinks of the sun, Drail nodded.

From the other side of the arena, four Skullan strode out across the sand. Tryst recognized the wave tattoo before anything else.

For the King had agreed to his son's wish, to reward the Hand of Victory with an exhibition game. That had surprised Tryst. He'd carefully marshalled his reasoning, but had not been called upon to explain.

Instead, the King had chosen the Black Tide, the Skullan team Drail had faced that disastrous first night. The team that had utterly devastated them.

Tryst found it hard to believe it was mere coincidence.

Athan surveyed the stands before surveying his opponents.

It was still early, yet the crowds were already swelling. The tale of these two teams meeting before, of the drubbing he'd bestowed, added spice to this rare delicacy. That the dust-dog claimed his grandfather had received this same honor also added spice.

"I'll break four bones in four minutes," Quentis grinned.

Athan planted his fist on the man's chest. "An exhibition game by royal decree," he hissed. "You break those bones, and the Prince will break ours."

"But –"

"Vent your spleen on the Wolf Pack in the second game. I will not lose favor in the Palace over your foolishness."

Quentis said no more. The look on his face, however, did not reassure Athan. He'd have to keep an eye on the man.

The game had yet to begin, and already the flaws in his own team were revealed. Athan would start seeking Quentis' replacement on the morrow.

Having labored at her new powder, Marra hurried through the streets to the Black Arena. Tryst had sent an escort, but she'd pretended not to know and left through a back way.

In truth, she didn't like staunch men escorting her

here and there. Mauric had been surprised when she'd once explained that to him. He'd insisted it was a mark of honor bestowed on women. A warranted courtesy, he told her.

She'd merely waved a hand at three Trumen females, all hurrying to their destinations alone. Poor Mauric had wrinkled his brow as if startled to even see them. "Those are just..."

"Trumen?" Marra asked drily.

He'd actually blushed. "Not everyone can afford such protection," he said. "And not everyone requires it."

"I don't require it," Marra had replied.

Truth was, she liked her independence. She liked walking the streets, going where she wished to go, when she wished to do so. Of course, there were parts of the city she would not roam alone, places to be avoided late at night. But everyone should avoid those parts – not just her. It made her feel equal to everyone else.

On the other hand, the Black Arena was not a place for Trumen. She realized that as she neared the gate, surrounded by Skullan spectators. Be confident, she reminded herself, and walked through without any hindrance.

Until Minister Charis stepped out of the shadows to block her way.

"Marra," he bowed. All her independence vanished on the spot. "The King desires your company. He requests that you watch from his own arena box."

Around her people glanced up in surprise, already seeing her different than they had but an instant before. They thought her honored, she realized.

She thought she was something else.

Charis extended his arm.

"I must deliver this to Drail," she plucked the crystal bottle from her pocket.

Charis signaled. An Elite Guard appeared, lifting the powder out of her fingers and stepping back into the shadows.

"Drail must have that," she called.

But the guard was gone, and Charis' arm waggled commandingly by her nose.

For a blink of the sun she hesitated. But there was no other option.

So she laid her hand atop his and went with him.

Lump waited outside the herb school.

He'd sent two toughs in guard uniforms to get the girl. He didn't relish actually killing her, but orders were orders, and it might make his life easier.

It was a good plan for its sheer simplicity. Logically, she should have leapt at the chance – women loved that sort of thoughtfulness. Turning down a prince's escort just shouldn't happen.

All the same, he wasn't surprised when the two returned with startled eyes and shoulders shrugging.

Tryst, Mauric, and Jason mounted the arena ramp behind an Elite Guard. At the top they were marched in the opposite direction from the royal box.

Mauric opened his mouth, but Tryst silenced him with a gesture.

The guard ahead moved with an odd gait, as if unused to the weapon at his side. Realizing the implication, Tryst turned to Jason – who made the same silencing gesture to him.

Through a doorway, past a second guard, and they found themselves in an arena box as far from the King as it was possible to be.

"With the King's compliments," the guard bowed, waving at a table ladened with food and ale. The guard withdrew.

The door swung shut behind him, latch clicking in place.

And the three exchanged looks.

Mauric broke the silence first. "It's not so bad. Have you not asked your father for your own suite here?"

"I asked – once – to hold a gathering of friends for the Gold Harbor Championship, where the revelries would not be hindered by my father's presence."

"So now he will not hinder our enjoyment."

Tryst moved to the rail, gazing out across the sandy field, to the distant royal box. "I think it is we who will not hinder Charis." He was unhappy, but not worried.

Not, that is, until he spied Marra in his father's box.

The trumpets startled Drail.

Blaring sounds from their long horns proclaimed the outset of the exhibition. And then the Judge – if one could call him that – marched to field center. The crowd overflowing the stands fell silent, waiting.

"By Royal invitation, the Trumen team from the Desert Flats, Drail and the Hand of Victory, shall demonstrate their skills today.

"Seven days past, the Hand foiled a daring attempt to murder our Prince Tryst. They did so in the midst of a comet game, and thus saved the heir to Missea.

"The King has requested the pleasure of watching their play here today, in the greatest place a comet team can play. Only one other Trumen team has ever held that honor."

Despite himself, despite his stomach's knot, Drail gazed up at the Red Storm banner swaying above him.

"That first team was granted the privilege by the young Prince at the time. The man who is now King Bactor – Ruler of all lands."

The resounding applause drowned Drail's harsh snort. Nothing made a desert man as skeptical as this Skullan claim that their dominion encompassed the Wavering Continent as well as their own.

He watched the man who must be the King step to the edge of the royal box, lifting a hand to the cheering crowd. The brilliance of his robes, the gleam of gold upon his head, dazzled Drail.

The cheers increased and the man stepped back.

And in doing so, revealed a girl almost tiny in comparison. She might have gone unnoticed if not for the long red hair and that stance he knew so well – a proud cloak to hide her nervousness.

Drail spun around. Tryst and his friends were still in the opposite box, far away from Marra.

Precisely what was Tryst up to?

"Today the Hand of Victory faces Missea's own Black Tide!"

As the Skullan team strode out across the field, the wave tattoo mocked Drail. Of course he must face the very team that had once crushed them as ants beneath a boot. The Skullan who had single-handedly defeated – no, humiliated – the entire Hand.

Slowly the cheers tapered off. Slowly the Judge marched to his place.

The Black Tide spread out in a line across the field. Turning, Drail saw that Manten, Olver, and Fallon had done the same. Fallon's eyes were wide in his face, but Manten actually leaned forward, relishing the moment.

Drail knew they were each there for a very different purpose. Yet whatever road had brought them to this point, the Hand of Victory now faced perhaps the strongest Skullan team in all of Missea. He could choose to feel Fallon's fear or Manten's eagerness.

His feet sprinted forward before his mind had caught up. Arm raised, he whirled to show his grin to the entire mass of spectators. Thousands of faces, all

Skullan, stared back.

And long before he reached the comet tail, the crowd roared their approval.

Marra saw Drail for a brief moment before Minister Charis pulled her back.

All she could think of was that she'd handed the powder to a guard. She might have still held it, opened it, and used it. Whatever influence the King was under, she could have ended it now.

But how could she have guessed she'd be this close to him?

Her eyes locked on Tryst's father. He seemed a normal Skullan, perhaps kinder to her than most. Still, she'd never known him before he'd been affected – if he'd been affected. She had no way to judge.

Charis had pulled her back from the rail, setting her in a chair. Seated, she couldn't see much of the field. Her last view was the Black Tide spreading out across the sand.

Fear slowly gnawed at her gut.

She didn't think the Skullan would purposely try to injure Drail and his men, although in truth Skullan could do that without effort. But the Prince was far across the field.

Drail would still do what he'd been asked to do – launch a comet ball at the Skullan King.

Tryst was supposed to be here, now. Tryst was supposed to do the deed himself, with a bit of revelry.

A son's teasing gesture with his father.

Drail had to see that – had to realize the implication. He had to abandon the scheme.

But he wouldn't. She just knew he wouldn't.

"COMET!"

The ball shot between the two lines of men.

Athan watched Drail leap for it, and suppressed his grin. Desert dogs were always so eager, so quick to run without strategy. The Black Tide intended to hold back, to give a show for the King and the crowd. It would be disappointing if this ended too soon.

Snatching the ball on the run, Drail darted away from the comet tail. Athan suddenly wondered if the Trumen, too, would try to prolong the game.

Too foolish, that. Surely Drail knew he couldn't win. There was no need for him to try to make the game longer.

The dust-dog darted between two of the Tide. His own teammates had to try to follow him, which meant being closer to the Skullan than they should want to be.

Athan spun on his heel, whirling to see Drail race toward the royal box with Quentis in hot pursuit. Drail lifted the ball, as if shooting.

And the Skullan barreled into him, snatching the comet while bashing his head with a forearm.

The leader of the Hand crashed to the sand as Quentis loped away, laughing. Quentis, Athan thought in fury, would be the Black Tide's downfall.

The desert dog rose to his knees, then a wobbly stand, as Quentis circled the edge of the field, holding the ball aloft and waving to the cheering spectators. At least he made no move to sink the ball. Athan himself had drilled it into his men to let the exhibition stretch on until he or the King signaled to finish it.

He ought to have told Quentis not to touch the Trumen as well.

To their credit, the other dust-dogs didn't rush to aid their leader. Instead they chased Quentis, who was too busy with his theatrics to feel the men behind him. The one with blond hair caught up and struck the ball from his grasp.

Quentis stumbled. He regained his balance in time to see the Trumen racing away with the sphere, and bellowed his rage. The noise thundered around that place designed to carry sound on the field to the highest tier. Athan knew it was coming before Quentis opened his mouth, and yet still felt the man's anger melt his bone marrow.

Even the crowd quieted.

They loved a bit of blood, he knew. But in a game of honor for Trumen heroes, injury and death should not be on the program. Yet Quentis' furious cry promised just such a spectacle.

Athan sprang forward, intending to intercept not the ball, but his teammate.

Spitting grit, Drail shoved himself away from the sand.

He saw Manten speed toward the comet tail. The vicious Skullan roared again, hurtling in pursuit. Drail feared that could be very bad for Manten.

So he leapt up, stumbling before he found his balance, and flew after them.

Drail had told the others that *he* needed to be the one to sink the ball. Galling to claim that, to let them think he must show off in the Black Arena. And not one of the Hand had blinked, not one had said a word. That had cost him more than anything else in this foolish scheme.

The sphere dust cover was not comet suet, but some sort of powder Marra had created as an antidote. The King, so the Prince insisted, was under an evil influence. This whole exhibition was Tryst's plan to save his father.

Drail had agreed, as much for Marra's sake as any reason. It was to be a friendly gesture, Drail tossing the ball to Tryst, who would catch it to the delight of the spectators and deliver the dose straight to his father's lap.

But Tryst was not in the royal box, and the Desert Crane only knew what that meant. Drail suspected that to deliberately hurl a comet at a King would be the death of him.

Yet he also knew this whole thing held Marra in its grasp, and he wanted her free. If it looked like an accident – bounced off a Skullan's arms perhaps – it could merely be a source of amusement. Maybe.

But if Manten or the others had a shot to sink the ball...

Drail sprinted across the field, infuriated to think he was more focused on getting the ball than saving his friend from a vengeful Skullan.

Marra crept to the railing.

Charis reached for her, and she slipped beneath his hand. "I can't see, First Minister," she murmured.

After two blinks, his hand lowered.

Pressing her solar plexus against the barrier, she stared at the tableau on the field. Drail was just rising from the sand, Manten hurtling towards the comet tail with the ball in his grasp and a monster of a Skullan giving chase. Gaining.

Marra clamped her mouth closed to keep from shouting as Manten launched the ball.

It sailed high in the air, in a perfect arc. All their hopes would sink with it.

And then the ball was snatched by the Black Tide leader. Marra started breathing again.

The pursuing Skullan barreled into Manten, elbow aimed at the Trumen's head. The elbow missed – but the desert gamesman hit the sand so hard he created a wave of grit.

The whole stadium exhaled when Manten sat up.

There was nothing to stop the Black Tide leader

from sinking the ball – yet he merely waited for Drail. And then threw – to spin it into the dirt at Drail's feet.

He was toying with them. The crowd burst into raucous cheers, loving the arrogant gesture. A Skullan gesture.

And when Drail snatched the ball from the sand, a new worry gripped her. She'd put a lot of powder on the ball, but how long would it last on the field of play? The extra vial she'd brought Drail was gone, taken by a guard she was very sure never delivered it. How much was needed to free King Bactor?

And even if they did somehow get this powder to the King, had she created a true cure in the first place?

What if all of this was for nothing?

Drail sprinted straight for her, ignoring the tail. Behind him the Skullan leader frowned, leaping into pursuit. He hadn't anticipated Drail's course, and didn't understand it.

That might save them all.

Marra locked eyes on Drail. Without Tryst here now, ready to catch the ball, the plan wouldn't work. Drail couldn't hurl it directly – surely he saw that.

Without conscious thought, she stretched her arms out over the rail to catch it.

Tryst leapt from the box onto the comet field. Landing awkwardly, pain shot up from his wrist to his elbow. He ignored it, rolled upright and ran.

As tempting as it was to sprint through the middle

of the arena, he circled the edge. Doing so made him look like an over-exuberant prince, a little the worse for his ale.

But to run through a heated comet match reeked of something more.

Tryst had expected Drail to abandon the plan. They'd have found another way, one risking his own skin and not that of friends. For Drail to do this now was suicide.

But there the gamesman was, making his second run for the royal box with a murderous Skullan on his heels. If Tryst couldn't stop him, he might at least deflect the worst of the retaliation. If he was in time.

If they'd even listen after his own father had exiled his son from his presence.

Athan trotted after the Trumen, his confusion increasing. Was the man trying to lead him away from the tail, to swing round for a clear run? If so he'd gone too far for the strategy to work – the rest of the Black Tide would easily block him.

Yet the dust-dog raced to the side. To the royal box, he realized, where his Brista stared down at him with such frantic eyes. She held her hands out in a seeming playful gesture, as if asking him to toss her the ball. But her face belied the movement.

The First Minister joined her at the rail, frowning.

Athan heard crowd reaction and glanced over his shoulder to see the Royal Heir himself leap to the field and run.

It made no sense. Nothing made sense.

Quentis shot into view, hurtling to cut Drail off. Quentis, he realized, would hold nothing back. Killing the Trumen would be satisfying sport to him.

That thought lent Athan speed.

Quentis dove for Drail, fists aimed for his spine. At the very least, the desert man would never walk again.

But whether by instinct or sheer luck, Drail veered at the last instant. Quentis flew past to thud into the sand. He struck hard and laid still.

Drail neared the royal box, preparing to throw the ball at the girl. Athan couldn't understand it – this was a royal exhibition and anyone could see the little Brista was afraid.

The Prince was still many steps away when the comet arced toward the box. The dust-dog fell as he threw, his eyes fastened on the ball.

An Elite Guard deflected it with a shield. The comet ball fell back to the pit. And a firestorm burst upon them.

Two guards leapt to the sand, blades drawn. The herb girl cried out, scrambling as if to leap after them, but the First Minister grabbed her arm.

And the King himself rose and stepped to the rail, scowling upon them all as the Royal Heir sprinted up shouting, "No!"

Athan plucked the ball from the sand.

Drail stared up at him, eyes so compelling. "Toss it

to the King," he whispered. "Now!"

Athan felt his mouth gape.

"Please! Before it's too late."

Later he could never fully explain why he did what he did. It might have been the look on the girl's face, or the way the Prince himself gestured toward the King.

Or after all, it may have been the honesty in Drail's eyes. That blasted honor Athan had always recognized – and resented – in the dust-dog's nature. Something he thought he himself had once had, before knuckling under to his father and changing his team's name.

The ball left his hands. Not a hard throw, but a gentle toss like he'd make to a small boy waving in the stands.

The King caught it instinctively and burst into spasmed sneezing.

Marra trembled beneath the Minister's grip.

The King's violent sneezes shook the box, holding everyone frozen. For something was happening to the King.

If the powder worked, he should be free of any influences by Minister Charis or Kratchett or Rain. Would they be able to tell?

The sneezing stopped with a burst of air, not from his lungs but his whole body. She winced away, and when she looked back –

There was no king at all. There was a – a *creature*.

Covered in hair like an animal's fur, his big eyes glared with malevolence. Intelligence.

The beast stood a third larger than the Skullan guards, perhaps more. His chest seemed twice as wide, his muscles twice as bulky and oddly placed.

Somehow he seemed familiar.

He turned a scowl on her. Two large curving teeth protruded from his mouth, the enamel tinged green.

"You interfering little herbist..."

The Terrin!

The stuffed toy Tryst had given her, the one supposedly from the Dim Continent. This creature looked just like him, except that a small toy covered in soft fur was very different from this Monster towering over the guards. Moisture dripped from the fangs, making it resemble a childhood nightmare more than a plaything.

And then it growled.

Guards, Charis, Drail and Tryst, even the gamesmen below had not moved until the growl.

The Terrin leapt towards her, yanking her arm.

Falling against the thing, she discovered its fur was harsh, grating against the skin. And the smell held a trace of musty earth, but beneath that, the stench of scorched bone.

She wondered, with a part of her mind that could still wonder, if that smell was some sort of commonality on the Dim Continent.

And then she fought.

Flailing wildly, Marra jerked back from it – but the thing's grasp on her arm was as iron. She tried Tryst's wrist release, circling her hand around its paw. No effect.

Hearing her own heartbeat pounding in her ears, she watched it back towards the door, dragging her with it. The other paw reaching for her.

Tryst leapt over the rail, landing in a crouch. He straightened, eyes on the thing, as behind him Drail jumped up, dangling for an instant till he swung his legs over. And then both men ceased moving.

They were afraid to move, she realized, because it held her. The creature would get away, and it would take her with it.

She knew she'd die if she left the Black Arena.

Marra kicked its leg hard. And kicked, and kicked. The Terrin flinched, reacting to the blows, yet gripped her tight. One more kick, in the same spot, as her hand again sped through the release move.

This time it worked. She was free.

For an instant the thing stared at her, and she at it. Tiny black eyes held intelligence, but she couldn't discern what emotions were within, if indeed it felt anything at all.

Hands snatched her away – Drail, she realized. She was yanked back against him, held safe. If it wanted her again it would need to pry her from the gamesman.

One guard finally drew his sword.

The Terrin whirled and fled through the door, its loping gait odd, its movement awkward. Yet it was gone in the blink of the sun.

"Stop him!" Charis barked at the guards, who belated chased after the creature.

Drail's grip tightened before turning her around. He said nothing, merely scanning her as if certain he'd find some injury. She found herself scanning him in the same way.

Tryst remained rooted, eyes locked on the doorway where the Terrin had vanished. "My father?" he asked. But she could see the knowledge reflected in his eyes. He knew.

The First Minister had fallen back to yield to Drail. He now seemed not a minister at all, but a shaken old man.

Charis only shook his head.

Drail leaned against the wall. And released a breath he'd seemingly held since that thing had first appeared.

He stood now in a waiting area below the pit of the Black Arena, idly rubbing a sore muscle. Before him Manten and Olver lay on healer tables, both being treated for strains and stress pain, while Tryst, possibly with a broken wrist, insisted on waiting.

Not 'Tryst', Drail admonished himself. 'Prince'. Better get used to calling him Prince.

Marra watched the healer work because the healer

had insisted. The woman had been Agben trained, and felt it would serve Marra to learn. When his Brista wrinkled her forehead at the wrong time, he surmised she was thinking not of herbs but of the Terrin.

Just as all of them were thinking of the Terrin.

Except for the healer, they were alone in the room. Two handfuls of guards waited outside the door, but for the moment they were alone.

"I swear it had green fangs," Manten told the mattress he lay upon, and then looked to Drail. "Is that possible? Green teeth?"

The healer snorted, and slapped Manten's shoulder. "You'll do, my fine fellow. Give it a full day's rest, and then stretch the muscle the following day."

She beckoned to Tryst. "Come sit, your Majesty."

Startled, the Prince was slow to move. "Call me Prince – not Majesty."

The Agben woman merely gestured again.

Tryst perched on the edge of the man-length table. And said not a word while she worked.

Shifting his position, Drail watched Marra. Evidently her lesson was over, for she left the healer's side to approach him.

"You are truly well?" she asked. He'd had a notion of having her rub that leaf and oil concoction on his arm – but realized his motivation was not to ease any pain.

"I'm well."

Another moment, and the healer stepped back. She

gave them all a last look, and left.

Tryst was rubbing his wrist. "I wanted to thank you," he said.

"You're welcome," Drail responded.

Pushing up from the table, Tryst met his eyes. Drail saw the sincerity – overlaid with some other emotion. "Thank you...for everything.

"Drail, Manten and Olver – you befriended a wretch in trouble when few would. You could easily have left me to those that pursued, and you never did. In return I lied to you. And after all that, you helped me again tonight."

The door opened, and a young guard entered. He marched up to Tryst, ignoring Drail and the others.

The guard sank to his knee. "Highness. First Minister Charis requests you return to the Palace."

Drail watched the Prince – seeing the flash of annoyance firmly suppressed, the decision reached. Tryst nodded his head.

And turned again to Drail. "I'm very grateful. Any favor that I may grant, now or in the future, you have only to ask." His eyes moved from man to man, making the promise individually. Manten grinned and nodded; Olver actually looked embarrassed.

From where she stood, Drail couldn't see Marra's reaction. But Tryst locked eyes on her for a long time, before spinning on his heel and following the guard out.

The door shut behind them.

"It seems we have the gratitude of Skullan royalty," Olver broke the silence. "You want to tell us just what by the Desert Crane happened tonight?"

So Drail told them.

Jason leaned so far forward he practically lay on the horse's back.

This will not help, he told himself, forcing his muscles to ease. His mind did not take the hint – it still whirred in a loop of fearful possibilities.

That would have to stop as well. For this was no quick sprint but a long journey, and though he hadn't told anyone, he strongly suspected where it led.

He pushed hard, but the twelve men with him, including Mauric, voiced no protests. Jason had lost time scouring the Elite Guard, seeking men he knew and trusted to chase this...thing. Being now staffed with fools and raw recruits, it had taken too long.

Tryst had expected to ride with them. Only Minister Charis himself was able to turn the Prince's mind. "You rule the Skullan Empire now," he'd stated, in a voice faintly trembling. "You cannot abandon your people."

And it had all flooded back. The training, the lessons drilled of state and governing. Monarch responsibility, which had always made Tryst grimace. Well, perhaps the boy had reason.

But he had stayed.

This – Terrin – had fled with no less than ten

others. Eight of the Elite Guard disappeared. They knew the count by the number of horses gone from the stables, one of which was the Brushfoot steed.

Jason had smashed a fist into a wall when told that. He should have asked questions, probed for the owner. For why would anyone stable such a giant beast with the King's finest? It was a work animal – far too tall and wide of back for practical riding by any man.

The trail led to that same road he and Mauric had followed four moons back. To the Nirr Provence, and he was sure, to Borden's harbor.

The Prince, now called Highness, was frantic to recover his father. As Tryst had once lain in false sleep, unaware and vulnerable, he now feared that same fate for his father. And though Jason doubted the King lay sleeping, he'd said nothing.

But he thought it far more likely that the King was dead.

Jason, Mauric, and the guard arrived at Borden Harbor to find only two ships anchored. Three others, including a large vessel everyone still talked about, had left the night before. A wild rumor told of a giant bear walking up the gangplank on its hind legs.

"Just crazy talk," the Dockmaster assured him. "'Twas old Gorgin, sir, who claims to have seen it. And Gorgin does like the bottle."

"Do you know where she was bound?"

"Most ships these last two years were from the Dim

Continent. Or so they say," came the answer. "Me, I don't know. They didn't act like other ships."

Jason and Mauric exchanged a look. "How so?" Jason asked softly.

"Ships need friends in port. Dockmasters like me, to get quick berths and fast papers. Tavern keepers, to eat better, mayhap gain a little tolerance for crew excess. Dock workers, warehouse owners. Most captains get to know fellows round here."

The Dockmaster spat on the ground.

"These lads kept to themselves."

It was all of a moon later when Marra left Kirth's house in the woods. She'd gone to seek help with a new tincture.

Well, truthfully, she could have waited for Kirth to return to the Agben School. She had not, because Marra rather liked the house in the woods. It seemed exactly the sort of house one should have.

She hadn't stepped ten paces when Drail appeared on the trail.

"They told me where to find you." He stood there surveying Kirth's home, the white-washed walls, the stacked stone chimney. "Now this is a house," he smiled.

Marra nodded. "It's the sort of place you ought to live." She cast a last fond look over her shoulder. "Did you need to see Kirth?"

He shook his head. "They told me where to find

you. We've just accepted a game tonight – in the warehouse district. We'll need some Birr Elixir. Or is it too short of time to make that?"

"I'll do it as soon as I get back."

He turned to walk with her. They left the clearing and started down the forest path.

"You came all this way just to tell me that?"

Drail nodded. "I'm glad I did. It's nice to escape the city walls."

The path widened so they could walk side by side. She realized how rarely that happened. Marra somehow always trailed the men when they'd walked across the desert, probably because she felt more comfortable that way.

"You like the woodland home as well?" His eyes swept the green trees appreciatively.

Marra sighed. "Someday, it's the sort of place I'd like to live."

"Surely you'll stay in the Palace?"

Surprised, she shook her head. "Tryst needed me to help with his father. That's finished now."

"He wouldn't kick you out. He's very grateful after all you did."

"After all *you* did," Marra shook her head. "I don't want to stay there."

Drail gave her a penetrating look. She frowned back, trying to puzzle out his thoughts.

"The Palace," she explained, "is not a home at all. It's an indoor city. There's no hearth, no privacy. Just lots of strangers and cold empty chambers."

"You'd really rather live in a house in the forest?"

She nodded, surprised he had to ask.

"I'm not sure when I will settle down." Drail stopped, turning to face her. "We may travel the Great Continent at some point. I'd like to see it."

"I'll go with you," she said. And then, worrying, she added, "If you'd like me to."

"I would like you to," he grinned. And he put an arm around her shoulders.

Together, they walked back to Missea.

Epilogue

TRYST PACED the council room. "I cannot accept that."

It was dark despite the morning hour, thanks to the east opening having been sealed along with the rest. Tryst was determined to fix that this afternoon.

"There is no trace," Minister Charis told him. "Your Majesty, we must..."

"Do not call me that!"

Jason stepped forward, laying a hand on his shoulder. "Tryst, my friend, we will scour the country. We'll sail to the Dim Continent itself, beating the ground till our quarry is forced to reveal itself. Whatever happens, we will discover the truth."

"He cannot be dead." Tryst meant it as a command, perhaps to the Great Goose himself. "My father is alive." His eyes locked onto Charis. "He must be alive."

Charis flashed a beseeching look to Jason. And then seemed to find his own strength.

"Your father could well be alive," the First Minister agreed. "But that doesn't alter the fact that Missea needs a king. It cannot wait night after night, moon after moon, for its ruler to return."

Looking to Jason for support, Tryst saw the Defense Master agreed with Charis.

"We will declare you ruler in trust. After all that has occurred," Charis continued, "some royal pageantry is in order. A formal coronation. Twill still be a period of mourning, but there will be light at the end of that dark path. Missea needs to move on, Highness. If – *when* King Bactor is found, you can easily abdicate in his favor."

My first royal decision, Tryst sighed. And I'm doing exactly what the Minister wants. Well, he would seek additional advisors on the morrow.

Or the day after that.

"No trace?" he heard himself asking again.

Jason squeezed his shoulder. "We know the very ship that Terrin-thing took. Everything indicates the Dim Continent as the destination. And there are so few ports there."

"That we're aware of," Tryst added bitterly.

"I doubt they'll use some hidden port. They've a good jump on us; they'll easily lose us once they set foot on dry ground."

"That is what I fear."

Jason went down on one knee before him. His action startled Tryst.

"My Liege, I swear to you I'll find the truth. I will not rest until then."

I really am King, Tryst breathed. It was not a welcome thought.

He'd always known the day would come, of course. But he'd expected to be much older, to have seen so much more, done so many things. He'd envisioned himself taking this responsibility as his father stood beside him hale and whole. In his hazy dreams, Tryst would be able to seek his father's council for years afterwards.

The last thing he wanted now was his closest friend absent during these early days. But it was necessary, he knew. He'd never fully trust a report from anyone other than Jason.

"There are people here I can trace," Jason rose to his feet again. "Leads to follow. Once that is done, we will pursue the beast to the Dim Continent."

"Surely my father is here. They wouldn't send him..." Tryst trailed off, realizing his father could very well be a continent away.

These same conspirators had sent him a continent away.

"If we cannot find King Bactor here, we will search the Dim Continent. Even if we do find him in Missea itself, we must still ascertain how deep this plot goes.

And if it is done – or moving to a new phase."

Tryst found his gaze wandering to the conference table, to the grain of the wood, the insets of carved marble. The tabletop represented the seven provinces, he realized. Odd that he'd never noticed that before.

Responsibility, his father had said. To consider all else before yourself, to shut your own little desires in a closed corner of your brain. Every choice, every decision must come from what is right for Missea, for the Skullan race.

And for the Trumen race.

"Go, my friend." His lips wouldn't quite form the smile he sought. "Seek my father. Seek the truth."

Jason nodded, respect in his eyes. His dimple appeared, as the Defense Master found the smile that eluded Tryst.

"I go as you will, my liege."

And when Jason strode out the door, Tryst felt truly alone.

He would not abandon his father. He would not leave him in some unnatural sleep, to wake on a continent far away. King Bactor would be found, and those that held him would be caught and punished.

Tryst vowed to discover the truth. All of it. And then the King's justice would be served in full measure.

End of Book 2

THE BIRR ELIXIR

Book 1 of The Legend of the Gamesmen

Marra never heard of Birr Elixir. But when Drail sees the potion in her dead mistress's book, she agrees to make it. Even lacking the right ingredient.

And after drinking it, Drail and his men defeat a Skullan team - something no one has ever done before. Marra is offered a place as his traveling potions mistress. Full of doubts of her own ability, she takes the chance to escape her slave-like existence.

Then her potions woke a man who was not supposed to wake.

Now every day draws more attention from the True Masters. And their motives – and morals – are not for the faint of heart.

If they discover the truth ...

.

THE DIM CONTINENT

Book 3 of The Legend of the Gamesmen
Series Finale

Agben taught the art of using herbs to heal or enhance. Yet Marra saw one woman's brews detect a passing prince and cloak a creature's true appearance. A forbidden discipline - and being wielded against Tryst's throne.

The key ingredient grows only on the Dim Continent.

Journeying with her mentor to this fabled place, she stumbles on another secret: that the Women of Agben include Terrin - the same hairy creatures that kidnapped a king. Now the trust that bound the two species together is rapidly corroding.

Marra doesn't know Prince Tryst has also pursued the traitors to this wild, dangerous land. Or that Drail travels with him, to provide gamesmen cover.

In a land of strange beings and dangerous animals, Marra, Tryst, and Drail must again pool their skills, this time not just to save themselves – but to save all their people. The fate of Skullan and Trumen alike depends on defeating a powerful enemy who has plotted their destruction for centuries.

The final battle looms in the evil heart of power – the Dim Continent.

ABOUT THE AUTHOR

Jo Sparkes, a well-known Century City Producer once said, *"...writes some of the best dialogue I've read."*

Jo graduated from Washington College, a small liberal arts college famous for its creative writing program, and went on to study with Robert Powell: a student of renowned teachers Lew Hunter and Richard Walter, head of UCLA's Screenwriting Program.

She's won a Kay Snow for her comedy script, 'Frank Retrieval', a Silver IPPY for 'The Birr Elixir', and BRAG Medallions for multiple books. A member of the Pro Football Writers Association, she was (unofficially) the first to interview Emmitt Smith when he came to the Arizona Cardinals.

Jo served as an adjunct teacher at the Film School at Scottsdale Community College, and even made a video of her most beloved lecture. Her book for writers and artists, "Feedback How to Give It How to Get It" has garnered strong praise.

When not diligently perfecting her craft, Jo can be found exploring her new home of Portland, Oregon, with her husband Ian, and their dog Oscar.